DROWNING

a novel
TOM HITCHCOCK

This is a work of fiction. Names, characters, businesses, places, events and incidents are either the products of the author's imagination or used in a fictitious manner. Any resemblance to actual persons, living or dead, or actual events is purely coincidental.

DROWNING. Copyright ©2021 by Tom Hitchcock.
All rights reserved.

Cover and Book Design by Susan Hitchcock
Author photograph by Susan Hitchcock

To Mark, who opens doors
that make the novels possible.

Also by Tom Hitchcock:

God Only Knows

Girl in the Painting

We Know Where You Live

Foreign Exchange

ACKNOWLEDGEMENTS

It's one thing to envision the outlines of a plot and think they may make a pretty good story. But an outline by itself isn't enough. Without a factual framework to flesh out the ideas, the premise is just a premise, not a novel. My premise involved a rescue at sea—off the coast of Florida to be precise—under mysterious, highly suspicious circumstances. I figured the Coast Guard would be involved in looking into it, of course, but that's as far as it went. A search filled in a few more blanks but nowhere near enough to build a credible story around the mechanics of an investigation.

I turned, as I have so often in the past, to my friend and invaluable resource, Deputy Chief Mark Foxworth of the Fernandina Beach Police Department. My request had a tinge of desperation: Mark, do you happen to know anyone whose occupation and expertise could fill in my factual framework? It was a shot in the dark, poke and hope.

Sure enough, Mark knew a guy ... who knew a guy. Without that guy, Randal Thompson, *Drowning,* as a novel, (pardon the pun) is dead in the water. As it has been with Mark and others, Randy's graciousness and generosity with his time was remarkable. Every time I thought I'd overdrawn my account with respect to questions, he assured me it was fine and helped usher me along to another plot element or twist.

To the extent that the crucial pieces of this book came together, it was due largely to my wife Susan—nonpareil collaborator, sounding board, and life partner. In addition to reading, proofreading, designing the cover, back cover and page layouts, she passes judgement on plot ideas as I float them (sorry) during our dog walks.

A friend, Elaine Laurent, agrees to read the raw product in batches of chapters, an objective guardrail on the novel's flow and pacing. Is she yawning, or turning pages? And speaking of patience, a special tribute to my sister-in-law and inspiration, Ellen—whose editorial voice and guidance carries the weight of having done this stuff at the highest levels, far above my pay grade.

He had no plan, in the same way a drowning man has no plan, in the same way a drowning man's survival imperative will drive him to clamber on top of a fellow victim, fighting to stay above water, fighting to stay alive.

1

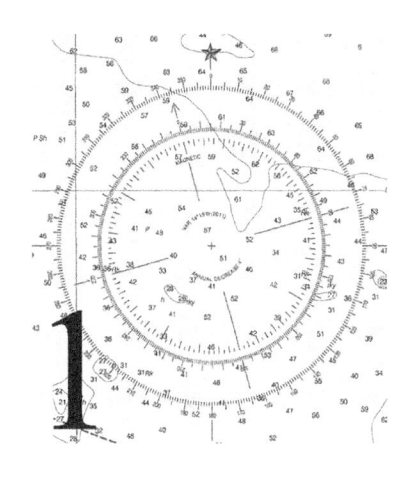

November 2018
At sea, off the Atlantic coast

Blake Wentworth appeared at the top of the companionway steps, his head and shoulders above the hatch, facing aft. Elbows resting on the cabin top, he stood, turning toward the wind from the northeast, taking note of how it had strengthened. He tucked his t-shirt into his shorts, pulling them up and straightening them. Tim Jameson, sitting behind the wheel at the aft end of the cockpit, took notice of Blake's wardrobe adjustment, attaching a significance to it that only fanned smoldering suspicions.

For Tim, already predisposed to believe that Blake's shorts had been lowered for the wrong reasons, Blake's whole demeanor suggested something sensual and libidinous, furtive, having taken place down below in the dark, just beyond the reach of Tim's eyesight and hearing, but not his imagination.

Blake moved aft and stood next to Tim, crooking his elbow around the backstay to brace against the boat's motion. The sky had darkened in the east, the last glow of the sun in the west streaked the sky and clouds in majestic shades of magenta and ochre.

"Breezing up," Blake said. "We should shorten soon. No hurry or panic with this boat, though. She's putting her shoulder right into it. We'll just help her ride a little easier, take in the headsail and put a reef in the main. That, and a little bitty staysail, and it will be like sitting in a recliner watching TV. It's why I love this boat."

Tim said nothing for a few moments. Then, "Guess that's not the only reason you love this boat, is it?"

"Okay, what's that mean?"

"You know exactly what the hell I mean. I must be crazy to let you two alone down below on my watch at night."

Blake looked off to the northeast. The swells seemed larger in the fading night, whitecaps curling down their face. He figured close to twenty knots, anyway, maybe a little more.

"This wind from the northeast should be fine if we want to change course," Tim said. "Am I right?"

"This wind's perfect for where we set out to go," Blake said. "What course change are you talking about?"

"We're gonna turn west. Toward the coast. Put in somewhere along Georgia or Florida. Put you ashore. This trip's over. Or at least your part of it is. I want you off my boat."

It was their fifth night at sea since they'd passed between the Virginia capes from the mouth of the Chesapeake, out on the open ocean, sailing southeast.

"Tim, man," Blake said, "You been taking some pops on the rum bottle or something? That where this cockamamie idea about doing a U-turn comes from?"

"No, goddammit. Fuck you! That's not what it is."

"Don't know what else it could be cause you're barking at the moon, dude."

"Bullshit. Trying to move the goalposts, right? Fancy footwork?"

Blake looked back out at the waves before turning to Tim. "Nope. I got nothing to hide. It's your boat. You and Lauren want to call it quits, I get no vote. But she does get a vote I assume, doesn't she? She with you on this? She wants to head back?"

"She will."

"Well, Tim, I'm not so sure. But for now, let's take in some sail."

Blake instructed Tim to turn the boat slightly to leeward. He loosened the headsail sheet and cranked the winding drum that wrapped the sail around the forestay like a window shade, leaving a smaller staysail still drawing. The boat's energy and motion eased.

"One more adjustment," Blake said. "Keep her to leeward, ease the main sheet, lock the wheel and then come up here and help me."

Tim seethed. This is my fucking boat, he thought. My wife, down below, who knows what's been going on between them for who knows how long? Now he's making accusations and giving me fucking orders? Fuck this! He eased the sheet, locked the wheel with the knurled black knob on the pedestal, and charged up onto the cabin top, sticking his chest into Blake's. He backed Blake toward the main boom, grabbing his shirt with two fists.

"You think I'm fucking blind and stupid? I want this fucking boat turned back toward land so I can dump you ashore. Got it?"

Blake bucked his forearms upward to knock Tim's hands aside, and jolted him, pushing back forcefully. Just then the boat careened sideways and down as the momentum of a large wave took hold. Tim tumbled backward off the cabin top into the cockpit. His head bounced hard off one of the large winches on the cockpit coaming. The sound of the impact was audible over the hiss and foaming of the rising waves.

In the cabin below, Lauren Jameson reached for handholds as she braced and staggered, stowing and securing anything loose. Minutes earlier, Blake had run his palms down her ribs and along her flanks. She pressed close to him, hooked her thumbs in his shorts and eased them down.

"No, stop," he hissed, wondering if the danger, the risk of Tim's proximity fifteen feet away and a flight of steps up in the cockpit was part of what turned her on. She was a package, this woman. "I've gotta go up on deck," he said. "Wind's picking up. Feel it?"

She breathed, "I can feel something picking up."

"Priorities, babe. Okay? Please? I need to you to make sure everything down here's secured. Can't have stuff flying around if the weather gets any worse." He cupped her ass cheek, caressed it, and turned to climb the companionway steps.

A few minutes later she heard the shouting and harsh words from the cabin top above her. Cursing, heavy footsteps and grunts. She looked out the companionway hatch opening just as Tim's body plummeted past, slamming into the lazarette bench cover and coaming. When his head hit the winch, his form went limp. He flopped like a rag doll and lay still, motionless, seemingly lifeless, except for the way the motion of the boat rolled him back and forth just slightly.

She darted up the steps and Blake flew down off the cabin top. "Tim!" she screamed. "Tim! Oh my God!"

"Holy Christ," Blake said. "I can't believe this!" He reached up quickly and sheeted home the mainsail to steady the boat. "Jesus, man. He really hit!"

"What happened? Did you—?"

"He came up after me. He knew, said he knew what you and I were up to. He was pissed off, screaming, grabbed me. Wanted us to turn back west, toward the coast, put in somewhere so he could throw me off the boat. I pushed him back, he lost his balance, I—." Blake was breathing hard. He placed his thumb and forefinger on Tim's carotid arteries. "C'mon, man! Jesus." He bent and put his ear to Tim's mouth, listening, feeling for breath. "Get me a light. Quick!"

Lauren rushed back up the steps with a flashlight. Blake shined it into Tim's eyes. The pupils were dilated and fixed. He pressed his fingers on the neck again feeling for a pulse. "Shit!"

"What? What!? Blake! Is he dead?

He looked at her with wide, panicked eyes. "God! I don't know. No pulse, no breathing." He raised his fist and pounded hard on

Tim's chest, once, reaching for the neck once again to check for a pulse. Then pounded again, in desperation.

"This isn't happening," Blake said. "Tell me this isn't happening. Jesus Christ!"

She screamed. "Blake! Talk to me! Is he dead?"

He met her eyes and sagged. "Yeah, I think so."

She stood and sucked in air and whirled. "Oh, dear lord in heaven." She sobbed, put her hands to her mouth and then knelt. "Oh, Tim, Tim, Tim, please ... please no, good God, please no."

Without a hand on the helm, the wind and waves began to have their way with the boat. It bucked and veered, heeling sharply with the strengthening wind gusts. Blake moved behind the wheel and adjusted the trim to steady the boat.

Lauren took Tim's hands and folded them on his chest, holding them. She looked down at Tim's face for a long moment, then at Blake, her eyes wide and red-rimmed. "This is a nightmare."

"It's way more than a nightmare," Blake said. "You wake up from a nightmare. We won't wake up from this." He ran his fingers back through his hair. She'd never seen him scared or rattled.

"What do we do now? Is this—? Some kind of ... what?"

Blake looked at her. "If two guys get in a physical confrontation, and one of them winds up dead, it's manslaughter."

"But it was an accident. Tell me it was."

"Hell yes, it was. But it doesn't matter. Understand? Still a crime. Five years, maybe ten."

"Are you kidding? How do you know this?"

Blake reached for her hand. "I just do, baby. You have to believe me."

"I can't lose you like that. I can't. I won't. No matter what. Why can't we just tell them he fell? He'd gone up the mast or something, a knot slipped, something gave way. He fell and hit his head."

Blake shook his head. "Did you see the accident? This fall from the mast?"

"Sure."

"Did I?"

"Yes. We both did."

"Let me tell you something. When you try to make up a story, it always falls apart. They ask you the same questions, over and over again, ask them in different ways, in different order. At some point, you're tired. You screw up, forget, make a mistake. They catch you. And when there's two people with a made-up story, it's even worse. No way you can keep it straight. Then they play you off against each other. Or ask you to take a polygraph. Any way you look at it, you're cooked. They got you for the crime, plus lying about it, which is an extra charge on top of the homicide."

She looked at him and realized there was a part of his life they hadn't covered yet. After a time, Blake said, "Listen, this isn't my call. He's your husband, it would be your decision. But there's another choice. Not a good one, I admit. Horrible. Maybe even unthinkable."

Lauren needed no prompting to leapfrog Blake's train of thought. "What difference does it make if it's not a good choice if it's our only choice?"

"We're over three-hundred miles offshore," Blake said, "two and-a-half, maybe three days away from a port. That's three days with Tim up in the V-berth, riding along with us."

"No, no. God, no. I just don't think I can deal with that."

"We put in somewhere," he said, "tie up, call the Coast Guard, report the incident. They come to get him, go over every detail, ask a hundred questions. Then the FBI takes their turn asking me another hundred questions. If I tell the truth about what happened, they'll arrest me, check my sheet, and I could be just a hop, skip and a jump away from a long stretch in federal prison."

"No."

"No what?"

"Not when there's the other way."

"Which is ... damn, Lauren! It's not up to me."

"We're both thinking it." She hissed: "Just say it!"

He looked over the side to the wavetops barreling along, at times no more than a foot below the toe rail. And then back at her. "That's it, then. Roll him over the side. Is that what we're saying?"

"Yes! My God, yes. What the hell do you think? But now, dammit. Right now, before I completely lose it and change my mind. Hear me?"

And so it was that neither he nor Lauren—minds clouded by panic in the midst of their cataclysm, in the dark of night, bracing to stay balanced in a stiff wind and a pitching boat—noticed that Tim's chest had begun to rise and fall, haltingly, almost imperceptibly, with the first faint stirrings of respirations. They believed he was dead and had reached an emotional point of no return.

Blake unhooked the two lifelines along the cockpit seat where Tim was lying. They lifted and pulled, grunting with the effort, dragging, shoving, until Tim was between the toe rail and coaming on the leeward, or lower edge of the boat. With the next lurch to leeward it was a simple matter to roll his inert form into the waves.

In five seconds, he was ten yards astern of the boat. And in those five seconds Lauren and Blake were struck with the horror of a realization, the price of muddled thinking and acting hastily. Integrated with Tim's life vest was a strobing, man-overboard distress light designed to activate automatically upon contact with water. They watched helplessly as the light on Tim's vest did what it was supposed to, the piercing staccato flash winking brightly as he bobbed farther astern. There was no thought of coming about to attempt to recover Tim's unconscious or lifeless body. Both knew that maneuvering alongside in rough seas, trying to secure it somehow and hoist it aboard a high-sided sailboat as the hull rolled and heaved, was not just a physical impossibility, it was also dangerous.

"Jesus," Lauren muttered.

"God*damn*," he said. "Stupid ass." He watched. The pulsating light drifted, now and then dropping below the mid-ocean wave heights churned by a twenty-knot wind. He grabbed her by the shoulders and turned her. "Look, we're out in the middle of the ocean, okay? Those things are only visible for a mile and a half. In this kind of sea, less than that. And the battery goes dead eventually. We're fine." He tilted her head up and looked into her eyes. "We're fine."

He looked astern again. "See? He's half-a-mile back and you can barely make out the light. You really have to be looking."

The notion that her husband of eight years had been reduced to a fading, flickering light on its way to oblivion was too much. She collapsed in a paroxysm of sobbing and despair, sagging into Blake's chest. "I can't believe this," she said. "He's gone. Just like that. My God. It's not what I wanted." She looked out over the water. "It's so dark, Blake. I'm scared. I want it to be light again."

He looked astern one last time. The blinking light was faint, dipping from view beneath the waves for long intervals. "Sun'll be up in ten hours. But for you and me I don't know when it's gonna be light again."

Had he bothered to look astern again, a few minutes later, he might have been able to see just over the very edge of the horizon and catch a quick glimpse of a tiny pinprick of light. Not blinking, steady. The masthead light of another vessel. Still far enough off to dip from view for long periods. And even if he'd seen it, it was way too far off to determine its heading.

2

Blake had placed his fingers on Tim's neck, feeling for a pulse. Finding none and reaching back through the years to his rudimentary first aid training, he had assumed the worst. That assumption plunged Lauren and him deeper into an abyss of desperation and panic. Based on a frantic and ill-founded assessment, he and Lauren had been foolhardy and irrational, prodded by hysteria. Blake had no way of knowing for sure whether Tim was clinically dead. The two of them had reached life-and-death decisions in the crush of the moment.

Serious head trauma can lead to ventricular defibrillation, a malfunction of the heart's electrical system and a component of cardiac arrest. That would have explained, amid a confused and panicked uncertainty, the absence of a carotid pulse and breathing so weak and shallow it was undetectable against the noise of waves and a strong wind blowing across the deck.

When Blake pounded his fist on Tim's chest, it was possible, though unlikely, that one of the blows corrected the heart's fibrillation and restored its normal contractions. Even among trained medical professionals, however, the practice, known as a precordial thump, has been discredited as unreliable and mostly ineffective. Had it worked on Tim, it would have been the sheerest, most improbable stroke of blind luck. Yet it may have. Somehow his heart regained a minimal level of pumping power, enough to keep him alive and his brain marginally viable.

The intervention of blind luck would have been in character with the sequence of events that followed, a chain of happenstance at some outer edge of improbability. For instance, the ocean water temperature in early November, three hundred miles out, at the latitude of the Florida-Georgia border, was 66 degrees Fahrenheit. When Blake and Lauren rolled Tim overboard into that water, the cold was just enough of a shock to arouse his nervous system into a higher level of consciousness. Between this heightened awareness and his life vest, he was able, barely, to keep his face out of the water.

Moreover, 66-degree water, though cold enough to deliver a shock, was not quite cold enough to be life-threatening in the short term. Under the best of circumstances, Tim could be expected to remain conscious for two hours and survive for some period beyond that. Conditions were less than optimal, however. The three to four-foot swells that tossed Tim around forced him to expend energy—and heat—paddling, clutching and pawing, despite his life vest, to keep his head and face out of the water.

Worse, the aftereffects of his head injury clouded his thinking, kept him confused and disoriented, and made him drowsy. Ominously, these were the very same complications of advancing hypothermia as its effects worsened. In Tim's case, he was compromised by his injury from the outset, even before hypothermia's symptoms set in.

And yet, strangely enough hypothermia has one tangential upside. In recent years, researchers had been exploring a therapy known as induced hypothermia to stave off brain damage in treating victims of cardiac arrest. As the body's core temperature drops, its metabolic processes wind down. As the core temperature continues to sink, those processes enter into a kind of suspended animation. Cells may be on their way to dying, eventually, but the progress is greatly slowed. Inside Tim's skull, hypothermia was mitigating the effects of the inflammation, bleeding and swelling around his brain resulting from his injury. It was also lessening the effects of his brain having been starved of oxygen over several minutes, when he lay unconscious in the boat, as Blake and Lauren agonized over what to do.

Those researchers, however, had the ability to keep conditions under tight controls. They could modulate a patient's core temperature according to meticulously timed protocols. Tim could not. He had been immersed, badly injured, in water cold enough to draw warmth from his body in steady, unrelenting increments. After an hour and a half, he could barely concentrate on the movements necessary to stay upright, and his head kept dropping as he struggled to stay awake. He'd been shivering badly but now was past that stage. Apathy claimed the lives of many hypothermia victims, but it was difficult to combat the sensation unless you were aware of it. Tim was aware of very little. He was sinking into unconsciousness, the sensation of slipping into a dark place, unable to fight it any longer.

Mac Crandall sat high up in the wheelhouse of the *Eleanor Beal*, a 76-ft. long-liner fishing boat out of Savannah. At the moment, he was intent on a large color chart plotter and the nearby screen of a 3D depth sounder. Easing along at five knots, he was comparing features on the sea floor with the boat's position on the chart. The last set had come up with a disappointing catch. The crew was not happy, nor was he. He needed to find the right axis along which to place the next set, twenty miles of lines with a baited hook dangling down every fifteen feet. Plotting where to find the concentrations of fish involved currents, prevailing winds, the presence of bait fish, bottom contours, what had worked in the past, and where. It was inexact, but his crew depended on him for the income that fed their families. Indeed, boat payments, gear, fuel, insurance, bait and maintenance all hinged on Mac coming up with the right formula. Thus, his intense focus on the two screens.

Avoiding other ships was also part of his duty. Every so often he glanced up at the radar screen and out over the expanse of darkened sea. An anomaly caught his eye. What the—? What is that? A flashing, bobbing strobe less than a hundred yards off the port bow. He reached for the switch to turn on a massive floodlight above him on the wheelhouse roof. Instinctively, he turned to port so that the strobing light was now off his starboard bow. He throttled back as he aimed the floodlight. Jesus! A figure in the water! How in the hell? Out here? He grabbed the mic on the PA system.

"Andy! Butch! Damn, guys! We got a man in the water. Just off the starboard bow! I got him on the leeward side. See him? Get the net over the side. Quick, now! C'mon." He slowed a bit more, keeping the floodlight trained, maneuvering the 200-ton vessel so it would drift slowly down on the victim without sweeping over him.

Andy and Butch slapped on life vests, threw the boarding net over the side and clipped themselves to the boat with safety harnesses. Climbing up over the gunwale and down the side, they waited, holding on to the net with one hand, reaching with the other. As Tim floated closer to the net, they stretched, gathering him under the arms, and pulled. He was unconscious, dead weight, hard as hell to handle. The boat rocked. Butch put his head and neck in the crook of Tim's armpit and lifted, pushing with his legs. Andy pulled up on the other arm. Greg, another crew member, leaned over the gunwale and grabbed Tim's shirt, pulling until he could reach the forearms. They worked with the urgency of knowing that some dark night in the middle of the fucking ocean it could be one of them. They all knew guys who'd disappeared beneath the waves, individually due to an accident or in groups when a boat went down.

They dragged Tim over the gunwale and laid him on the deck. Mac came scrambling down the ladder alongside the wheelhouse. "Christ! Take it easy with him." He'd studied hypothermia extensively and knew that the gentle handling of victims was paramount. He knew also that a victim was not dead until, as the saying went, he was warm and dead. And, too, that warming had to be done slowly.

Mac checked Tim's carotid arteries and felt a faint pulse. Tim's hands were ice cold. "Okay, he said, "this guy's in rough shape but he's still alive. Carry him inside, gently, get the wet clothes off, and towel him down. Wrap some blankets around him, a few extra around his head and chest. He's gotta get warm slow, got it? Slow. I'm gonna call the Coast Guard."

The HH-60 Jayhawk helicopter flew east out of Jacksonville at 190 knots, vectoring on a course that would take it to a rendezvous with the *Eleanor Beal*, hove-to and drifting three hundred miles off the coast of Florida. Tying in GPS coordinates and AIS technology made it relatively easy to find one another, even in the dark of night. Mac Crandall flipped on a strobing masthead light as a visual beacon that guided the chopper pilots in from ten miles away.

Hovering above the *Eleanor Beal*, the helicopter crew lowered a rescue basket to her deck. The Coast Guard crew knew that Crandall and his hands were competent in securing a victim in the basket. When they gestured with a thumbs up, the winch aboard the helicopter lifted Tim until he could be gathered in through the hatch and attended to by a Coast Guard crew member, Kelly, who was trained as an advanced life support clinician. She and another medic ministered to Tim, gathering vital signs. Kelly hopscotched a stethoscope around his chest, while the other medic took his temperature with a forehead thermometer and clipped a pulse oximeter to his forefinger. Kelly yelled sharply in Tim's face, took a fold of skin and pinched it hard, and then shined a bright penlight back and forth between each eye.

Their preliminary assessment would characterize Tim's condition as critical. His heartbeat was weak and irregular, the oxygen level in his blood was low, his body temperature was 90.7 degrees F. He was comatose; no response to pain or loud noise. His pupils were dilated, of different sizes, and only marginally reactive to light. Before swaddling Tim in a specially designed, insulated hypothermia wrap, Kelly attached electrodes to his chest. The zig-zagging green lines on the monitor just above their eye-level told them what they pretty much suspected about Tim's heart. They were 90 minutes out from a Level-I trauma center in Jacksonville. Kelly phoned in their initial findings to a trauma nurse on duty in the ER. As the helicopter drew closer to the trauma center, Tim's EKG readings would be transmitted as well.

Kelly understood the heartbeat and breathing parts of the equation: second stage hypothermia could account for that. In theory, as Tim's core temperature warmed, those indications should improve. She was troubled, however, by his neurological symptoms. His temperature was warming enough by now so that he should have scored better on the Glasgow Coma Scale. His indications were those of someone who had suffered a traumatic brain injury, not just a moderate case of hypothermia.

Tim was in a no-man's-land between life and death. On-call and standing by at the trauma center were neurologists, cardiologists, pulmonologists, radiologists, and trauma and ER specialists, all backed by a platoon of nurses, interns, residents, technicians and fellowship candidates. He would be delivered into the hands of those who could save his life, sustain it perhaps, unveil the clinical causes underlying his condition. But none of them could explain what had happened to him, or how.

Ultimately, that would be left to Tim. But for the moment, Tim wasn't talking. And how much longer that would continue was in God's hands, or whatever force shuffled the cards in the realm of improbable fortune.

3

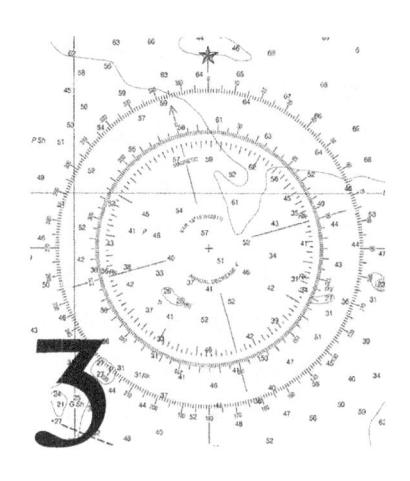

To the east, the sky lightened in stages sufficient to ease the spirit of anyone weighed down by fatigue from an all-night tumult of waves and wind. Both were more stressful and intimidating in the dark. But in the case of Lauren Jameson, the fatigue was layered over with a suffocating dread. The wind and motion of the sea moderated as it grew light, normally elements of relief and deliverance. Yet for someone who had been party to the sudden death of a crewmember, a husband, and had helped roll her spouse's body into the sea nine hours earlier, the new light served only to illuminate the extent of the torment that lay ahead of her.

The wind had eased enough to allow the spread of more sail. Blake moved about the boat, shaking a reef out of the mainsail and unfurling the large headsail. When he had finished adjusting the trim of those sails, the boat responded to the added horsepower, settling into the task for which it was designed, knifing through the waves with a sense of purpose and an easy motion.

Lauren was at the helm, making minor adjustments to sync the boat's course with the sail trim. Blake always thought she had a natural feel for it, a rarity. A light touch on the wheel, keeping the sails full as she responded to slight changes in the wind's direction and variations between gusts and lulls, feeling them as they happened.

Their eyes met. In the morning light she looked haunted, pale and drawn. Stricken. He sat beside her on the locker seat behind the wheel and gently nudged her over, replacing her hand on the wheel with his. "I'll take it," he said. "You need to go below and get some food, and rest."

"How?" She asked. "How am I just supposed to go and close my eyes and try not to see the replay of the worst, most horrible moment of my whole life?" Tears ran down her cheeks.

"Lauren, listen. Listening?" He tilted her chin, raised her face to his. "We're a thousand miles from Vieques, six days sailing. I've sailed places doing long tricks at the wheel, but I can't do this by myself. We're going to have to do it in shifts, and you're going to need some sleep. Sorry. No other choice."

She was quiet for a few moments. "Why so far? Why can't we put in someplace closer and rest for a few days?"

"Like where?"

"I don't know. Somewhere in the Bahamas."

"It's a foreign country. We'd have to clear customs and immigration. You bring the ship's papers ashore with you. The boat is registered to a Mr. and Ms. Jameson. My passport indicates I'm not Mr. Jameson. Where is Mr. Jameson?"

"He was called home on business," she said. "We put in at Jacksonville and he flew home from there."

"Really? Lauren, remember last night when we talked about stories falling apart? You're talking to a Bahamian immigration officer. You're scared, nervous. Tired. He sees that. He's trained. What kind of business is Mr. Jameson in? Where did he fly to? Is he planning on rejoining you here? You screw up or flub one answer, that's it. Game over. He's got a couple standing in front of him, no husband. What's he supposed to think? They take us to different rooms. Then the game's really over. A lot of questions, from Bahamian cops and maybe U.S. cops, or Coast Guard, and no good answers."

"Okay, all right already. I get it." Silence, only the sound of water sluicing alongside the boat. "What about Florida?" she said. "Somewhere, just to get off this fucking boat. Dry land. A real shower."

"You and Tim wanted to do blue-water sailing," Blake said. "Remember? A voyage, you said. This is part of it."

"That was before it turned into a living, breathing nightmare." She was too wired and upset to make rational choices or reason with. Her complaints sounded too close to whining. And pretending that stopping somewhere would fix what they'd done, angered him. He was as exhausted and stressed as she was.

He hissed. "Listen, goddammit. There's no point in second-guessing and beating the shit out of ourselves over this. We made a decision, a choice, and it's done. Okay?" He shouted. "Hear me? It's done! Over! And here's something else you probably don't know. Still listening?"

"Yeah."

"Good. When any kind of injury or accident takes place aboard a boat, like what happened to Tim, the captain or the owner is supposed to report it to the Coast Guard. It's the law. And if you don't report it, you're up shit's creek. And that's on top of me most likely being guilty of involuntary manslaughter, and one or both us being guilty of getting rid of evidence of a crime."

She looked over the side and for a brief second wondered if she should just climb up on the railing, grab a stay, and jump.

"Ever been in prison?" Blake asked.

"No."

"I have. And believe me, however you feel about this boat right now? It's like an ice cream and cake birthday party compared to prison."

He ran his hands along her shoulders, comforting her, trying to cut through the despair taking her down into a deep cavern. "Why don't we do this," he said. "Let's get some more miles under the keel, okay? Another day or so south? That puts us on a latitude of Fort Pierce or Stuart or somewhere down there. For now, I think it might be good for us to be farther away from—"

"From where we dumped Tim overboard? Go ahead, you can say it."

"God, give me a break. Yeah, that's what I was going to say. But what I meant was, all we can do is try to be smart about what comes next. If we get a ways farther south, and we still think it seems smart—I don't know why we would—then maybe we can turn west and pull in somewhere along there."

She sagged. "Okay. I'm sorry."

"Now c'mon. Go below, please? Just close your eyes. Try to rest." He pulled her close. But there was a resistance, a stiffness. She stood and shuffled toward the companionway steps. She looked back at him as she grabbed the handholds and made her way down.

The Coast Guard held a conference call between senior officers in Jacksonville and Miami. At issue was what the response should be to the individual, who they had started calling John Doe, recovered at sea by the long-liner vessel *Eleanor Beal* and subsequently flown to the trauma center in Jacksonville. Reports from the trauma center were that his condition, though slightly improved, was still precarious.

There were periods of silence during the call as the officers reflected on the dearth of facts. No distress or Mayday calls. No distraught relative or loved one calling to report a missing family member. No inquiries from friends to report him overdue at some expected destination. No ancillary or explanatory event, before or after the long-liner boat called, reporting that they'd plucked John Doe from the ocean, half dead, three-hundred miles out.

The doctors in Jacksonville reported that a CAT scan and MRIs showed he'd suffered a serious brain injury. He was still comatose and unresponsive. The crew of the *Eleanor Beal* reported all they knew, which was very little. The victim was wearing a life vest equipped with a strobe. How? Why? Was he a single-hander who fell overboard, suffering a head injury as he fell? Or did the head injury result from foul play, other people on board a boat with him? But then why the life vest and the strobe? It didn't add up.

The Coast Guard officials had no choice but to make assumptions. They had to go with the single-hander-gone-overboard theory. Another assumption posited that he had to have gone overboard somewhere within a reasonable distance of the *Eleanor Beal*. The *Eleanor Beal* was on the outer edge of the Gulfstream when they recovered John Doe. At that location, the Gulfstream travels northward at about three knots. If John Doe had been in the water any more than five hours, he'd probably be dead. So, moderate hypothermia, figure three hours in the water, maybe less, times three knots, means he might have gone in the water somewhere ten miles south of the *Eleanor Beal*, drifting north till they found him. A scientific wild-ass guess they called it. The officers consulted a chart, which told them nothing, except where the rough outlines of a search area would be.

They hesitated. Helicopter searches were ruinously expensive, contingent items they couldn't budget for without shortchanging the other mandates piled on their plate: drug interdiction, anti-terrorist efforts, anti-pollution policing. Yet there was no choice but to organize one. Soon. But looking for what? Where? The solution they devised was a compromise. Two search and rescue helicopters, HH-60s, one out of Brunswick, Georgia and one out of Ponce De Leon, 160 miles down the coast, would fly pie-shaped patterns. Three hundred miles east-northeast, turn south for a hundred miles, then 300 miles back west to base. With a range of 800 miles, the aircraft would have a hundred miles worth of fuel to spare. It was a great deal of money to spend looking over a vast expanse of ocean without a clear idea of what anyone expected to find. For lack of anything more specific, the crews were told that a clue to what they might be looking for was an abandoned vessel, adrift. Or something.

In the meantime, the Coast Guard issued one of its periodic Notice to Mariners. Disseminated online or as a print publication, the notice urged mariners in the Atlantic coast region to be on the lookout for a vessel adrift, unmanned or abandoned. Officials also issued a press release with bare-bones details of the incident, asking anyone with information to please come forward. It ran in a few smaller papers up and down the coast.

The chopper out of Brunswick, designated Search Engine 1 for this mission, queried a container ship inbound to Savannah. They'd seen nothing. But then the crews of container ships rarely ever looked. Search Engine 2, the southernmost of the two, asked the same of a worse-for-the-wear coastwise freighter out of Puerto Rico, bound for Charleston. The same. No. Nada. Sorry.

Among the challenges for crews on these missions was maintaining focus while looking out at an expanse of ocean for hours at a time, at one-thousand feet. They were trained, though, to fight through it. Their job was saving lives. Search Engine 2 had been on its southbound leg for 80 miles when a pilot pointed straight ahead and spoke into the helicopter intercom. "Sailboat up ahead. We'll take it down to 600 feet and slow to hover when we get astern of 'em."

Lauren was taking another turn at *Breezeway's* wheel, steering a southeasterly course, in a sixteen-knot breeze from the northeast. The boat was on a port tack, sailing a beam reach, very nearly an optimum point of sail.

In addition to a versatile sail plan, the *Breezeway* had a kind of broad-shouldered musculature to her that kept her tracking and steady in moderate winds like today, or balanced and sure-footed when the wind piped up and the waves steepened and churned with white caps. A crew could adjust her sails and count on the strength of her design and architecture to keep her head, and her feet, in wind and waves that would have their way with lesser boats. Along the length of her hull, beneath the water, was a full keel. Like feathers on an arrow shaft, the longer the keel, the straighter and truer a boat sailed. The balance between sails and keel and an oversized rudder let Lauren keep *Breezeway* on a steady course with minimal effort.

Wearing a bikini top and white shorts, she heard a faint clatter, an unfamiliar rasping and throbbing from behind her. She turned and saw the unmistakable white and orange graphics of a Coast Guard helicopter ranging in from behind as it slowed.

"Damn," said one of the crew members. "Look at *this*. Check it *out*."

"Blake!" she yelled. "Blake! Coast Guard!" She looked back up, petrified. "Jesus Christ."

He leaped to the top of the companionway steps. "Holy fuck. What do they want?"

The VHF radio receiver rang out with an insistent, authoritative voice over the air. "Southbound sailing vessel, this is Coast Guard helicopter. Do you copy?"

Blake grabbed the handheld VHF. Standing in the companionway hatch, looking up as he answered: "Coast Guard, this is southbound sailing vessel. Copy." Normally he would have included the vessel name in his response, but didn't.

"Roger, Captain," came the reply. "We're conducting a search of this area. Have you seen or run across any abandoned vessel, one that might have been adrift? Not under command?"

One did not simply sail past a boat that seemed abandoned or in distress. Blake assumed that was understood and kept the reply succinct. "No sir. We have not."

"Okay Captain. We'd like you to keep your eye out and report to us if you do see anything like that. Copy?"

"Roger. Yes, sir."

"May I have the name of your vessel please?"

He and Lauren flashed panicked glances back and forth. The boat's name on the transom was hidden by the inflatable dinghy secured to it. For a split-second Blake considered fabricating a name, but then thought of his own cautions about making things up. "Breezeway," he said.

Silence from the Coast Guard radio. What did that mean? What? Oh my God.

Then, "Roger, Captain. Just the two of you aboard?"

"Yes, sir."

"Where are you bound?"

"Virgin Islands."

"Long way from here, Captain."

"Yes, sir."

"Be safe. Roger and out."

The helicopter was nearing bingo fuel level. The crew was tired and bored. One of them wrote down the boat name as "Beezeweigh," scribbling on a form on a clipboard, which he tossed to one side. The helicopter banked and turned west toward Ponce De Leon. Another hour and forty-five till Miller time.

As the helicopter clattered away to the west, Lauren put her hand to her forehead and then ran it down her face. "Oh, man. What was that all about?"

"I don't know," Blake said.

"Let's take a guess, worst case."

"Hell, who knows? Worst case? Might have something to do with Tim. If I had to take a wild guess, the fact that they're looking for an abandoned boat means that if they found Tim—if they found him—

they think he was a single-hander who went overboard. That's a big if. Really jumping to a conclusion."

"Or maybe not."

"Right. Maybe not."

He looked out over the waves. "Still want to pull in somewhere in Florida?"

"No."

"Listen, Vieques is kind of an out-of-the-way place. Esperanza's a small town on the south coast. Not much happening, not a real favorite with the cruisers. It's U.S. territory, no customs, no immigration. People leave you alone. Good place to close the door behind you."

"So, we're hiding out. Not exactly what we had planned for this trip, is it?"

"Not really hiding out," he said. "More like, I don't know. Like ..."

"A sanctuary?"

"Yeah, that's it. A sanctuary. Catch our breath, rest up for awhile. Decide what or where we might want to go next."

She let her head drop. "Okay. Sounds good. A sanctuary."

"Yeah. Now go get some rest, okay? I mean it. We've got some miles in front of us. I can do a lot of it, but you'll have to spell me every now and then."

She stood in the companionway opening before descending the steps. "Blake, are we going to be all right?"

"I think so."

"You mean you hope so."

"Whatever you say. I mean I don't know, but I sure as hell hope so."

TOM HITCHCOCK

4

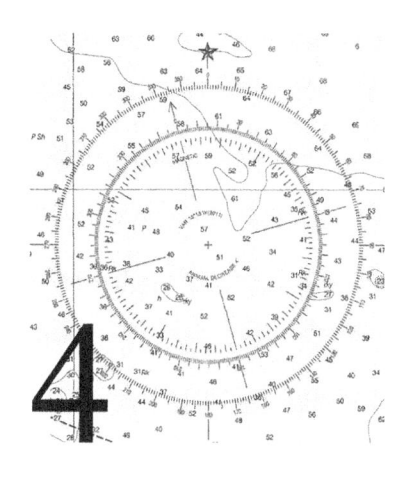

Eight months earlier
April, Tilghman Island, Maryland

Blake Wentworth looked up as he walked between rows of boats supported on jack stands. The boats were raised to heights that allowed their owners access to the curvature of their hulls and their undersides, portions not easily reached or inaccessible once a boat had been lowered into the water. It was early April, and the buzz of activity was a rite of Spring. Boat owners around the Chesapeake Bay bent to the tasks of prepping their vessels for a full season afloat, accompanied by the smells of paint and fiberglass resin.

Blake saw tan thighs disappearing up into a pair of short jean cutoffs. "Looking good!" he called out. A woman stood above him on plank scaffolds. Stationed between a-frame ladders, the planks spanned the length of a 37-ft. Island Packet sailboat.

She looked down, pausing from the chore of buffing out the wax on the hull between deck and waterline, and saw bleached, tousled hair, a smile, sunglasses, tan shoulders and arms in a ragged t-shirt.

"Thanks." She was unsure if he meant the hull, or her.

Blake was the boatyard honcho in a close-to-the-bone marina whose facilities paralleled a narrow channel separating the northern part of a peninsula from a small island to the south.

He bent under the scaffold planks. "See you got the bottom painted. That's the hard part." He looked up through the planks along her legs. "I've seen you around before. Beautiful boat."

A man came around from the stern of the boat. He held rags, strips of masking tape and small paint brushes. Blake turned. "Hey, you're Mr.–

"Jameson, Tim ... Jameson."

"Right. Nice to meet you, Tim. Just telling your wife, Ms. Jameson I'm guessing? She's beautiful. The boat, I mean. You know. Sorry. What I mean is, you can tell she's a vessel built for the sea."

The woman clambered down an a-frame ladder. Blake had gotten her attention. "Hi," she said, smiling, "I'm Lauren."

"Lauren, hi. I'm Blake. It's a pleasure to meet you and Tim." Blake walked out from underneath the planks and ladders and took a wider perspective of the boat, shaking his head as he walked. "Like I was saying, she's purpose-built that boat. Meant to take on the open ocean. So many of these cookie-cutter sloops, high aspect rigs, fancy-schmancy keels, racer-cruisers they call them. But they aren't either one. They're great for a 12-knot wind out on the Bay, a cruise from St. Michaels to Annapolis, big deal. Half the time you see them with their sails furled anyway: too tender for twenty knots or too boring for eight knots. Either too much wind or not enough, or it's blowing in the wrong direction. I never understood the point of it."

He continued circling the boat. Lauren followed; Tim lagged behind just a little. "But not this lady. Look at her. Look at those aft sections." He held his hands out as if cupping them. "Beautiful. I'd take her anywhere. But hell, she's not my boat, so why am I even talking like that? Sorry. I sure do admire her though."

Lauren edged a little closer. Anyone looking closely would have seen that her eyes shone, just a bit. She had a faint, crooked smile on her face. "It's funny you should mention that ... Blake, you said?"

"Right. Blake Wentworth. Mention what?"

"My husband and I have been considering, that is, talking about venturing out someday. Sailing off somewhere, the Caribbean, I guess. That's one of the reasons we bought this boat."

"Well," Blake said, "you got off on a good start making the right decision with the boat. It's what she's built for."

Tim Jameson stepped forward to weigh in. "We also liked the amount of room below. Plus, Island Packets hold their value. And let's just say Lauren's a little more gung-ho on this cruising adventure than I am."

"Sounds almost like a right-brain, left-brain kind of thing," Blake said.

Tim chuckled. "I run an accounting firm in Easton."

"Ah, well, okay. Guess that explains some of it." Blake said. "But still, with that cutter rig and full keel I imagine there might be times when she's a little sluggish in light air. On the Bay that's a lot of the time."

Tim stiffened a little. "Yeah, maybe."

Blake adjusted quickly to correct the inadvertent faux pas of slighting another man's boat. "On the other hand, when it really pipes up, that's when you see what she's made of. I bet that's when you're really proud of her. If you ever go on that voyage of yours, you'll be glad you've got—what's her name? *Breezeway*? great name— you'll be glad you've got *Breezeway* under you. I've been out in some heavy weather in those other kind of boats, the racer-cruiser Clorox-bottle types. Some are okay. But sometimes you're hanging on, wishing you were somewhere else."

Tim said, "Sounds like you've been there."

"Every now and again I have," Blake said.

"Where?" Lauren said. "Can I ask?"

Blake let out a deep breath. "Let's see. Bunch of times back and forth between the Caribbean and New York, and Boston. Those were boat deliveries. Couple of races: Newport to Bermuda. Once Newport to Cowes, England. That's damn near three-thousand miles. That might be about it. I'll think of a few more."

"We're you ever scared?" Lauren said.

"Scared? Oh ... well. Yeah, maybe. Not terrified or anything. More like a little uptight or nervous. A few times. Sometimes the weather definitely gets your attention. But I'll tell you what else you feel. You never feel more alive. A billion stars. Big white caps coming by the boat at two a.m. You and Mother Nature. And she's in charge. No sensation like it. And when you lower your anchor into water so clear you can see thirty feet to the bottom, there's no feeling like that either."

The description pulsed through Lauren. She turned to Tim. Tim said to Blake, "You had experienced people on board, I'm sure."

"Yeah, of course," he said. "It's how you earn your spurs, I guess. I learned from them. Paid attention. It's a matter of confidence. After a while you know what you can do, what you can handle."

The owner of the boatyard leaned out the door of the office. "Blake! Phone call."

"Okay! Right there!" He turned back to Tim and Lauren. "Great meeting you guys. You've got a helluva boat. Hope she takes you wherever you want to go." He turned as he trotted back to the office. "See you around."

That evening Tim and Lauren sat at an outdoor table in one of the restaurants alongside the narrow waterway that made Tilghman Island an island. The server had arrived with beers and left with their orders. A full day of physical labor on the boat had left them pleasantly tired, and hungry.

They sipped beers in silence. Which was odd, and out of character given the occasion. Ordinarily there would have been a conversational agenda filled with items and details pertaining to the boat. But there was a catalyst for the silence, an undercurrent, a topic Lauren was straining at the leash to raise, but held back. At least for the moment. Tim could sense it, feel it coming. The topic had come up before, intermittently, never with any satisfactory conclusion.

When the silence finally became too pronounced, Lauren spoke up. "I thought Blake was nice, didn't you?"

"I did, yes."

"It was incredible what he said about our boat."

"Which part? The part about being sluggish in light air?"

"No," she said. "You know what I mean. About her being built for the sea, how he'd take her anywhere."

"We knew that about the boat when we bought her."

"Yeah, but the difference is he could, we can't, or won't." The words bit, yet Tim had just helped Lauren make a point, to climb a mountain she'd been up before. "Don't you see?" she implored. "He wasn't saying anything that's not true or that we didn't know already. She's probably a little too robust for the Bay, that she wouldn't point as high as a sloop. And let's face it, off the wind in light air, she is pretty sluggish. She's out of her element on a July day on the Chesapeake."

"I know that."

She looked at him. "We both do. It was the whole point with *Breezeway*. Someday we'd venture out, fulfill a dream. Wasn't it a dream for both of us?"

"You know it was."

"Was?"

"'Is, I mean. Still is, of course.'"

"We bought her three years ago."

"I'm aware of that."

Their order came, a temporary lull in the sparring that in the past had led nowhere. "This will be our fourth season with her on the Bay," Lauren said. "When people head to the Caribbean, they go in the fall. You know the saying: 'If not now, when?'"

"This discussion always comes back to the same dilemma," he said. "We agree it's risky to just take off sailing on the ocean without having done it before. Even Blake said that. People do it, but it's not smart, or safe. You hear horror stories. So how do you get the experience?"

Lauren smiled. "You buy it. And take it with you."

"What are you talking about?"

"We hire Blake."

"What?"

"We pay him to sail along on the first leg. From the Chesapeake to a destination in the Caribbean. He coaches, teaches, we pay attention and learn."

"Why would he do that?"

"What do you think he makes in a month at the boatyard? Fifteen bucks an hour, if that? Say, times forty–"

"Less taxes."

"Right. So, what? Fifteen hundred a month, give or take. We pay him something like two-thousand, in cash, tax free, plus airfare home."

"Wow. This is a new one. Are you serious?"

"Completely serious. And it's not really new, not unusual at all. People hire captains to go along with them for part of a blue water trip. I did a Google search. All kinds of listings turned up."

"Yeah, I've seen them. The thing is, the guys you're talking about are licensed captains."

"Those licensed captains start at $400 a day."

He shook his head. "We don't even know this guy."

"Agreed. But we're not adopting him. And besides, we've got plenty of time to get to know him better. If we're not comfortable, we back away."

They paused, each marshaling the next rejoinder. "I think" Lauren said, aligning the front and rear sights of her logic, "that we have to look at this as tuition. A cram course in blue water sailing. One we agree we need before we set off on our own, and one we can afford."

"Assuming he wants to go along."
"Of course."
"How will we know that?"
"Ask him."

TOM HITCHCOCK

5

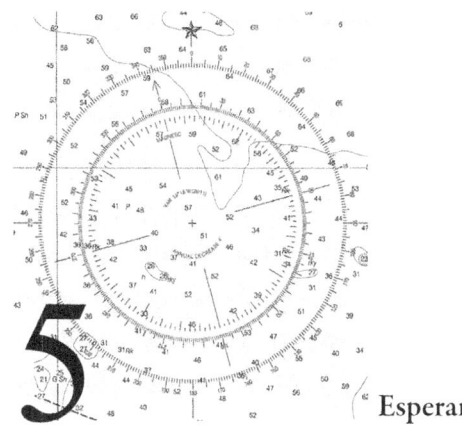

November
Esperanza anchorage, Vieques, PR

The passage between the main island of Puerto Rico and Vieques channeled the wind, funneling it in a way that gave it a freshened kick, powering *Breezeway* southwest through the strait. But as they rounded the southwest headland of Vieques and turned east toward the anchorage at Esperanza, the wind dropped. *Breezeway* slowed. They were now in the lee of the island.

Blake reacted without hesitation to the boat's dawdling pace. "Time for the engine," he said. "I think we've done enough sailing, don't you? It'll take us another hour at least to get there at this rate. I'm done. Let's step on the gas, get the hook down and get ashore. I need a burger and a beer or two or three." He looked at Lauren. "What do you think?"

She smiled wanly and nodded. "Sounds wonderful."

Blake guided the boat between the two islets that formed a doorway to one portion of the anchorage. He noticed two white mooring balls ahead. Securing the boat to one of these was a simple matter of picking up the mooring line and dropping the loop over a cleat on the boat. Far less labor intensive and more secure than anchoring, the nominal nightly fee was well worth it in the short term. "Let's pick up a mooring. We owe it to ourselves at least for a few nights."

"Done," she said, though most likely she would be paying for it.

Notwithstanding the fact that a seagoing boat is, in its entirety, inanimate—the sum total of its engineered functionality—it is not at all uncommon for the owner, or a crew that has spent time aboard the vessel, to bestow it with a persona, a human characteristic viewed with a certain fondness and loyalty. Thus, when *Breezeway* swung gently on the mooring ball, when her sails and gear, the knees and stringers of the hull, were relieved of their duties of harnessing the wind and leaning into tons of oncoming water, it was easy to imagine that she'd come to a well-deserved rest. Blake turned off the engine, and it was quiet. They were one: Blake, Lauren, and *Breezeway*.

The two sailors sagged with fatigue. Physical and mental strain, the oppressive presence of guilt, had weighed on them, beaten them down: The cumulative psychic toll of having cast another human being, Lauren's husband, into a darkened, wave-tossed sea. It was impossible to look back and not see it for the profoundly shameful transgression it was. Viewed through one lens, the episode, best case, was a tragic lapse, judgment distorted by panic and confusion and the belief that Tim was already dead. Through another lens, it was an irredeemable act of callous, self-absorbed expediency that would shock and horrify most decent people.

Lauren collapsed into Blake's arms. "My God, I'm so tired. I just—"

He held her, stroked her hair, and said nothing. He was limp, drained by the emotional trauma, the lack of sleep, jerking awake in the cabin below in the few hours of his off watch, reliving the nightmare when he was supposed to be sleeping.

"Let's go get some dry land under our feet," he said. "I know a great place to chill, get something to eat and a few beers, then it's only a short walk to a nice beach with showers—a real, hot shower. Sound good?"

"Sounds way better than good."

Blake untethered the dinghy from the harness that had secured it to the transom, wrestling and maneuvering it into the water. He attached the small outboard, getting it started after some tinkering and half a dozen pulls. They set off for the dock jutting out from the small town's waterfront.

The restaurant was a popular place along the main street, open air and facing out over the harbor's blue and azure water. Their food orders had come and gone, and they sat with beer mugs half full. Amid the prolonged silences that had accompanied the meal, Blake attempted morale-boosting small talk. "That was good," he said. "I really enjoyed it. We were overdue for an infusion of junk food."

She had neither the will nor the energy for idle patter. Actually, the food was average, but it did hit the spot after thirteen days of improvised fare thrown together from canned goods, dry stores and pre-packaged foods. When it was only the two of them on the last leg to reach Vieques, they ate just to stave off hunger before collapsing and trying to catch a few hours' sleep.

She sipped her beer and said, finally, "I've gotta call my parents."

"Okay, I figured that. Do we need to talk about it?"

"I don't know. Why? Talk about it how?"

"Nothing. Just that we don't want to drop any breadcrumbs that could lead people—you know, the wrong people—right to our doorstep. We have to be careful."

"You mean I have to be careful, right? You don't think I know that?"

"I do," he said. "Sorry. It's just that you're tired, hell we're both tired. They may want to know all kinds of details. So, tiptoe your way through those. Okay? That's all."

"Okay. Be right back." She walked over to a railing that ran alongside The Malecon, a promenade that fronted the beach on one side and faced the shops, restaurants and smaller hotels on the other. Dialing as she walked, she took deep breaths, several in fact. Her mother answered.

"Hi, Mom, it's me, Lauren," she said.

"Lauren? Oh my God. I can't believe it. Are you there?" Her mother called out to Lauren's father, "Elliott! It's Lauren! She's calling from, wherever. Doesn't matter. She's safe, thank God! Aren't you?"

"Yeah, mom. Everyone's fine. We're here. Puerto Rico." She kept the geographical details to a minimum.

"So, your big adventure. Is it what you expected? Tell me."

Lauren looked around. "It's beautiful. Exotic. We just had lunch at this really funky place, all kinds of cruising people and expatriates. I'm overlooking a gorgeous beach right now. A whole other world." Only part of that was true.

"And Tim?" her mother asked. "He's doing well? And your other friend? What's his name? Drake?"

Lauren didn't correct her. "Yes, they're both fine."

"I can't wait to get your pictures on Facebook," her mother said. Lauren was quiet for a few moments. "Lauren? Sweetie?"

"Ah, I don't know. Facebook? Do I have to? God, it's so ... so, I don't know."

"So what? We want to see where you are. You and Tim and Drake in your tropical paradise."

"Who's we, Mom. Your friends? Dad?"

"Yeah! So? What's wrong with that?"

"Nothing, I guess."

"Can't wait to see them."

"Okay. I'll, um, do what I can. Right now we all need some sleep. Just wanted to check in and let you know we're all right."

"I'm glad to hear your voice, sweetie. Glad you're okay."

"Thanks, mom. I'll call you soon. I love you." As she hung up, she looked out over the water and allowed her shoulders to collapse in a spasm of quiet sobs.

DROWNING

When Blake and Lauren eventually returned to the boat, they made straight for the bunks in the v-berth and collapsed, falling onto them. And slept for twelve hours. When they had both awakened the next day, Blake reached for her, enfolding her in his arms. She welcomed the comforting sensation of an embrace, but it soon became apparent that Blake's cuddling had an agenda, an added, unspoken urgency.

He inched closer, positioning himself for the leadup to the next stages of intimacy.

At one point not so long ago, she would have encouraged Blake's advances. But not this time. "Wait," she said. "No, please. Let's not. I can't."

"Okay," he said. "You all right?"

"Yeah, I'm fine. It's just—"

"Just what?"

"Too, um, soon or something. Know what I mean?"

"I guess," he said, "sort of."

She sank back, wondering why Blake couldn't transcend the carnal yearnings of this moment and try to comprehend the larger issues. "The memory's too fresh," she said, "too awful. God, Blake, it's still right there, instant replay in my head."

"Lauren, you and I made love many times behind Tim's back."

"That was different! He wasn't dead. I could compartmentalize our affair when we were back in Maryland."

"Compartmentalize," he said. "I don't know what that means."

"It means keeping things separate, putting things in different drawers mentally. But now I can't compartmentalize helping you roll his corpse overboard into the ocean and then having sex with you in this v-berth a week later. Don't you get it?"

By now whatever intentions Blake had a few minutes ago had faded. From the outset, a large part of the attraction between he and Lauren had been the free-ranging raucousness of the sex. They had taken each other to new frontiers. Now, though, it seemed possible that a door was closing on that part of it.

"Listen," she said. "I heard an expression once in D.C. This guy said something about 'dancing on a grave.' It was a figure of speech. It meant taking too much joy in someone's defeat. But that's what I'd feel like now if we made love: like dancing on Tim's grave, celebrating somehow." She dropped her head as a tear ran down her cheek. "I don't know where our marriage was headed. Nowhere good, probably. But for God's sake, wherever it was going I never wanted him dead."

It was quiet for a few moments. The boat rocked slightly; a breeze blew down through the partially opened hatch above their heads.

"I'm sorry," he said. "I should have realized."

She took his hand and held it. "We just need to work through this. We need some time, that's all."

He sat up, smiling. "Let's get cleaned up, go ashore and get some breakfast. What do you say?"

She smiled too. He didn't mention who would be paying for it.

Six people surrounded Tim Jameson's bed in an ICU in the UF Health Trauma Center. Two were Special Agents from the Jacksonville office of the Coast Guard Investigative Service. Three were physicians, and one was an ICU nurse. An array of monitors framed Tim's bed. Tim was comatose, unable to eat. An IV tube supplied his nutrition; a ventilator assisted his limited breathing ability.

The physicians and agents stood back just a bit as the nurse circled around the bed, checking and adjusting equipment, eyeing the monitors.

"Is it just me," said Troy Barrett, one of the Special Agents, "or does he seem a little better than when I was here a few days ago?"

Jenna Yang was an ICU hospitalist, a physician dedicated to the singular task of overseeing and coordinating the care of ICU patients with the cadre of specialists involved. "He is slightly better," she said.

"Better being relative. But you're right. His core body temperature is back to normal and his breathing is better. We may be able to take him off the ventilator soon. I'd like to see a more robust heart rate, but it's steady, better than it's been."

"Still no idea who he is?" asked Joel Robertson, another of the doctors, a trauma specialist.

"No sir," Barrett said. "We've put out notices, announcements, press releases, PSAs, searched thousands of square miles of ocean—nothing. And it doesn't look like our John Doe's gonna be talking any time soon. Am I right?"

Yang looked at the third doctor. "This is Dr. Nichols," she said, "a neurologist. You want to take this one Doc?"

"Um, sure," Nichols said. "So, the patient suffered a severe brain injury, which we pretty much all know." He set up an iPad on the overbed table at the foot of Tim's bed, swiping through images. "These are MRI and CT scan images from the night he was admitted, and these are from two days ago." He turned to the two CGSI special agents. "It may be hard for you to interpret what these mean exactly, but suffice it to say John Doe is lucky he's alive."

Pointing to dark blotches with the point of a pen, he said, "These are areas of bleeding and severe swelling, inflammation. Here you can see areas of trauma, damage to brain tissue. Under certain circumstances, those injuries would be enough to cause death."

"Why didn't they?" asked the other special agent.

"Dr. Robertson and I have a theory, not much more than that. We can share it with you in a few minutes. But in the meantime, let's talk about John Doe's prognosis."

Barrett was hesitant. "Right here?"

"I'm pretty sure he can't hear us." Nichols said. "At any rate, this is an EEG readout, results from an electroencephalogram done earlier today. Again, may be hard for you to make sense of some of it, but these are brain waves, electrical impulses the brain emits. These patterns are very abnormal, indicative of a brain struggling to repair itself. And finally, there are tests we do to measure the depth and severity of a coma. Low is not good, higher is better."

"How did John Doe score?"

He came in at a three when he was admitted. That's very low. He's really not much better than that now. Taken together, the prognosis for this patient typically would be very poor."

It was quiet for a few moments. Until Robertson looked at Nichols and said, "Except."

Barrett said, "Except what, doc?"

"Dr. Nichols and I theorize that hypothermia may have helped John Doe." Robertson explained how physicians have been treating some cardiac arrest victims with induced hypothermia to reduce damage to the brain from the lack of oxygen. "We think as John Doe's body started to cool and hypothermia set in, it was like putting an ice pack on an injury. It slowed everything down, slowed the blood flow, mitigated the inflammation and tissue damage."

"The dichotomy is this," said Nichols. "If he'd been in the water another hour or so the hypothermia might well have killed him. But if his body hadn't been chilled by the hypothermia, the effects of the brain injury almost certainly would have killed him."

As a group they turned toward the patient, reading their own respective tea leaves, each contingent grappling with its own questions and concerns.

Facing Dr. Nichols, Barrett said, "Doc, I know you're not a medical examiner, and I'm sorry to ask this, but is there any way you can venture any kind of theory—a guess, even? Anything at all about what might have caused this brain injury?"

"Agent Barrett—"

"Troy, please."

"Okay, Troy. At one time I had an interest in forensic neurology. I've dabbled in it, kept current with the literature. I've been called in to consult on investigations. I can offer guesses only, but it's all off the record as long as you're okay with that."

"I'm fine with it. We have nothing else at this point."

Nichols walked toward the bed. "John Doe suffered an especially nasty contusion on the lower right rear of his skull. When I see the bleeding and swelling resulting from it, it's hard to imagine any average person generating the leverage and power needed to hit someone that hard, especially on a boat in the middle of the ocean. I mean, it would have to have been a big swing with something pretty heavy. Plus, when I've seen trauma from blunt instrument assaults, they're mostly blows that come down on the top or side of the head. And the bruising in this case is in a circular, diffused pattern. Bottom line, I don't know what hit his head."

"Could he have fallen?"

"That's as plausible as a deliberate assault, I suppose. Would have to be a helluva fall, though, from some height. But we're just guessing now anyway. No point in that."

"And there's no way of knowing when, or if, he ever wakes up."

"No. You hear stories of people suddenly coming awake with full command of their senses. It does happen, I guess, but I tend to discount the miracle aspects of those accounts. Even if John Doe does finally regain consciousness, more than likely he'd need weeks or months of therapy to achieve even minimal levels of cognition. But mostly patients like this lapse into persistent vegetative states, or, sadly, eventually pass away. In the absence of any family, who knows where this will end up?"

Troy Barrett and Neal Franklin, his CGIS special agent colleague, made their way out of the Trauma Center complex in silence. Silence reigned as well during the five-minute drive to the Coast Guard sector office in Jacksonville. Both were lost in thought, turning over theories and scenarios.

When they reached the office and gravitated toward the coffee maker, Barrett finally asked, "Well, partner, you got it figured out yet?"

"Sure I do," said Franklin. "But I'm keeping it to myself."

Barrett laughed. "C'mon. Share it with me."

"All kidding aside," Franklin said, "what about this? John Doe climbs up the mast. He's got some kind of problem aloft. The weather was a little rough that night. He falls, the boat is heeled over to leeward. He hits his head on something on the deck–"

"Like what?"

"I don't know. A winch?"

"Interesting, that could explain the–"

"Great minds thing alike."

"How's he wind up overboard?"

"He's out cold. The deck is pitching. He slides under the lifeline into the water."

"Going up the mast might explain why he wasn't hooked to a safety harness."

"Good point. Plus the life vest and the strobe."

"The thing is," Barrett said, "if anything like your theory happened, I'm not really sure what we're investigating. There's no crime here if this was an accident, a single-hander falling overboard off his own boat."

"Or, there might be a crime," Franklin said, "and we just don't know it yet."

"A riddle, wrapped in a mystery, inside an enigma."

"Somebody famous say that?"

"Yeah," Barrett said. "Churchill."

"Thought so."

For all the panicked bumbling aboard *Breezeway* in those chaotic few moments, for all the impulsive, haphazard decision-making, the irony was that if Blake and Lauren had deliberately set out to mystify and confound investigators, they could not have done a better job. They were horror-struck when the strobe on Tim's life vest activated, a blunder with potentially disastrous consequences. Yet the strobe and life vest were what had Barrett and Franklin scratching their heads, unable to make them fit into any scenario involving a crime.

"Well," Franklin said, "maybe we'll get lucky and John Doe'll wake up and tell us what happened."

"There's that, but there's also the fact that John Doe didn't live in a bubble."

"Meaning ..."

"Meaning damn near everybody, no matter what, has family or friends, neighbors, co-workers, something. They call it a web of relationships."

"So?"

"So, nobody just disappears down a hole from that web without somebody wondering what happened to the guy, eventually."

"So we wait," Franklin said, "for John Doe to get his wake-up call, or for his ex-wife to start down the warpath looking for her alimony checks."

"Yeah. Something like that."

6

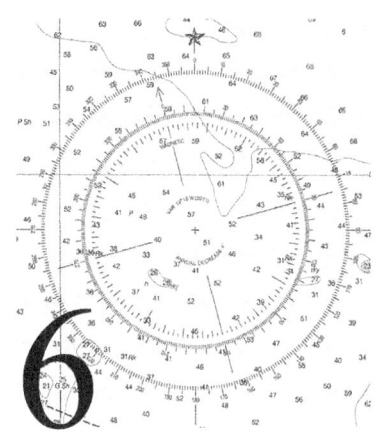

Eight months earlier
April, Tilghman Island, Maryland

The three of them, Tim, Lauren and Blake, sat around a high-top table set apart in a far corner of the bar. Lauren divvied up the last of the beer in a pitcher among their three glasses and held the empty up as a signal to the bartender to bring another.

They'd been talking about sailing, but the totality of Tim and Lauren's experience paled alongside Blake's. His stories and insights slowly took center stage. And that was fine with Lauren; it suited where she wanted to steer the conversation in the first place. In the subtle, delicate minuet of male egos that often wafts just below the surface in these situations, Tim was only grudgingly drawn into the salty, authoritative ring of Blake's accounts.

Tim and Lauren were not armchair sailors. But during most of the sailing season on the Chesapeake Bay, conditions ranged from moderate to placid. A reasonably well-found boat in capable hands was rarely in real danger. On occasion, vicious thunderstorms with blasts of high winds would roar across the Bay. As intense and frightening as they could be, they were usually short-lived. Other times, those storms were precursors of cold fronts, whose passage was ushered in by nor'westers, strong winds that whipped the Bay into a froth of steep, choppy waves. But a boat with the heft and muscle of *Breezeway* could take almost any of it in stride.

And none of it compared to surfing down the face of thirty-foot combers in a Force 8 gale in the North Atlantic, fighting for hours on end, as Blake told it, to keep the boat from yawing sideways. His style of storytelling was low-key, shrugging as he related episodes that sounded hair-raising to the average ear. His unaffected, what-the-hell tone gave his accounts an added layer of unintended drama, unnerving and compelling at the same time. Even Tim, his reticence notwithstanding, recalled with pride Blake's evaluation that he would go anywhere on *Breezeway*. A guy who'd done what he'd done, saying that about his boat, touched something in him. Like the owner of an untested thoroughbred languishing in its stall, Tim felt a sudden push to put *Breezeway* through her paces, to let her finally show her mettle on the open ocean.

Neither Tim nor Lauren shared a desire to battle gales in the North Atlantic. But Lauren, especially, was pulled to the sense of adventure underlying the next best thing, accompanied by the reassurance of sailing with someone who had been there and done that.

It was quiet for a moment after the new pitcher came and glasses were refilled. "So," Blake said, "enough war stories. I've been in bars with blue water sailors where the waves get bigger and the wind blows harder every time somebody tells one of them." He smiled.

Lauren looked at Tim and then down at her beer glass for second. "I guess that brings us to why we're here," she said. "A few days ago, you said you'd go anywhere aboard *Breezeway*. We want to take you up on that. We want to take her from here to the Caribbean, outside, with you along as captain, or whatever, on the first leg. The idea being that you're our training wheels, till we can get up and ride on our own." She pinched her shoulders up and grinned at Blake. "Does that sound too ridiculous?"

Blake looked at her over the rim of his glass as he drained about a third of it. "No," he said, "not too ridiculous. Depending."

"Depending on what?" Tim said.

"Depending on details," Blake answered. "Lots of details. Like, for instance, is this going to be a paying gig?"

"Yes, of course," Lauren said. "Of course."

"That's good to know," he replied. "But we should talk actual numbers before we waste much time on anything else. You understand."

Tim cleared his throat. "We understand. I like numbers. We're proposing a two-thousand dollar fee, we pay all expenses, for a two or three-week voyage to a destination in the Caribbean, and we pay your airfare home."

Blake took another sip. "So, let's figure 18 days, just to split the difference. I'm your training wheels, like you say, but it's pretty much a 24 hour-a-day job." He got out his phone and started punching numbers into a calculator. "Twenty-four hours times 18 days is 430 hours, roughly. Divide 2,000 by 430 hours and, let's see, that comes to less than five bucks an hour."

"It'll be cash, tax-free," Tim said.

"Tim, my tax bracket is somewhere way down here," Blake said, motioning downward with his palm. "Doesn't make much difference."

"And there's the airfare," Lauren said.

"None of that goes in my pocket, can't spend it. All it does is get me home."

Tim and Lauren cast their eyes downward, into their beer glasses.

"Look, guys, you have to remember, I used to go on boat delivery trips. I know what captains used to charge."

Tim said, "I assume you have a captain's license?"

"Used to, 50-Ton Master. But I let it expire."

Tim was surprised. "Really?"

"Yeah. They're good for five years, but when it comes time to renew it costs money and there's a bunch of red tape hassles. I wasn't using it so I couldn't see the point." There was another reason Blake had forfeited his license, but he barely knew these people and figured his past was his business.

Tim thought for a moment. "When you went on those boat delivery trips, were you ever the captain?"

"No," Blake said. "It takes a lot of sea time and a Near Coastal license for that. Plus you need the contacts. Insurance companies are real careful."

"So you weren't making what the captain made," Tim said. Lauren was quiet. She hated bargaining, but Tim was in his element now. "And I'm guessing two thousand is more than you make in two or three weeks at the marina," Tim added.

Blake nodded. "True. But I also get to sleep in a nice dry, warm, motionless bed every night. Eight hours straight if I want. I can eat burgers, or pizza, or bacon and eggs at a table that's not moving." It was quiet again. Finally, Blake said, "The thing is, guys, I'm not gonna work for five dollars an hour. Sorry. If we were talking twice that, somewhere around four-thousand, say, that starts to make it worth my while."

"Oh, Blake," Lauren said, "that's just not in our budget." Disappointment resonated in her voice. Blake did some quick mental calculations. Tim had mentioned his ownership of an accounting firm. Not hard to imagine that situation putting him in a very comfortable income bracket. Blake wasn't sure exactly what Lauren did, but he knew where they lived and was familiar with the dwelling—a handsome waterfront home newly built just a few years ago. He knew as well that their 37-ft. Island Packet would go for about $400,000 on the open market. Of course his asking price was within their budget. They were just trying to get him on the cheap.

"Why don't we try this," Tim said. He punched some numbers into the calculator in his phone. "Why don't we split the difference, make it three thousand, and put a time limit on the number of days, like 15. That brings the hourly rate up. And if we assume that not every day will be a 24-hour shift—after all, you'll be sleeping part of that time—I think that makes it a fairer deal."

Blake narrowed his eyes. They were right in one respect. Three grand was a helluva lot more than he made in two weeks at the boatyard. And there was a fair amount of drudgery and sameness about his work. The trip would be a good change in scenery. He looked at Lauren—in more ways than one, he thought.

"Okay," Blake said. "You're right. Getting close to fair. So for now we'll say we have a deal on the money part of it." He reached over to shake Tim's hand. "I'm good with that. But there's a lot of details to get straight, lot of work to do."

"I'm sure," Tim said.

"Like, let's start with when you were thinking of going."

"Oh my God," Lauren said. "There's a ton of loose ends we'd have to tie up. But we'll go along with whatever you think is best. Isn't that the whole point?"

"I guess. But we can't go any time soon no matter what. This is the busy season at the yard. Darryl would shoot me if I bailed now. And by June it's getting on to hurricane season. Especially if you want to go the offshore route. Have to be crazy to go then, or really any time before October. I'd look at early November."

Lauren was beaming. "This is so awesome. A date, something to shoot for." She reached over, squeezed Tim's hand and raised her glass in a toast. "To *Breezeway*," she said, "and to us. May she carry us safely to lower latitudes."

Blake smiled as he looked back and forth at the two of them. "You know, the thing about a trip like this, it helps a lot if the crew is simpatico. It's a long time in cramped space. Something to think about."

"You know what Blake?" Lauren said. "I've just got this feeling." She smiled, a dazzling wide smile. "Something tells me we're gonna be fine. Maybe even better than fine."

Nine months later
December, UF Health Trauma Center, Jacksonville, Florida

A nurse hovered around Tim's bed in the ICU, checking, making notes in an iPad, adjusting the tubes that delivered nourishment, fluids and oxygen to Tim's inert form. Scanning the neon-tinted numbers and graphs on monitors mounted above and beside the bed, she happened to look down for a brief second at Tim's face. His eyes were open. She stopped, stunned, and then leaned over closer to his face.

"Sir!" she shouted, not knowing how to address him. She got nose-to-nose with him, yelling,

"Sir! Hello? Can you hear me?" Tim's eyes were fixed, glazed, staring straight up, showing no sign of recognition or reaction. She grabbed a penlight and shined it directly into each eye. His pupils reacted, sluggishly, then his eyelids closed again.

"Damn," she breathed, reaching for her phone to call Dr. Nichol's answering service.

7

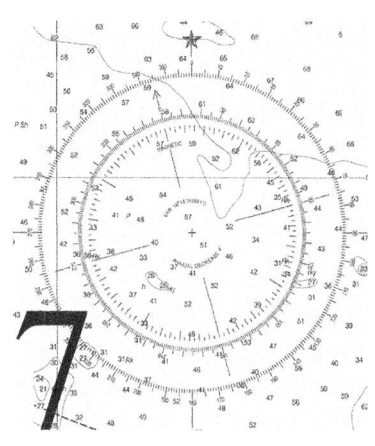

December
Esperanza anchorage, Vieques, PR

Blake was schooling Lauren in the fine points of inspecting and maintaining the myriad components of a sailboat's gear. It was now, during downtime, he said, when attention to detail would save you heartbreak or even disaster when underway in a stiff breeze and waves rising higher than your head as you stood behind the wheel.

"There's always something waiting to break," he said, "and it'll happen at the worst possible time. Take care of the gear, it'll take care of you." He took her on a tour of snap shackles and screw pin shackles, and the halyards, sheets and wire rope connections that formed the sinew of *Breezeway's* running and standing rigging. He showed her how to lubricate winches, check halyards and sheets for wear, change them end for end if necessary. How to check the engine oil, how to bleed air from the diesel fuel lines, and how to change a fuel filter. Unfurl the sails and look for signs of wear or chafing—you can't always just spring for a new mainsail or jib, but at least you know it's something that needs attention—sooner rather than later. "*Breezeway's* a tough lady," he said, "but salt and wind and physics always take their toll. No boat is bulletproof. Check everything, all the time, assume the worst, and you might be okay."

Lauren came up through the companionway with two cold beers. The tutorial in boat maintenance had reached an appropriate time for a break. Blake's conditional benediction of "you might be okay" assumed an eventual transfer of *Breezeway's* stewardship from his hands to Lauren's. When, or under what circumstances, was unknown, and as yet hadn't been brought up.

His original deal with Tim and Lauren had specified a tenure of fifteen days. He and Lauren were long past that point by now. He could only imagine how his boss at the boatyard was reacting to his extended absence, no doubt embarking on a search for his replacement. And though Blake had collected one half of his fee upfront, before departing Tilghman Island, the other half was still outstanding. But because Lauren had been footing all the bills for their sustenance since arriving in Vieques, he was in no position to raise the topic of the remainder of his unpaid fee.

He and Lauren were in an emotional and financial no man's land. They hadn't bothered to look ahead to envision how the last act of their lust and infatuation would play out. But now it was here, minus Tim. And neither of them had a script. The lack of one made for periods of dead air, like now. Until Lauren could no longer pretend she hadn't heard what Blake revealed in the crucible of those moments the morning following their calamity, when his patience had worn thin with her second thoughts. She looked at him evenly: "What you said out there, when we were off of Florida, was it true? You were really in prison?"

It was something he should have been prepared for but wasn't. She had obviously stored it away and chose now to raise the issue.

"Yeah," he said, "I was."

"You never mentioned that to us."

"Didn't think I needed to. Would it have made a difference?"

"I don't know. Might have to Tim."

"Well now I guess it doesn't, does it."

She tilted her head. "Depends. Are you dangerous?"

"Dangerously naïve, maybe," he said. "That's about it."

"What did you do?"

"I didn't do anything. I did a boat delivery with the wrong people, that's all."

"The dog ate my homework kind of thing?"

"No, not that simple. I hooked up with these two guys. They needed a third hand to deliver a 47-foot Beneteau from Fort Lauderdale to Annapolis. They offered me a lot, too much. Even airfare to get there. I should have figured something wasn't right. We pull into the marina in Annapolis and DEA's waiting for us. Somebody ratted on somebody. It took the dogs about two minutes to find the cocaine. Twenty kilos. A million and a half, maybe two million street value. Next thing I know guys in blue windbreakers are leading me away in cuffs."

"You didn't know?"

"Nope. I didn't. God's truth. It's not that hard to bury forty pounds of cocaine on a 47-foot boat."

"Jeeze. Wrong place at the wrong time."

"That's it. My father got me a good lawyer. Why I don't know. These days he wants nothing to do with me. The lawyer managed to convince them I wasn't in on the delivery. They had the other guys under surveillance, but I never showed up on the tapes. But I still had to do time. Made a plea deal, accessory to drug trafficking. Two years in the Federal Correctional Institution, McKean, Pennsylvania. That's the real story behind what happened to my captain's license, in case you were wondering. Anyway, I did sixteen months and got paroled."

Lauren was quiet. "Want another beer?"

"Sure."

When she came back up into the cockpit, she bounced, reanimated by something. "So what was it like? Prison."

He looked at her and thought, what kind of question is that? It was prison. "My lawyer hired this guy, an ex-con, a prison consultant. He made his living off guys like me, people who were fresh meat, scared, and no idea what to expect. He schooled me in the code of conduct. There is one, believe it or not. I was lucky in a way. McKean was a medium-security joint. Not too many hard cases, mostly drug offenses like mine, or embezzlers, money launderers, corrupt politicians, that kind of stuff. But you still had to learn to stay inside the guard rails to avoid trouble."

"Like what?"

"Like, keep to yourself, don't gamble or do drugs, don't accept any favors, don't stare at another con, show respect, don't bitch about your sentence, don't go into another guy's cell unless you're invited, whatever food you're not gonna eat offer it to whoever might want it, never reach across another guy's tray, lift weights, work out, don't back down from a fight, keep your distance from the guards, never, ever snitch, whatever you saw you didn't see anything, and so on. The law of the jungle."

Lauren took a swig of beer. "Okay, here goes. A dumb question: no sex?"

"What? No, of course not."

"No conjugal visits?"

"No. They didn't have those. And besides I had no one to conjugate with."

She laughed. "So …"

"So yeah. That answer your question?"

"Think so. It was kind of like we are now."

"Right, but for sixteen months."

"Whoa. I don't think I could last that long."

"I didn't have a choice," he said.

"But now you do."

"Didn't know it was my choice. It never really was."

She stood from her side of the cockpit and moved next to him. "Oh, come on. It was mutual, you know that. You could have had me any time you wanted. I couldn't stop you."

"What about now?"
"Try me."
"A conjugal visit?"
"Yeah," she breathed. "A conjugal visit." She stood and pulled off her t-shirt. Unbuttoning her shorts, she backed down the companionway steps, lapsing into a melodramatic breathlessness. "Oh, baby," she said, "I've missed you so much."

He caught on, picking up his lines in the script. "You sure you haven't fucked any other guys?" He pulled her close, roughly.

"No, no! I swear I haven't," she said, dropping her shorts. "Just you, baby. I only want you."

Her creativity electrified him. He pushed her backward into the v-berth, stripping off his shirt and shorts, and lunged. She guided him in, and it was off to the races—boisterous, unrestrained, frenzied. The voltage of pent-up desire heightened by unrelieved tension. When it finally wound down, it left them gasping, drenched, chests heaving. He flopped over on his back. They both gazed up at the ceiling of the v-berth, pondering the implications of this spontaneous burst of passion.

Blake wondered about her metaphor, that having sex would be the equivalent of "dancing on Tim's grave." How did she square that with the play-act sex involving a conjugal prison visit? Her thoughts paralleled his. Where did that wantonness come from? Why? She knew enough about Blake to know he wasn't husband material. But damn, the chemistry, the torrid sex. She'd been married long enough, though, to know that torrid sex counted only for so much, and at any rate with Tim it never really approached that description.

She needed Blake until she was capable of managing the boat on her own. More than that, she needed him as a hedge against being alone. Tropical paradise notwithstanding, for a woman to captain a sailboat on her own in the Caribbean was not without some degree of risk.

Blake, being of limited means, needed the financial sustenance of Lauren's access to the Jameson's bank account. It had crossed their minds, too, in the days since the incident at sea, that there was a mutual dependence stemming from the very real possibility that they'd been co-participants in serious crimes. As long as they were together, they could be reasonably sure one was not preparing to sell out the other in the hopes of cutting in line for a better deal. Once they'd gone their separate ways, however, that possibility would always be a wild card.

A few days later, they'd taken the dinghy ashore for errands. Interspersed with the errands was an interlude for a few beers at the local waterfront bar and hangout. Along with tourists, cruisers like Blake and Lauren, whether anchored out for two days or two months, were regular patrons.

With the Christmas season approaching, the bar's sound system was featuring a selection of holiday music, much of it with a distinctly Caribbean flavor, reggae or an energized salsa beat. The effect on Lauren was twofold, an odd mixture of homesickness and nostalgia, coupled with a delight in the contrast between the two styles of music. Traditional Christmas music at home was mostly slow, maudlin and mopey, ground into one's consciousness through years of endless repetition. And at this time of year in those latitudes the days grew shorter and darker, and colder.

Here, with bright sun and warm breezes rustling palm fronds, the Christmas music made you want to get up and dance. The two sensations sloshed back and forth in her. This setting was something she'd dreamed of—a bar populated with boaters and expatriates who had opted out of the life where she'd just come from. Yet some of the sloshing recalled holidays with Tim, her family, close friends, fireplaces, Christmas trees. It was oddly incongruent. This was where she wanted to be, but not at the expense of the trauma that had amputated her so totally from anything and everything familiar.

She and Blake sipped the last of their beers, lost in the buzz of the music and the ambiance. Blake felt a slap on his shoulder. He turned.

"Jesus, if it isn't my old shipmate Blake," the backslapper said. "Of all the places to run into you. Man, I can't believe it. How the hell have you been?"

Blake pivoted, paused, and did a hesitant homie handshake with the guy, palm to palm, fingers wrapped around the back of the hand. "Dude, man, it's good to see you." He couldn't remember the guy's name.

"So, what are you doin' here?" backslapper said.

"Just chillin'," Blake said. "Trying to figure out which way's next. You know how it goes."

"I do. Totally." The backslapper turned to Lauren. "And who's this fine young thing?"

Blake stiffened a bit. "The lady's name is Lauren. If you talk to her at all, tip your hat when you do so and keep it respectful. I insist."

"Okay, well, yes sir," backslapper said. "I get it."

"Good."

Wow, thought Lauren. Chivalrous, authoritative, and hellacious in bed. Too bad his earning potential would always be so limited.

"You here on a boat?" backslapper asked.

"Yeah."

"Which one?"

Blake nodded out toward the anchorage. "The cutter rig, over there."

"Nice," backslapper said. "Yours?"

"Nope, fraid not."

"Oh. You doin' a charter gig?"

Blake's instincts from federal prison kicked in. "Dude, you're asking a whole lot of questions, but the problem is I don't know who I'm talking to. I don't even recall your name."

"Oh, right. Sorry about that," backslapper said. "Andy. Andy Fallon."

"Nice seeing you again, Andy," Blake said. "Recognized the face, just couldn't connect it with a name."

Lauren just smiled, faintly.

Blake turned the interrogatory around. "So what are you up to these days, Andy?"

"Ah, same stuff. Boat deliveries mostly. Just got done with one: Norfolk to St. Croix. I'm lookin' for a trip back north, but it's the wrong time of year goin' that way. But I'll hang out for a while. Somethin'll shake loose. You been there, right?"

"Yes, I have," Blake said, and then was quiet. Clearly, Andy was not going to learn more about Blake and his lady friend. Blake's reticence was almost awkward. Andy tried to cut through the stillness by shifting the focus to a neutral topic, one he figured would be of interest to any sailor who transited the Eastern Seaboard on the way back and forth between the Caribbean or the Bahamas.

"Um, anyway. So, don't know how long you've been here, but did you guys hear about the dude they found off Florida?"

Blake, in prison mode, turned slowly. "No. What dude?" Lauren felt an electric jolt shoot through her innards.

"Yeah, some guy. I heard a long-liner picked him up. He was half-dead. Christ, they were three-hundred miles offshore. Middle of fuckin'—oops, sorry—middle of nowhere, middle of the night. Goddam miracle."

Blake put his hand on Lauren's knee. He looked at Andy. "Where'd you hear this?"

"I heard it from a couple guys. Coast Guard sent out a Notice to Mariners, and broadcast advisories all over the place. 'Be on the lookout for this, the lookout for that.' One guy I know saw it in the paper in Brunswick."

Lauren thought back to the Coast Guard helicopter that had swooped down on them less than two days after the fact. Good god.

"Shit," said Andy, "you never know. Where in the hell a guy like that comes from, floats up out of nowhere. Last I heard he was still breathin', but who knows? Anyway, it's some story isn't it?"

"It is," Blake said. He dug out dollar bills to lay on the bar. They were his but coming from near the bottom of a diminishing pile. "Listen, Andy, it was good seeing you again. We've gotta be going. Hope you don't mind."

"No, no, gotta get goin' myself." He reached out to shake Blake's hand, "Till next time." He watched Blake and his sinewy lady friend walk away. Their departure was abrupt, out of character with the camaraderie prevalent among sailors and cruisers who reunite by chance and commune with one another in waterfront bars the length and breadth of the Caribbean and around the world. The couple's body language seemed oddly tense as they walked away. At one point she gestured with her hands as if agitated or upset.

Weird.

TOM HITCHCOCK

8

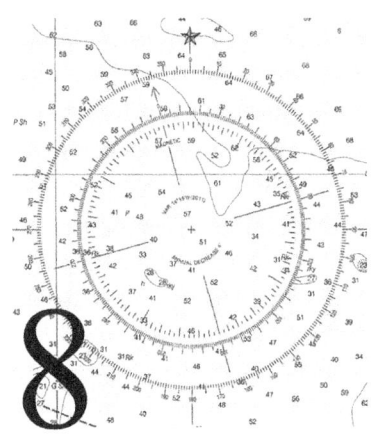

December
Easton, Eastern Shore of Maryland

A warm, soft light shone out through the windows of the accounting firm of Jameson and Cox. Inside, Christmas music sifted through muted bits of conversations. Against a backdrop of holiday decorations and two tables filled with crab and oyster hors d'oeuvres, the quiet clinks of wineglasses set the tone for a festive gathering. It was the firm's annual Christmas party, the first in many years at which Tim and Lauren Jameson had not graced the occasion as hosts.

Present were a handful of valued clients as well as Jameson and Cox staff. Almost all the clients knew of Tim and Lauren's plans to embark on a blue water trip south to the Caribbean. He'd made careful preparations to elevate two of the staff CPAs to partner status. In meetings with key clients before his departure, Tim had assured them that passing the baton between his oversight of their account and the management of their business would be seamless. Besides, he told them, he'd most likely be back in less than a year.

Some of them were uneasy. Over the years Tim Jameson had saved them thousands in taxes and helped them make decisions that built their businesses. Still, changing an accounting firm would be a disruptive undertaking, the logistics justified only when left with no other choice.

So, imagine the discomfiture of one of those clients when, in the course of normal holiday-gathering patter, he asked Dennis Cox, casually, "What have you heard from Tim? He enjoying life in some balmy anchorage somewhere?" And Dennis, after clearing his throat, replied, "Actually, um, we haven't heard from him."

The client cocked his head. "What? Really? That's odd isn't it?"

"Yes, it is. Disconcerting."

"Disconcerting is a good word for it," the client said. "What about Lauren?"

"Likewise, I'm afraid."

The client swirled the wine in his glass and took what could only be termed a gulp, more than a holiday-gathering sip. He was lost for a moment, sorting through the implications of what he'd just heard. "Has anybody heard from either one of them, as far as you know?"

"I don't know."

"I mean, it's the holidays. You don't call your partners and co-workers with holiday wishes? Family? Let everyone know you're okay?"

"Yeah, you'd think," Dennis said.

"Are you concerned?"

"A little. But then I keep in mind that the point was to get away. Sail over the horizon. Maybe checking with the office isn't part of that."

"Not even the Facebook nonsense? Twitter? That stuff?"

Dennis shook his head. "Tim thinks it's all nonsense too. I don't know about Lauren."

The client shifted from one foot to the other. "What about his family?"

"His father passed away a few years ago. I know his mother's had some health issues. I think he has a sister in Ohio."

The client edged over to the table with the wine, refilled his glass, and moved back to face Dennis. "You know, Dennis, Tim has a whole archive of institutional memory about my business. I'm betting some of these other clients are in the same position."

"We have digital and written records," Dennis said. "Tim spent hours briefing Kathleen and me on each client's account. And I was involved in a lot of the work on your business."

"It's just not the same."

"I realize that. But you're acting like he's missing in action or something. They went on a sailing trip, a voyage to the Caribbean, not the ends of the earth."

"Whatever. But if I were in your shoes, I think I'd be more proactive. Just saying."

Dennis put one hand in his pants pocket, cradling his glass with the other, looking at an ersatz Christmas tree in one corner, draped with decorations the staff pulled out of a box in the basement. "Away in the Manger" droned over the sound system. He bristled at the notion of a client telling him how to run the firm. Yet that client represented nine percent of the firm's revenue. If he infected other clients with his fears, it could trigger a gradual exodus.

The client sensed that Dennis was in a tough spot. "All I know," he said, "or think I know, is that under normal circumstances damn near anyone in their situation would contact their family or colleagues and let them know they were all right, especially at this time of year. Yes?"

"Yes."

"Okay. A few phone calls couldn't hurt."

Kathleen Sanders, the newly appointed partner, had drawn within earshot of the conversation. She smiled faintly when they turned to her. It would be reckless, she determined, like a loosed bowling ball, to hint at the whisperings she'd heard from farther south, near the tip of the Bay Hundred peninsula.

December, UF Health Trauma Center
Jacksonville, Florida

Agents Barrett and Franklin stood at the foot of Tim Jameson's bed in the Trauma Center ICU. They'd been called there by Dr. Nichols, the neurologist charged with monitoring Tim's care.

"So, Doc," Barrett said, "you called cause you've got news?"

"I do," Nichols said.

"Good news? Bad news? In-between news?"

Nichols smiled. "A little bit of good news, with a generous helping of in-between."

"In our business," Franklin said, "we'll take whatever we can get."

"The problem," Nichols said, "is there are so many shades of grey. I could have three different neurologists standing here and we'd get three different assessments. The brain is by far the most complex of God's designs."

Barrett turned to him. "You believe in God, Doc?"

Nichols paused. "I believe you can't study something as powerful and wondrous as the human brain and not entertain some notion that its designer meant for us to use it for higher purposes."

"Like?"

"Like trying to puzzle together what's happened to this man's brain, how nature, or God, will see him through it."

"God aside, Doc, what do you think?" Franklin said. "You called us here."

"I think our John Doe may be transitioning through two phases of consciousness. One's called wakefulness, the other awareness. His pupils are responding to light, he blinks when we touch his eyelids, and he responds to what we call painful stimuli—he opens his eyes. And sometimes he opens his eyes spontaneously."

"That's good," Barrett said.

"It is," Nichols said," It's the early stages of wakefulness. But here's where it gets complicated. You could snap your fingers right in front of his eyes, yell out his name, but he'll remain unfocused. His eyes are open, but he's not seeing or hearing, or responding. That's the in-between news. From here he could progress to what's called a minimally conscious state, transitioning to awareness, where he can respond to directives or questions that require him to think, like 'hold up your thumb' or 'nod your head if you're hungry.' Or, he could remain static, lapsing into a persistent vegetative state. Progressing through stages of a minimally conscious state and increasing awareness would be the most hopeful prognosis."

"And how likely do you think that is, Doc?" Barrett asked.

"I don't really know," Nichols said. "But I like the odds. He's made progress, the imaging shows signs of improvement, he's relatively young, and Dr. Robertson and I still like our theory of how the cold water helped mitigate the effects of the injury and the inflammation. I only wish we knew if he'd stopped breathing for any length of time."

Barrett jotted notes. Franklin tilted his head and said, "No way of knowing, but how's that important?"

"Any damage to the brain is worsened if it's been deprived of oxygen concurrent with an injury. The prospects for recovery are usually diminished."

"Well," Barrett said, "we don't know that, we don't know what happened to him. We don't know if or when he'll recover enough to tell us what happened."

"Doc," Franklin said, "how long will John Doe stay here in your ICU?"

"I'd say if he keeps progressing, he'll be transferred to a rehab facility soon. But he'll remain under my care."

Barrett finished jotting. "And only God and the fates know whether that'll happen."

"Correct."

"You'll call us with any noteworthy changes?"

"Of course."

"Thanks, Doc," Franklin said. They shook hands all around as the agents made their way out.

December – Esperanza, Vieques, PR

The lights along Esperanza's waterfront reflected across the water, soft and shimmering, dancing, as if accompanying the music drifting out over the anchored boats. Since Lauren and Blake arrived here, they'd been enchanted by the setting. As of their encounter with Andy the backslapper that afternoon, however, they were no longer enchanted. They were spooked.

Blake broke the pensive silence with one phrase: "How's your French?"

"Excuse me?"

"I said, how's your French?"

"Okay, I guess. Why?"

"You speak it?"

"Ca va. Pourquoi?" she responded.

"Excellent. Not sure what that means, but it's where we need to go. Soon as we can leave. Next three, four days."

"Where?"

"Guadeloupe. French West Indies."

"Why there?"

"I think we need to pull the door closed behind us, get some distance between us and what Andy and people like him may have heard."

Lauren thought back to what seemed like a marathon sail to get here, to Vieques. "How far is it?"

"Not far at all. Less than 300 miles. Two days, maybe not even that."

"If it's that close, how does it put enough distance behind us?"

Blake smiled. "It's not so much how far in mileage, but how far away it is culturally from places like here or the BVIs or the Bahamas."

"I don't get it."

"The Virgin Islands and the Bahamas attract a lot of U.S. sailors.

The islands are close, not too challenging, and everybody speaks English and takes U.S. dollars—suits the comfort level of a certain kind of aspiring or fledgling cruiser. That means you run into more people from up and down the East Coast, more chance of running into someone like Andy, who might've heard what he heard. I don't like the odds."

"You said French ... French how?"

"Guadeloupe is part of France, they call it a department. The people there are French citizens. They're friendly, very nice really, but most of them either can't or don't want to speak English. It's either French or Creole. If you ask whether they speak English, they just smile and shrug: 'Désolé, je ne parle Anglais.'"

"Sorry, I don't speak English."

"That's it! It's one of the few phrases I picked up. And they aren't really that sorry."

"So if it's part of France, what about customs, immigration, all that? Thought you said that's a problem."

"Normally, yeah. Not so much in Guadeloupe. That's the other beautiful part of this plan. There's a few customs check-in spots that are kind of relaxed. They put them in cafes or stores. Fill in a form on a desktop, print it, and get the owner of the business to stamp it."

Her eyes met his. He was taking her on the next leg of the adventure. She had little choice but to trust him, at least for now.

He took her hands. "You'll love it. It's got more of an international flair. Yachts from all over the world." He swept his arm toward the Esperanza shoreline. "Half these places could be in St. Thomas or on some cheesy Key West street with Jimmy Buffet music playing. Same vibe, people singing 'Cheeseburger in Paradise' thinking it's really cool. In Guadeloupe, if the wind changes and it gets too rolly you pull up the hook and move. The next anchorage is gorgeous and has a wonderful boulangerie ashore."

"And no Jimmy Buffet music."

"Right." He smiled. "No Jimmy Buffet music." He pulled her close. "Wanna play conjugal visit?"

"No," she said. "No need for that. Let's just be Lauren and Blake. The way it used to be. I couldn't get enough of it."

9

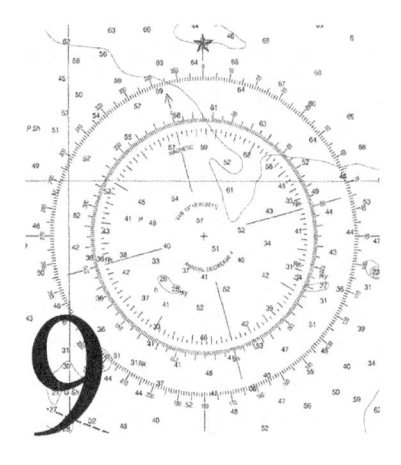

Six months earlier
June, Tilghman Island, Maryland

Tim, Lauren and Blake stood in *Breezeway's* cockpit. As it was buffeted by the wind, the boat yawed back and forth in its slip, pulled up short by the dock lines straining to keep it centered and away from the pilings.

Bright white clouds raced across a deep blue sky, driven by stiff gusts of wind. This was the kind of weather the three of them had looked forward to, with varying degrees of enthusiasm.

A front had passed through overnight, bringing with it the signature robust wind out of the northwest, blustery, insistent, building and pushing serrated ranks of foaming waves across the Chesapeake Bay. This day was to be a combination boot camp, training exercise and evaluation.

The Bay's configuration—shallow and narrow—was such that a 20-plus knot wind created waves that were steep and choppy. They came in closely stacked rows and broke sharply, offering little or no relief between one narrow trough and the abrupt wall of the next crest. When that wall met the bow of a boat traveling to windward, sheets of stinging spray would cascade aft, pounding at anything they met, whether gear or crew members.

Most boaters, sailors or power boaters, experienced and otherwise, opted to stay home under these conditions. Boating was supposed to be about pleasure. And unless there was no choice other than to brave it, no pleasure was to be had in churning through the washing-machine conditions that could kick up on a day like this. The pounding and thrashing was as much a mental strain as a physical one. A boat like *Breezeway* was more than equal to it, but Blake knew there might well come a time at sea when there would be no choice but to carry on and tough it out. Staying home would not be an option. He wanted to see how Tim and Lauren stood up to it.

When, after a time and the usual routine of preparations, Blake asked, "So, all ready to go?" Tim and Lauren looked around, unsure, sensing they might be missing something.

"Guess so," Tim said.

"Well, guessing isn't good in a wind like this. So let me help. If you know this already, just say so. But what we need to do is reef the main while we're still here in the slip. Lot easier in here, now, then it is out there, later. Remember that. Assume the worst. Err on the side of caution, isn't that what they say? It's a lot easier to let more sail out if you're underpowered than it is to take it in when you're overpowered."

They climbed up on the cabin top as Tim and Lauren reacquainted themselves with the reefing gear and how it worked. "You guys will need to know how to do this in the dark, when it's blowing," Blake said, "so keep going over it. Reefing is your friend. Sometimes we'd do it just as a precaution when the sun went down if we thought the wind was going to kick up."

Tim and Lauren undid the ties that secured the mainsail to the boom. Tim clambered back down into the cockpit to raise the sail by means of a winch on the cabin top. When it was two-thirds of the way up the mast, Blake called out, "That's good."

Tim climbed back up. "How deep you think we should reef it?"

Blake put his hands on his hips, looking around, up at the wind indicators spinning hard at the top of the mast. "Let's start with two. Like I said, always easier to let more out than it is to take it in if you guessed wrong."

They had to put the second of two grommets around a hook on the boom, tie off the excess sailcloth, and tighten the small lines at the rear of the sail, the clew, where it met the after part of the boom. The effect, when they eventually raised it, would be a triangle of sail shrunken to about half of its original proportions.

As they circled around the boom, tucking, tying, adjusting, the boat took a sudden lurch in a gust. Lauren lost her balance and staggered backward slightly. Blake caught her around the waist and pulled, steadying her. When she'd regained her balance, he held on. Tim was on the other side of the boom.

Blake looked down at her, she grabbed his wrist and held it around her waist. He loosened, slowly, backing up. "Sorry. I–"

"It's fine," she said, meeting his eyes. "It's okay, believe me."

They moved apart, eyes lingering on each other's. Tim came around the mast. "Not something we ever did. We either stayed home or had a clusterfuck experience trying to reef out on the water, which happened maybe once or twice."

Blake's glance kept gravitating toward Lauren, who returned it in a sidelong way, unobtrusive but there, questioning, intrigued, wondering.

Maneuvering out of the slip was an adventure in itself. Once out of the marina and through the channel markers leading out into the Bay proper, the force of the wind made its presence known. As they passed the last of the day markers, Blake called out: "Turn her up into the wind, Tim. Lauren, crank up that sail." The sail flapped and flailed as it made its way up the mast. "Okay, fall off a little Tim. You know how to do this." Tim did indeed. Tim looked at Blake and made a throat-cutting motion. Blake nodded, Tim reached over and cut the engine.

Breezeway settled into a slot, hobby-horsing through the waves.

"Let's roll out the staysail," Blake called out. Lauren brought a winch handle. Without prompting, Tim pointed the boat a bit higher into the wind. The sheet wound around the winch, which drew and unfurled the smaller sail aft as Lauren cranked. Tim eased away from the wind just a bit and the two sails popped as they filled. Blake looked at them both and smiled, holding up two thumbs. *Breezeway* powered forward, glancing off the walls of the waves, digging in as she rose over some of them or piled into others.

Blake moved aft and settled in next to Tim, who was grappling with the wheel, ducking the occasional sheets of spray while trying to hold the boat steady as wind and waves tried to wrest control of her. "Jesus!" Tim exclaimed.

Blake laughed out loud. "What'd I tell you, Tim? Look at her. *Breezeway's* in her element. She reminds me of a retriever chasing a tennis ball out through the waves. Keeps going no matter what."

Blake watched Tim's handling of a boat being buffeted by wind and waves. It was only natural that *Breezeway* would swerve and yaw as she made her way to windward. The difference was how a person at the helm would handle those brief detours.

Tim was fighting the helm, oversteering, overreacting to the veering to and fro. *Breezeway's* steering was half a beat behind the force of the water or the wind. When Tim wrenched the wheel to bring the head back on course, he overcorrected, the boat lagging in response, coming too far up into the wind on one hand, and then falling too far off when he overcompensated in the other direction.

Lauren sat up high on the windward coaming, watching, smiling, shoulders back, with her forearms and wrists wrapped around a lifeline as a brace against the sharp downhill slope to leeward. Her eyes made their way to Blake's, penetrating, searching. Tim was preoccupied with negotiating *Breezeway* through the phalanx of waves that rolled past in an endless succession.

Blake was hesitant to point out Tim's steering deficiencies in front of Lauren. They were headed west across the Bay, as close to the northwest wind as they could sail. When they'd reached a point not quite halfway to the Western Shore, Blake motioned to Lauren. "Your turn at the helm," he said. "You need to take your lumps too. There'll come a time when it's howling and rocking and rolling but you'll still have to take a shift."

Lauren worked her way to the helm seat as Tim moved out from behind the wheel. The contrast between her aptitude for steering in heavy weather and Tim's made itself plain within moments. Despite the heaving and pitching, she kept a light touch on the wheel, allowing the bow to veer off, knowing instinctively that the boat's physics would begin a self-correction. Patiently, gradually, she would turn the wheel in increments, letting the correction happen without too much interference from the rudder.

She had a sense for the gusts and variations in wind direction, making minor adjustments to account for them. The boat's head held a relatively steady course, noticeably different than the zig-zagging when Tim was steering.

Blake watched, marveling at her feel for steering a vessel displacing ten tons of water through a tumult of waves and wind. "That's the ticket Lauren," he said, choosing to use her demonstration as an example for Tim. "Don't cramp her, let her find the way, nice light touch. Good job. Pinch up in the gusts, fall off in the lulls. Not too many lulls today, though. Mostly gusts." He turned to Tim. "There's a balance between the keel, the sails and the rudder. It's what I was saying before. Be conservative with your sail area, makes it easier to keep her up on her feet and easier to hold her steady in heavy air." What he left unmentioned was that Lauren seemed to have mastered the principle. If anything, the wind had sharpened as they reached the middle of the Bay. Lauren absorbed the added velocity with her elbows and hands. She stood, bracing a leg to leeward, holding the wheel as a steadying brake, adjusting, looking up at the curvature of the sails. Blake leaned over and loosened the main sheet. *Breezeway's* motion eased as she resumed her purposeful lunging to the west.

Later that afternoon, after having traversed the Bay and sailed back on a rollicking downwind ride, Tim and Lauren circled the boat, tying off dock lines. Tim gravitated aft, securing lines to the cleats near the transom. As Lauren stood, having tied off the bow cleats, Blake faced her. "I'm impressed," he said. "The way you handled the boat out there? Kind of amazing. You're a natural. Got saltwater in your veins. Born to it, or something."

She smiled. "You bring it out in me. Or something."

He turned to look back aft at Tim, stuck his hands in his pockets, and took a deep breath. "That's what I'm afraid of," he said. "The something."

"Why are you afraid? I'm not."

Blake looked at her. "Things get complicated. It changes lives."

"Doesn't have to, if you're careful and smart. As long as you don't confuse lust with love. No violins, no bouquets, swearing oaths to everlasting love. Just two people who want to have sex. No complications, no expectations. Keep a lid on it."

"How do you know so much about it?"

Lauren bristled. "What kind of question is that? I've seen the way you look at me. But if I have to draw you a map, you're not as interesting as I thought you were."

Blake looked back at Tim puttering around the cockpit, coiling lines, hosing down gear. "There's, um, Tim."

"Yeah? When you were looking up through the scaffold that day, checking out my thighs, were you thinking of Tim?"

"No."

"Tell me what you were thinking of."

"What you'd look like with those cut-off jeans down around your knees."

"Ooohh, you bad boy." She reached and unbuttoned the top button of her shorts. "Gonna call me?"

"Count on it."

10

January 2019
Eastern Shore of Maryland

Maya Jameson drove out of the rental car facility at Baltimore Washington International airport. Having just arrived on a flight from Cleveland, she followed the signs that would take her south and east, across the Chesapeake Bay Bridge, drawing closer toward her childhood home. When she reached the opposite side of the Bay, she saw the familiar sign: "Welcome to Maryland's Eastern Shore."

She'd taken a provisional week off from her job in Lorain, Ohio to travel here. The trip was in response to a contact from Dennis Cox, Tim Jameson's partner at the accounting firm. Her mother, Pauline, whose concern for Maya's brother was growing with each passing week, had also urged her to come. They were two of the people closest to Tim and Lauren, the ones who were at first mystified and then alarmed by the total absence of communication from the couple.

Early on, neither Dennis nor Pauline felt they knew Lauren's parents well enough to trespass into that relationship, inquiring whether they'd heard from Lauren. As the weeks went by, however, Dennis called them to express his concern about not having heard from Tim. Lauren's mother, Sarah, said she'd heard from Lauren three times, once by phone shortly after they'd arrived in Vieques. The second through an email a few weeks later. Then, sometime around Christmas, another phone call to report they were leaving Vieques to sail to the French West Indies. Sarah was surprised and disappointed at the infrequency of the contacts. She felt let down because she'd anticipated many more Facebook posts with photos and updates. She'd looked forward to sharing the posts with her circle of friends. She wasn't sure of the exact location of the French West Indies, and in each of the contacts Lauren had assured her that Tim was "fine."

With that skeletal backdrop as a starting point, Maya arrived on the Eastern Shore with the hope of finding some reasonable explanation why her brother and his sailing companions had slipped so far off the radar screen. She exited Route 50 just north of Easton, branching off onto a road that paralleled the Miles River. At the end of a lane leading back toward the river, her mother's home was tucked along its banks. It was her first stop on a mission without a clear beginning, and no indication of where it might end.

Their father had passed away a few years ago, struck down by a sudden heart attack. Their mother lived alone. Her father's assets were such that Pauline could manage the costs of keeping a home on the water, a home of sufficient age that it demanded a more or less constant regimen of maintenance. She and her mother greeted one another with the urgency of the moment. They hadn't seen each other in too long, and the man who they both cherished, one as a son the other as a brother, had somehow drifted beyond their grasp, out into a realm of eerie radio silence.

Pauline was one of those feisty, wiry women who, despite the onset of minor health problems, refused to accept the limitations of age. Though some thought there was a time stamp on her ability to manage life here on the water, or the demands of daily life generally, Pauline scoffed at them.

At the same time, Tim had never been far off, and had acted as a backstop who could step in when some task was too much for

Pauline, though she was loath to admit it. For the moment, though, Tim was not around. His unexplained absence drained some of her reassurance and energy.

After dinner, Pauline and Maya settled near a wood stove that basked the interior with a comforting warmth. "Tomorrow morning I'm going to see Dennis Cox," Maya said. "From our conversations I'm not sure how much he can help, but it's a starting point."

Pauline's eyes rose to meet Maya's. They glowed in the reflection of the flames. "What could have happened to him? Why wouldn't he call or get in touch somehow?" She stared back at the fire. "And why the hell wouldn't Lauren or her snotty parents have been in touch?" There was a cultural gulf between the two families, a frosty residue stemming from circumstances surrounding Tim and Lauren's wedding arrangements nearly ten years ago. Neither set of parents had ever felt compelled to reach across that divide to smooth the waters, and contact between them ranged from minimal to nonexistent.

"I know, Mama," said Maya. So far her imaginings hadn't entertained any possibility other than Tim had simply been negligent, though that was so out of character for him it was wishful thinking bordering on delusion. She refused, both on her own emotional level as well as a verbal one with Pauline, to discuss or even consider the notion that Tim hadn't been in touch because he was incapacitated somehow: injured, or worse. Still, the thought hung there, unspoken, dreaded, too frightening to confront—just yet.

Besides, how did any of it square with Lauren reporting that Tim was fine? It defied logic that if something had befallen Tim, she and the other guy would simply depart for the French West Indies. Didn't it? How could that be? Wouldn't they have made their way home or summoned family members if Tim had met with some calamity? Of course. Nothing else made sense. That was all Maya and her mother could hang on to as the room went silent.

Darkness came early at this time of year. As it settled in, both women felt the cumulative fatigue of mounting stress and worry. They agreed it would be an early-to-bed evening, though neither of them looked forward to another dark night, alone with unwelcome thoughts.

Maya awoke the next morning to the sounds of shotgun blasts echoing from blinds in the surrounding creeks and coves. The reports gave her pause for a few brief moments until the sounds stirred familiar recollections. The Eastern Shore was a mecca of waterfowl hunting in nearly all its forms. Indeed, the town of Easton hosted a waterfowl festival every November that drew tens of thousands of enthusiasts from across the country.

As the sky lightened slowly, she tracked the patterns of gunshots. Some sounded like faint pops, coming from far off. Others were sharper, issuing from a creek or farm field just a few hundred yards away. The shots came in bunches, as hunters in a blind zeroed in on a flock of inbound birds, then went silent for long periods.

She'd moved away from the area shortly after college, following a trend common among young people in the region. The insularity and provincialism that tourists and transplants found so attractive held little appeal for someone ready to embark on a career or looking for broader horizons. Job opportunities were few, limited primarily to low-wage, low-promise positions in the tourism or hospitality industries.

Tim had solved that problem by going to work for and eventually buying into the accounting practice of a CPA nearing retirement. The retiring CPA had been a fixture in the Easton business community, as had Tim's father. They were business and social contemporaries. The Jameson name was well-known. Those factors reduced what might have been otherwise insurmountable barriers to an outsider seeking to launch a firm from scratch.

Maya left the Eastern Shore on a wave of idealism. During high school she had become caught up in the swirl of politics and current events. She was consumed by the news stories surrounding politicians and opinion shapers. Drawn somehow to opinion shapers on the leftward side of the spectrum, she became passionate about the causes of social justice and equality. When it came time to narrow down college choices, she honed-in on Oberlin College in Ohio. Oberlin had long been known as an epicenter of progressive thought. Its policies on issues ranging from co-ed dorms to minority admissions were seen as radical, decades ahead of any similar institution. Students held seats on the college's governing bodies. Oberlin was where she wanted to go.

Her father, Lawrence Jameson, an investment advisor with a roster of wealthy, old-money clients, was horrified and resolutely opposed. It so happened, though, that Maya's academic rank placed her third in her high school class. She was also a standout lacrosse player. Pauline had been a marcher and protester back in the '70s, a strident advocate of women's rights. She would not stand by and watch Maya's ambitions be thwarted by outmoded notions of a patriarch calling the shots. Between Maya's academic and athletic achievements, scholarships would make the tuition reasonable, comfortably within the means of the Jameson family. Pauline went to the wall with Lawrence, presenting him with a fait accompli: If Maya wanted to attend Oberlin College, it shall be so.

In four years, Maya had become immersed in progressive ideology. She saw most things through the lenses of class struggle and identity politics. There were the oppressed, and there were the oppressors. That simple.

When she came home on vacations, she and Lawrence would engage in spirited but civil ideological debates. Lawrence always believed that the superiority of his ideology was embodied in the story of his family's struggle, their journey from poverty to prosperity. It turned out that Lawrence's great, great, great, grandfather had come from Ireland to the Eastern Shore in the mid-1840s, fleeing the potato famine. The price of his passage was an indenture, obligating him to work on a farm for five years. Indentured servitude had become more closely regulated by then, so at the end of five years he was duly freed from his contract and granted a small plot of land to work. The price of the grant was a share of the product from that land with the grantee. The share would gradually diminish until the day Darragh Jameson could claim clear title to 60 acres of land between McDaniel and Claiborne, Maryland. It took years of backbreaking labor and heartbreaking setbacks, but the Jameson family had gone from starving, penniless peasants to landowners.

Through succeeding generations, the Jameson bloodline advanced from dirt farmers, to merchants, to traders, to rumrunners, to minor politicians, to bankers, and finally, investment advisors who nurtured the wealth of families whose ancestors may have owned the indentures of Lawrence's family. To Lawrence, the saga proved that America was the land of opportunity.

Maya would counter by pointing to the generations of black families who'd been on the Eastern Shore long before her father's ancestors arrived, who were owned, not indentured. They'd arrived on slave ships, bought and sold, forever bound to work for nothing except living in a hovel with scraps of food and subject to whatever degradation their owner or master chose to visit upon them at any moment.

Even after the Civil War, when presumably the slaves were emancipated, few had access to land ownership opportunities, a small plot of their own to farm, say, or a chance to earn their way out of poverty and servitude. Their existence was reduced to working for subsistence wages on workboats plying the Bay for crabs or oysters, or piecework shucking oysters in miserable conditions with no benefits of any kind.

Shortly after the turn of the century, a resurgence of the Ku Klux Klan made life dangerous for African Americans on the Eastern Shore. As late as the mid-80s, a gang of racists on Tilghman Island burned a cross on the lawn of a black family who'd recently moved there from Virginia. "Your Irish ancestors ever come up against something like that?" Maya asked.

Lawrence was quiet. Maya wasn't finished. "Right now," she said, "there are hundreds of Latinos working in chicken processing plants up and down the Eastern Shore—in Salisbury, in Parksley and Melfa in Virginia. Same thing. Appalling conditions, grinding poverty. Think any of them will ever get a chance to own anything? No matter how hard they work?"

"A lot of them are here illegally," Lawrence said.

"So were your ancestors, strictly speaking. Captains used to pack them aboard ships in Galway and Shannon. Off you go, no visa, no papers, nothing legal except admission as a source of cheap labor for landowners here in the colonies. Just like the mules from Mexico. What's the difference?"

Lawrence was quiet.

"I'll tell you," she said. "The difference was they were white. Your ancestors were white. But, oh my God, they were also ... Catholic! Bloody papists! Irish immigrants got kicked around and spat upon by the WASPs for decades. But you're okay with it because they finally, grudgingly, let you into the club. You and the Jews and the Italians, Eastern Europeans—melting pot my ass. They wanted you for the labor: mines, factories, sweatshops. And the exploiters had no intention of sharing any of it with you. But you were all white, to a degree, kind of, and you were obnoxious and insistent enough to elbow your way into the club. And now you want to close the door behind you because the recent aspirants are of a different color, or talk funny, or have weird names."

"How much am I paying a year for this?" Lawrence asked.

Maya laughed. "Wait'll you hear the next iteration of it. According to one school of thought, not only were you and your fellow Irishmen here illegally, but so was every white person who set foot on these shores up until 1875. That's when the first real immigration rules were passed. And even they were aimed at keeping Chinese immigrants out, not Europeans."

"When you say, 'school of thought,' are you referring to your school?"

"Not really. What I'm talking about is when the Pilgrims showed up at Plymouth Rock, and the other colonists in Jamestown, they just pulled up in ships, anchored, rowed ashore, stepped out and decided this was their new home. No documents, no claims, nothing. Problem was, other people already lived here, by the thousands. That makes the Pilgrims our first illegal immigrants. Jefferson buys the Louisiana purchase from France, but it wasn't France's to sell. There was a whole vast civilization out there. So the government spent the next 100 years engaged in a massive campaign of ethnic cleansing, which, by the way, is now classified as a crime against humanity. In fact, the Nazis took a page out of our playbook when they set out to exterminate another race in Europe."

"I didn't know that."

"Historical fact. It's been documented. I can show you."

Lawrence shook his head. "No, that's okay. Is this what passes for scholarship in today's academic circles?"

"Well," she replied, "they say history is written by the winners. Two of our founding fathers owned hundreds of slaves between them. Andrew Jackson forcibly deported 80,000 Indians from their ancestral homes. Those white men are icons to many, portraits on our currency. But if you asked the Indians and the slaves to recount their version of 18th and 19th century history, you'd get a very different version than what we grew up with. Doubt if they see the white guys on dollar bills as heroes."

Lawrence had come to admire his daughter's ardent activism, if not totally buying into the underlying ideology. He thought back to the outraged idealism of his day. How the edge of it gets gradually dulled over the years as the realization sets in that the roulette wheel always seems fixed in favor of a certain class. Fighting it seems pointless. Better just to move over to their other side of the table. What a shame.

To the sound of a few more early-morning shotgun reports, Maya stretched, pulling the quilt up under her chin against the chill. Another ten minutes wouldn't hurt, why not luxuriate a while longer till the rising sun warmed things, even a little? She thought back to those debates with her father. How she treasured the memory of them now, and how she missed the good-natured fencing with him.

At Oberlin she had met a fiery, impassioned ideologue whose righteous anger and intellect enthralled her. Owen was mad at a lot of things, a serious guy. They became a couple, though no prospect of marriage ever came up. He judged it a bourgeois institution, frivolous, shackling people to outmoded traditions—like, it turned out, monogamy.

After graduation, Owen got Maya a staff job with a congressman whose district included much of Lorain, Ohio, not far from Oberlin. Lorain was a poster child for the hollowing out of America's industrial base. Once the home of steel mills, automobile plants and shipbuilders, Lorain had seen a steady exodus of manufacturing jobs as the companies decamped for Asia and Latin America. The economic dislocation left a crumbling landscape of urban decay.

Maya's idealism began to corrode one night when the congressman, a shining light of progressivism with a national profile, attempted a fumbling, groping, pathetic attempt at seducing her. She would have laughed were she not so surprised and horrified. She quit a few days later. Her absence from the staff only created more room for Owen to try his luck among the flock of wide-eyed college interns working on the congressman's campaign, many of them from Oberlin. She retuned home one night a few weeks later to find Owen in bed with one of them.

She'd been cured forever of any notion that fervor or stridency or so-called passion were attractive or romantic. Owen was a jerk, and the congressman was a pathetic, aging hypocrite.

Eventually she found a job in Lorain with a faith-based organization whose mission was coming to the rescue of people with urgent food or housing issues. This was the ragged edge, not of ideology but of reality. Rhetoric and zeal meant little to these people. They were hungry or about to be homeless. All Maya and her co-workers were doing were putting band-aids on a cascading economic crisis that was ravaging hundreds of towns like Lorain. But at least they were making small differences. It was tangible, down in the trenches, not sitting around in coffeehouses talking a big game, playing at being a radical.

On the other hand, she'd been with the food and housing assistance program for three years now. The pay was lousy with no prospect of getting better. As she lay in bed that morning in her parents' home, listening to the volleys of shotguns, she realized how much she missed the things that comprised a unique way of life on the Eastern Shore. Granted, in many ways it was parochial and clannish, but it was where she'd grown up. Her family was a charter member of the clans. To some extent the parochialism came from fending off modernity, preserving a way of life they all knew wouldn't last forever.

The grey, depressing decay of Lorain was wearing her down. Maybe it was time to reorient. Pauline, despite her pretense of rugged independence, would need help with the house. Maya could take some of what she'd learned in Ohio and perhaps apply it with a similar organization here. In pockets dotted around Talbot and Dorchester and Caroline counties, there was ample need for it. The opioid epidemic had swept across the Eastern Shore, much as it had in Lorain and other places where the economic casino had left people hopeless and destitute.

This morning she had an appointment first thing with Dennis Cox. After that she'd head south to Tilghman Island and start asking around. Tilghman Islanders were congenitally suspicious of strangers nosing around, asking questions. But her name and her brother's weren't totally unfamiliar. Tim and Lauren had a home there, and in recent years a steady influx of outsiders had diluted the trademark Tilghman Island xenophobia.

TOM HITCHCOCK

11

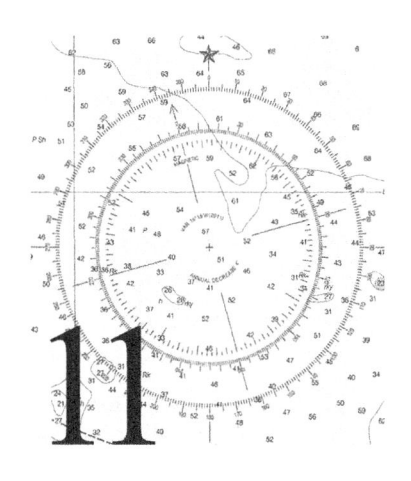

Maya left her morning meeting with Dennis Cox in Easton and headed south down Route 33, along the spine of the Bay Hundred peninsula. At the peninsula's tail end was Tilghman Island. She arrived just in time to be greeted by warning bells, gates and flashing lights bringing traffic to a stop. The signals were in preparation for the Knapp's Narrows drawbridge to begin opening—a slow, some said agonizing, ascent to a vertical position, allowing boats to traverse the waterway beneath it. The bridge was something of an attraction to tourists, little more than a time-wasting annoyance to many local residents.

Following the slow-motion ritual of the bridge opening and closing, she drove across it and took the first left onto a small road that ran alongside that Narrows. A hundred yards later, she turned left again into the gravel and hard-packed lot of a boatyard. Arranged in crowded rows were ranks of boats raised in jack stands, sitting idle during winter storage. Working vessels outnumbered pleasure craft. Here and there, men clad in coveralls and hooded sweatshirts labored underneath boats—painting, replacing, adjusting, fiberglassing—coaxing yet another season out of a boat they depended on to put food on their family's table.

Maya parked between the bows of two raised-up boats. As she got out, her attention was drawn to a man handling the wand of a power washer. He was circling under a boat suspended above a small rectangle of water by means of two slings, wielding the power washer to blast the hull clean of barnacles. Maya watched from a respectful distance. To shield himself from the detritus of barnacle shells, gunk and water, he wore a foul-weather gear outfit and long rubber gloves.

At length, the man completed the cleansing. He looked over at Maya, up at the dripping boat hull, and considered his options: talking to an attractive young woman or manipulating the travel lift to guide the boat to its own set of jack stands. He decided on the former.

"Hi," he said, smiling with some effort. "Can I help you?"

"I hope so," she said. "My name is Maya Jameson. I'm trying to find out what might have happened to my brother, Tim Jameson. I understand he and his wife Lauren have stored their boat here over the winter?" She motioned tentatively around her at the other boats.

"Jameson," the man said. "Jameson. Yeah, I know who you mean. Owns a nice sailboat. An Island Packet. Sure, that's right. Kept it here over the winter."

Maya pulled out her phone and swiped up a photo of Tim and Lauren, smiling, raising glasses, in *Breezeway's* cockpit. The man peered at the photo. "Hell, yes. That's them." He looked back at Maya with wide eyes. "Shit! Pardon my French, ma'am, but they're the ones who sailed off into the sunset with my yard manager, Blake. You see this stuff I'm doing? Supposed to be his job. He told me he'd only be gone ten days, two weeks, then he'd come back. That was two months ago. Well, I haven't seen or heard from him since they left. Now I'm stuck doin' this shit. Um, sorry."

Maya looked down. Tears leaked down her cheeks. "Ohh, ma'am," the man said. "Please. You okay? My name's Darryl. Want to come in the office? Warmer in there. C'mon with me." He ushered her through an inner and outer door, past a docile, welcoming Chocolate Lab in the passageway. The dog stood and looked up at her with hopeful eyes as she passed. Once inside a cramped office, Darryl gestured, "Please, have a seat."

Maya composed herself, raised her head, determined to stifle as many signs of distress as she could. It was quiet, Darryl figuring the woman would take the lead as necessary. She looked around. The office was crammed with product and parts manuals packed onto shelves and desks: hoses, belts, bronze fittings scattered about; large oyster shells serving as ash trays; windows brown and caked with dirt, cigarette smoke and salt; a piston and connecting rod over in one corner; a gallon of antifouling paint in another. It was a working man's boatyard. No one cared about amenities.

"The reason I drove to Tilghman," Maya said, "and came here, is that no one's heard from my brother since they left. His wife's been in touch with her parents maybe three times, that's it. We can't figure out what's going on."

"Wish I could help," Darryl said. "But like I told you I ain't heard squat from Blake. Way I heard it, your brother and his wife were hell-bent on going off on a sailing voyage. Problem was, they were greenhorns when it came to blue water, needed an experienced hand to show 'em the ropes. So I guess they got to know Blake and hired him to go along on the first leg, wherever that was."

Maya looked out through a yellowed window. "If you don't mind my asking, how well do you know this Blake?"

"I didn't put him through a background check if that's what you mean. He showed up here one day looking for a job as a yard jockey, anything. It so happened I needed a guy and so ... yeah. Knew his way around boats, that's for sure. Worked hard, showed up on time, did his job and then some. I was glad to have him. When we get somebody like that here, we don't ask too many questions."

"Um, how long has he worked here—or, had he worked here? Can I ask?"

"Let's see," Darryl said, thinking back. "He showed up here

around this time last winter. That'd make it a year or so, give or take."

Maya smiled and unfolded her hands. "I don't know why I even asked. Not like I know what I'm looking for, not some detective or anything. I'm just groping, you know? Wish I knew where to start."

Darryl sat back in his chair. "Tell you what I'd do."

"What?"

"I'd check with the Coast Guard. There's a station right over in Oxford. Maybe there's been a report, or, I don't know, something. Never know. Sorry I can't be more help."

"No, no, I appreciate your time. If I wrote down my contact information, would you reach out to me if you heard from Blake?"

"Course. No problem. But I'm not holdin' my breath."

She stood, walked out through the door, stopping to pet the Lab. "What's his name?"

"It's a she."

"Oh."

"Really want to know?"

"Sure. Why not?"

"Mystery."

Maya pulled out of the boatyard and made her way a few blocks to the west, toward a newer collection of homes, many of them built facing west out over the Bay, overlooking massive banks of stone riprap as a buffer against foul weather and waves coming in from the west. She found Tim and Lauren's address and stopped out front. The houses seemed mostly unoccupied save for one next door from which a faint light shone from inside.

In almost any other circumstance, Maya would have hung back from nosing around a house or a property that wasn't hers. Now she tossed hesitancy aside and walked up the short driveway, venturing onto the small porch, peering in through the windows. Seeing nothing that would pull back the veil on what had happened to her brother, she made her way around the back of the house, cupping the side of her face with her hands as she squinted inside.

Soon she heard, unmistakably, the opening and closing of a door from the adjacent house. She looked to see a woman walking toward her, gathering a heavy sweater around her as she strode through a fence opening, smiling uncertainly. "Hi!" the woman called out. "Is there something I can help you with?"

Maya moved toward her, smiling. "I'd like to think so, but somehow I doubt it."

"Oh, well, I'm sorry to hear that. I'm Shirley Fontaine, Tim and Lauren's neighbor. They're away for the time being."

"I know," Maya said. "I'm Maya Jameson, Tim's sister."

"Oh! Oh my gosh! I'm so glad to meet you." They shook hands warmly. Low, gray clouds scudded across the sky as a stiffening wind kicked up white caps out on the water. "How's a cup of hot tea sound? Can you join me?"

"Sounds wonderful. Yes, thank you."

They hunched their shoulders, ducking inside Shirley's house, pulling the door shut as the wind pushed it behind them. "Whew! January," Shirley said, "not exactly prime time to be living here. Anyway, welcome."

The inside was cozy and warm, a sanctuary against the wind that had begun to rattle the back of the house. Shirley placed a pot over a flame, rubbing her hands together as she smiled at Maya. The bonhomie began to fade ever so slightly as they waited for the water to boil, and to get down to the meat of the matter of why they both knew Maya was here. When they were seated near a gas heater in the living room, Maya said, as an entree, "It's so nice to meet a neighbor of Tim and Lauren's."

Shirley smiled, and said nothing. Maya looked at her and said, "I'm here trying to get to the bottom of what might have happened to Tim. None of his coworkers or family have heard anything from him since the three of them left on their so-called voyage. You can imagine that we're concerned. Beyond concerned, really. Edging toward panic."

Shirley looked down into her teacup.

"Did you know Tim and Lauren well?" Maya asked.

"No, not well," Shirley said. "Or—wait, I take that back. Yes. I think I knew them well, or pretty well anyway. Hard to say."

"Okay. I'm here looking for something to cling to, a ledge to set up camp and start climbing. Know what I mean? What the hell happened to them?"

Shirley was quiet again. She looked at Maya. "I don't know whether to put this out there or not."

"Put what?"

"There were rumors, umm, nobody seemed to know firsthand"

"Know what?"

"Well, some people thought that Lauren and Blake were, well, you know … involved."

Maya tired of the innuendo. "Involved? You mean, like screwing?"

"Yeah. Like screwing. An affair. Some said it was hot and heavy."

Maya felt her face flush. "God. You're kidding. How low-rent. How trashy." She felt a wave of humiliation and revulsion on behalf of Tim.

"Blake's a good-looking man," Shirley said. "Have to say, lots of women took notice."

"Lauren was married to a successful man. Blake was a boatyard slug. How does that happen?"

"I don't know. We can't know for sure that it did, I guess."

"Yeah, guess I shouldn't assume the worst based on rumors. I haven't been back in a while, but I remember enough about the Eastern Shore to know how tongues wag. Lot of busybodies. Like you said, rumors. But that doesn't stop them from being spread."

Shirley sipped her tea. "That's true. On the other hand—I hope I'm not out of line in saying this, Maya—but over the years, lot of the time it turns out there's a basis for the rumors. Problem is, this is a small town, surrounded by other small towns. You know that. There's no anonymity, no crowd to get lost in, no place to hide. People see things, notice things. Like on the days when Lauren went to Washington for her work? A few times Blake took that day off from the boatyard. For whatever it's worth."

Maya thought back over what little she knew of Tim and Lauren's relationship. Whenever they'd been together, she came away with the impression that Lauren was a free spirit, that Tim liked that about her but served as a brake on her impulses. She never knew precisely what Lauren did, only a general outline. Including that her work it took her to Washington, D.C. periodically, as Shirley confirmed. And, according to Tim, the work paid well.

Maya recalled a conversation a few years ago in which Lauren described her line of work. She'd called herself a communications consultant, which was far too broad and vague for what she did. "Spin doctor" was a crude but more appropriate label, she said. Lauren manipulated words, twisting them, altering their meaning or arrangement just enough so that what seemed like a clear dividing line between fact and truth was instead blurred, turned on its head. The clarity and moral high ground of one position could be warped, fed through a salad blender of words until the average person might no longer be sure what was clear or what was true. She wrote speeches, talking points, position papers, blogs, press releases, op-eds—a cascade of words and ideas peddled to reporters and journalists or fed to friendly websites.

Lauren only smiled when Maya asked her if it paid as well as she suspected. "I work for people whose compensation hinges on having their voices heard—and prevail. There's a lot at stake for them. I get paid accordingly."

Maya finished her tea, thanking Shirley for her time and hospitality. The lowering sky was ushering in a somber January darkness earlier than usual. She had to take her leave and head back to Easton. What would she tell Pauline? All she had learned was that most likely Lauren had been cheating on Tim with the guy they took with them on a sailboat out into the middle of the ocean. It was enough to give her pause, even let flashes of chilling thoughts intrude. But she resisted letting the pulp-novel side of her imagination run away with her. She decided against mentioning it to her mother. What would be the point?

But what about tomorrow when she drove to Oxford to talk to the Coast Guard? Would they care about that part of it? Might she look foolish? Possibly. She had no facts, after all, only rumors. And she had no idea what her approach to the officials would yield, if anything. Better just to lay out the facts as she knew them: a married couple leaves on a voyage accompanied by a single man, and no one's heard from the husband, her brother, since. Let them decide where to take it from there.

12

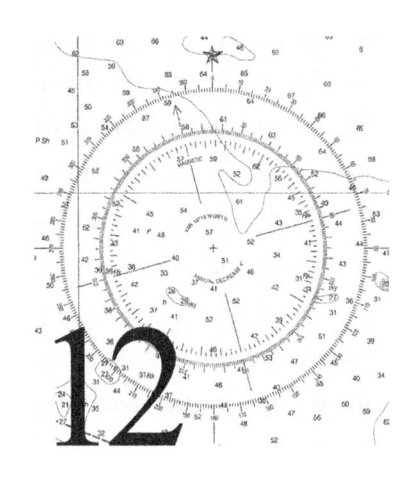

January 2019
Eastern Shore of Maryland

Maya's contact with the Coast Guardsmen in Oxford sparked a process that swept her inquiry upstream, along a chain of investigative protocols. The account of her brother's inexplicable silence since setting sail two months ago, along with her hints of an untoward relationship among the three voyagers, prompted her interviewer to contact the Coast Guard Investigative Service's Resident Agent Office in Baltimore.

That office began looking for matches among reported incidents—distress calls, rescues, recovered vessels or bodies—in the Coast Guard's LANTAREA, a truncated name for Atlantic Area. The RAO in Baltimore also cross-checked for possible matches in two databases: the NCIC and the Marine Information for Safety and Law Enforcement (MISLE).

Next, the Baltimore office networked with its counterparts in the CGIS Chesapeake Region Office in Portsmouth, Virginia. From there, the content and tone of the inquiries pushed their way across someone's radar in the CGIS's Southeast Region office in Miami, who then forwarded it to the Jacksonville CGIS office, where it happened to cross the desks of agents Troy Barrett and Neal Franklin.

Franklin was looking at the incoming messages that drifted across his screen, like the nondescript images of fish floating past on a vessel's fish finder. He watched until he saw the message come in from Miami. He jumped forward in his chair. "Fish on! Fish on!" he yelled out, like a mate on a fishing boat heralding the bite of what the anglers had been waiting for.

Barrett turned in his chair. "What the hell's that mean?"

"TB," Franklin said, "look here! A woman from Maryland reports her brother went off sailing, in early November, headed to the Caribbean with his wife and somebody else. Nobody in the family, no one, has heard from the guy since."

Barrett turned back to his monitor.

"Look at the description," Franklin said. "Early thirties, dark hair, medium build. That could be our John Doe."

Barrett turned and after checking a list, calmly punched in the phone number of the RAO in Baltimore. When a voice answered he said, "Good afternoon, sir. This is Chief Warrant Officer Barrett of the CGIS office in Jacksonville."

Barrett went on to explain how he and his colleague had been investigating an incident, the rescue of a so-far-anonymous victim out at sea. The inquiry originating in Baltimore had just reached their office, he said, and believing it highly relevant to their investigation, they would very much like to speak with the young woman who filed the report with the Oxford station.

The next day Barrett was on a flight to Baltimore. He was greeted by a GCIS counterpart, and together they drove to the Eastern Shore to meet with Maya Jameson. Sitting in Pauline's living room, Barrett explained why he was here, how Maya's report had unexpectedly opened a door on a case that had baffled him and his fellow investigators. After he pieced together the elements of her report with the events surrounding the rescue at sea, he unfolded an iPad Pro and turned it toward Maya. "Is this your brother?"

Maya put the back of her hand to her face. She turned quickly to gauge Pauline's wide-eyed shock. "Yes," she gulped. "That's him. My God, what happened to him?

"I–

"Where is he? Is he alive? Oh … God." She sank onto her knees before the photo that portrayed Tim's condition, which rarely changed in any noticeable way.

Barrett hung his head briefly, looked at his Baltimore colleague, and answered. "Right now, Ms. Jameson, he's a patient in a rehab facility in Jacksonville. And yes, he's alive. But he suffered a severe head injury. How, we don't know. He was rescued at sea, as I said, at the latitude of the Georgia-Florida border, roughly three hundred miles out." Barrett swiped to a page on the iPad showing a chart, pointing to the spot where Tim had been picked up by the long-liner.

Pauline looked at the expanse of ocean. Her voice grew steely. "He was just … floating? All by himself? Not on a boat?"

"No ma'am. He was unconscious from the head injury. In a coma. It was a miracle that vessel happened to be there when it was. A miracle they were able to see him in the dark."

"Oh dear God," Pauline said, shuddering at the image of her son floating, unconscious, helpless and alone, in a dark, forbidding emptiness of ocean.

"How did he get there?" Maya asked. "Did he fall off their boat?"

"We don't know."

She followed up: "Did they hit him in the head and push him over? Is that what happened?"

"We don't know that either. But I'm curious why you'd ask."

Maya shot her eyes quickly toward Pauline, then back to Barrett. "When the time's right."

"Okay. Well, if Tim could tell us we'd know, but he can't."

"Because he's in a coma."

"Correct."

Pauline's eyes misted over. "Will he ever wake up?"

Barrett demurred. "The doctors believe he's improving, showing more signs, faint signs of awareness. It was touch and go at first. He spent weeks in an ICU in a Jacksonville trauma center. But now he's stabilized enough so they transferred him to a rehab facility. They're encouraged, but it's complicated."

"You talk to his doctors?" Maya said.

Barrett nodded. "All the time."

"In person?"

"Sometimes."

"So you've seen him. Been with him."

"Yes."

Maya stood and demanded, "I want to see him too. I want to see my brother."

"Completely understandable, Ms. Jameson."

"When?"

"That's up to you. As soon as you'd like. I can have Agent Franklin from our office there to meet you. But it would be better if you could hang with me here, if only for another day. I need to stay around to conduct some interviews, get an idea of who's what in all this. If you could give me some guidance, get me started in the right direction, it may help us get to the bottom of what happened to your brother that much sooner." He reached out and took her hand. "I've been by his side off and on since November. I think he's okay for another couple days, at least."

She sagged. "Okay, not tomorrow then. Next day, Thursday. That's it."

"Fine," Barrett said. "Lots to do in the next 36 hours. I'm going to Tilghman Island first thing in the morning. Talk to me about what you know, who you think might help us."

Maya looked up from the iPad screen into Barrett's face.

Agent Barrett drove into the boatyard lot alongside the Narrows. He parked in what he guessed was a permissible spot and got out. Dressed for the weather, he looked around and headed for what he assumed must be the office. He eased his way in, hearing voices, through two sets of doors. A man sat behind a desk; two others sat in chairs along the wall.

Conversation stopped the second he walked in. Barrett had that air about him. He wasn't here to talk about getting work done on his boat. "Good morning," he said. "My name is Chief Warrant Officer Barrett." He drew a badge holder from his jacket pocket and opened it. "I'm with the Coast Guard Investigative Service. I'd like to speak to whoever's in charge, please."

The two hangers-on in the chairs stood. "See ya later, Darryl," said one. "Gotta get goin'." The long history of Tilghman Island was rife with contentious relationships between law enforcement and those who made their living on the water. Cutting corners was the natural order of things, many watermen believed, and they played games of cat and mouse with marine police cops and the Coast Guard, the "law" as they were known. The two men in the boatyard office were acting on a lifetime of conditioned response when in the company of the law: put distance between you and them, especially those from a heavyweight outfit like CGIS.

"Sorry," said Barrett. "Didn't mean to intrude. Are you the owner?"

The man behind the desk laughed "No, the bank is. I just work here. Ahh, not really. I'm Darryl Cummings. What can I help you with?"

Barrett began by telling Cummings which office he was from. The reason he was here on the Eastern Shore, he said, was that a bulletin originating in Baltimore had come across their desks in Jacksonville. The bulletin had to do with a young woman who had filed the maritime version of a missing persons report with the Coast Guard station in Oxford, Maryland.

"The woman who filed the report said she did so at your recommendation," Barrett said.

"Holy shit!" Cummings said. "That's right. It was me. She was in here a few days ago askin' after her ... brother, I think. Never gave it another thought, but now here you are already? Damn. 'Scuse my language."

"It's fine. It was Maya Jameson."

"Yup. That's her."

"Her brother is Tim Jameson."

"Right again. He and his wife winter-stored their boat here, oh, two, three seasons maybe." Cummings spun in his chair, opened a file cabinet drawer and miraculously withdrew one file folder from a tossed salad of records. "Let's see," he said.

For Barrett he was able to pin down the year, make, model, name and sail plan of the boat, along with its Maryland registration number.

"Can I get a copy of that somehow?" Barrett said.

"Ah, just take it. Don't really need it."

"That's great. Thank you." Barrett showed Darryl a photo of the two of them, Tim and Lauren, aboard the boat. "Is this them?"

"Sure is."

"Okay. Now, what about a guy named Blake? Blake Wentworth."

"Oh, that S.O.B."

"What?"

"Said he'd be gone ten days, two weeks. Never showed up again after he sailed off with them other two."

"With the Jamesons."

"Damn right. Now I'm stuck doin' all the grunt work around here till I find somebody else. Hard to keep up with everything."

"Did you know he had an arrest record?"

"No, but I ain't surprised. More than a few young boys around here had brushes with the law."

"This was more than a brush. Did a year and a half of federal time on a major drug arrest. He got off light. Could've been more."

"All I know," Cummings said, "was he did his job while he was here. Knew boats inside and out. Showed up every day. I'm not set up to run background checks on people."

"Well, that's okay. By now we know all we really need to know about his background. But what about this part of it: Were you aware he may have been involved—sexually, that is—with Lauren—Ms. Jameson?"

"You mean did I ever see it with my own eyes? No. But I heard all the whispers. Some of the boys joked about it. I don't guess it was any secret. I just don't pay much attention unless it affects my business here."

Barrett jotted on a pad. "Did this Blake person ever mention his plans to accompany the Jamesons?"

"Not till a few weeks before they left. We were comin' up on our slow season, they were payin' him more than I could, so I said what the hell, go ahead. Just make sure you're back here before Thanksgiving. Said he would. But now of course he ain't, and I'm stuck." Cummings looked out a window made translucent by accumulated grime as Barrett finished jotting. "So, if you can tell me, what's goin' on with this? I can't imagine they send someone like you all the way up here over hanky-panky."

"No," Barrett said. He hesitated a few moments. "We're investigating how or why Mr. Jameson wound up floating, near dead, three-hundred miles off the Georgia coast. Mr. Wentworth and Ms. Jameson, instead of reporting the incident, returning to land and cooperating with authorities, have all but disappeared from view. We'd like to discover their whereabouts and ask them some questions."

"Bad business."

Barrett handed him a card. "Thanks for your time and cooperation, Mr. Cummings. If you think of anything else, will you get in touch with my office?"

"Course." Christ, Cummings thought, what's ol' Blake got himself into? I wanted to warn him. Should have. That kind of shit never comes to no good.

Agent Barrett made his way to Shirley Fontaine's home, Tim and Lauren's neighbor. She offered little more than a reprise of what she'd told Maya. She put stock in the rumors, she said, believing that the weight of evidence made them credible.

A third stop took him to the marina across the Narrows where Tim and Lauren kept their boat during sailing season. With more amenities, including a pool and restaurant on site, it was a decided upgrade from the bare-bones, utilitarian slips available at the other boatyard. Barrett spoke to dock hands at the in-season marina who witnessed the couple, plus Blake, embark on sailing trips of varying lengths, preliminaries, it turned out, to the eventual departure.

"When they left finally," he asked one of them, "did you know for sure they were leaving for the Caribbean?"

"No doubt," he answered. "They'd been buying new gear and loading up on provisions and supplies. It's all they talked about. Hell, everyone knew. They left here at night to catch a strong ebb headed south and a good forecast. Only Blake could have talked them into that."

Barrett's final stop on the way back to his hotel in Easton that afternoon was at the Jameson and Cox office. There he learned that Dennis Cox had been in contact with Lauren's parents. Her mother had expressed both resentment and concern at the paucity of communication from Lauren. The calls, plus one email, had been cryptic, Lauren reporting only that Tim was "fine." And that soon they would be headed to the "French West Indies." That was the long and short of it.

In his room that night, he did a Google search on the French West Indies. They were "departments" of France. That was probably good. And the FBI had a legal attaché office on Guadeloupe. Another plus.

The next day, Barrett and Maya boarded a Southwest flight from Baltimore to Jacksonville. Maya gazed out the window until her eyelids grew heavy.

Doodling on his iPad Pro, Barrett used his Apple Pencil to organize a loose framework of where the investigation had progressed. God, he loved this thing. No typing, just draw, write, scribble, like on a yellow pad. He completed a fragmented picture: a diagram, really, with notes, arrows, names—and question marks. Way more than they had before, for sure, but still too many blind spots. And with the victim lying in a coma, too few answers. And with no real clue exactly where his crewmates had gone, or what had happened aboard the boat, it wasn't even clear even what to call them: Persons of interest? Suspects? Perpetrators? What the hell were they? *Where* the hell were they?

Did something ugly happen aboard the Island Packet that night? It seemed so. He closed the iPad. Find out what, he thought, then prove it. Good luck. Unless ... the crewmates happened to screw up somewhere along the line. Or he and his partner got more breaks like the sister coming forward.

But training taught the two of them not to wait, or hope, but to make their own breaks. During a phone conversation while Barrett waited for the flight from BWI, the two agents agreed they still had a couple of ways to pry something loose.

13

Maya moved through the door into Tim's room, edging tentatively across the floor toward his bedside. Barrett, Franklin and Dr. Nichols followed at a respectful distance. As she drew closer, she pulled the tips of her fingers up to her face. Not knowing what to expect, she was unprepared for the wasted emptiness of Tim's physical appearance. He'd barely survived a life-threatening trauma, the aftermath of which had rendered him helpless, confined to a hospital bed, unconscious, nourished by tubes, imprisoned by a coma. The assaults on his system had clearly exacted a disturbing toll.

She turned. "Can I touch him?"

"Please do," Nichols said.

"Can he hear me?"

"He might. Give it a try."

She leaned closer and took his hand. "Tim, it's me, Maya. I've come to see you. We've been worried about you. These nice people brought me here." She turned to Nichols, who nodded and motioned her to keep going. "Looks like you've been through a rough time," she said. "But it's okay now. I'm going to take care of you."

Tim slowly rolled his head toward the sound of her voice, opened his eyes and struggled to focus. His eyes slowly centered, moved back and forth, becoming less glassy and vacant, until he looked directly into her eyes. He sighed deeply and groaned as his fingers tightened ever so slightly on her hand. His eyes filled with tears. An attempt to say something resulted in a grunt, first one then another. His grip on her hand tightened to a squeeze. He sunk back with the effort but kept his eyes locked on hers. The tears spilled over, running down his cheeks.

"Hallelujah," said Nichols. "What once was lost has now been found."

Franklin and Barrett exchanged a long look. "One step at a time," Barrett said, "one step at a time."

Pauline placed the phone receiver back in its cavity. The call had come from Maya, from Jacksonville, to relay the news of Tim's condition. It was a blend of better-than-might-be-expected with "it'll really be an uphill struggle from here."

She stood and paced, and stewed. And as she stewed her internal thermostat, one that fueled her reserves of energy, brought her to a low boil. She wondered why she hadn't heard from Lauren's parents. Why in God's name weren't they as worried about their daughter as she'd been about her son? It was unnatural, inexcusable she thought, that they hadn't at least checked in with her to find out if she'd heard anything.

The steam overcame any reticence Pauline may have had in pounding on someone's door. She picked up the phone and dialed. Sarah Forsyth, Lauren' mother, answered.

"Hello?"

"Sarah?"

"Yes."

"Sarah, hi. It's Pauline Jameson."

Sarah's voice caught. "Uh–oh! Pauline! My God. Hi, how are you!

"Well, I could say fine, but I guess I'm not."

Sarah was quiet. "Oh, I'm sorry."

To Pauline it seemed perfunctory. But she ignored the perceived slight of the tone and shifted gears. "Have you heard from Lauren?"

"Yes, yes, I have. But not nearly as often as I'd like. We're anxious to hear all about her big adventure but so far she's been mostly incommunicado. A few calls, an email. I'm really disappointed." A moment or two of dead air. "Have you heard from Tim?"

"I have," Pauline said, "but not directly. It seems he's been in a coma."

"What? What are you saying?"

"He's lying in a hospital bed as we speak, Sarah, in Jacksonville, Florida."

"Good Lord. I can't believe this. How?"

"Lauren hasn't told you anything?"

"No, as I said, she's barely been in contact."

"Maybe there's a reason."

Sarah stiffened just a notch and paused. "I don't know what you mean."

"Here's what I mean. Tim was rescued 300 miles at sea, at night, unconscious, floating all by himself. He'd suffered a severe head injury. He was barely alive."

"Dear God, Pauline. I don't know what ... it must be so ..."

"Excruciating? Horrifying? Yes, all those things." Pauline's accumulated anguish simmered. "But I can't imagine what it must be like to be on your end of the phone, wondering what Lauren's role in this might have been. She's his wife! Where is she? Why isn't she with him?"

Pauline's forceful implications caught Sarah off guard. She tried to regain her balance with a delaying action. "Pauline, how sure are you of all this? Where did this information come from?"

"From the Coast Guard Investigative Service, who's been here visiting and asking questions for the last two days. They're conducting an investigation of what might have happened to Tim. And from my daughter Maya, who's at Tim's bedside in Jacksonville right now. I spoke to her just a little while ago. She told me that, unexpectedly, Tim had just awakened. It's possible he responded to her voice and showed the first signs of awareness since he'd been rescued, left for dead, from the middle of the ocean two and a half months ago." Pauline leaned harder on the last half of that sentence.

Sarah tried to corral her wits as an uncertain dread took hold. Her husband was Elliot Forsyth, a charter member of Washington's white shoe legal establishment. He'd represented clients in the crossfires of Senate hearings, and in the crucibles of justice department prosecutions. From him, she had absorbed enough instinctual caution over the years to sense when it was time to pull up the drawbridge.

"Pauline," she said, "I think it would be helpful if we could be certain of all the facts before reaching any conclusions."

"I'm just telling you what I know, Sarah. Somehow my son wound up clinging to his life in an ICU, and your daughter is nowhere to be seen. Right now, Sarah, I'm pretty damned certain of those facts." She ended the call unceremoniously.

As she sat, breathing heavily, feeling unsatisfied that she hadn't been more forceful in extracting her pound of rhetorical flesh from Sarah, Pauline's eyes stopped on a copy of the *Washington Post* lying on the coffee table.

She recalled how in the months leading up to Tim and Lauren's marriage, the couple had been drawn to an enchanting Eastern Shore wedding venue: an elegant country inn tucked back in a picture postcard cove. The Forsyths were not persuaded. Yes, it was charming, but it wasn't Washington—not the Willard, or the Hay Adams. The nearby accommodations, they said, were uneven, mostly not up to standard. And it was too far to drive: Ninety minutes from the Beltway and Reagan National; two-plus hours to the Northern Virginia suburbs or Dulles International. Many of the Forsyths' guests would be the type of people who had to catch flights the next morning. A drive of that distance plus Beltway traffic made the logistics untenable.

The Forsyths pressed hard for a ceremony at St. John's Episcopal Church, on Lafayette Square a block from the White House; the reception at the Hay-Adams Hotel, just another short block away. The parents, whose time in Washington made them skilled practitioners in the art of twisting arms, prevailed. Not to mention they were paying the bills. And so the Jamesons and their guests would make the drive across the Bay into the Alice-in-Wonderland maze of Washington D.C. traffic, and pay outrageous prices for hotel rooms.

Pauline had a distinct recollection of the reception and the subtle but unmistakable gulf between the two sets of guests. Though it was never voiced openly, the Jamesons and their crowd were the rubes from the Eastern Shore—a quaint, charming place, suitable for a second home on the water maybe, but far away, culturally and temperamentally, from the centers of gravity and whirlwinds of power where the Forsyths and their guests circulated.

The memory simmered, tiny blueish flames heating the resentment. She picked up the *Post*, scanning the names of reporters associated with certain kinds of stories. What would one of them do with the tale of a Washington power couple whose daughter had vanished following a mysterious boating accident at sea involving her husband, this same daughter rumored to be involved in an adulterous relationship with the third member of the crew. A few of the reporters' names seemed likely. But maybe not just yet, she thought. No rush. The story wasn't going anywhere.

While Barrett was returning from Maryland, Franklin, based on a hunch, sought out footage recorded by a search helicopter's camera, one of two aircraft dispatched shortly after Tim's rescue at sea. As one of the helicopters had approached and then hovered astern of *Breezeway* that day, its camera was recording the scene using Forward Looking Infrared technology. FLIR technology captures the heat emitted from a source, like a human body, and converts it to digital images. The range of heat values shows up as shades of white, grey and black, not unlike a negative produced in the old style of film processing.

As the footage showed the helicopter's approach to the boat, Franklin hit the pause button a few times to freeze-frame full-size images of the hull, mast, and sails. He captured a frame each time as a separate file that could be printed or viewed on a monitor. Now he and Barrett were studying them on a high-resolution monitor. The larger scale images clearly showed a cutter-rigged sailboat under way. From promotional material and yacht brokerage photos, Barrett had a whole library of photography showcasing Island Packet yachts.

"Damn if that's not the same make of boat," Franklin said. "Tell by the aft sections, the teak, the bowsprit."

Barrett pulled out the record of the Jameson's storage intervals at Darryl Cummings' boatyard. "Yeah, that's it," he said. "2013 Island Packet, 37 feet, cutter rigged, name of *Breezeway*. Maryland registration. That's gotta be them."

The images taken from closer to the boat showed a person behind the wheel wearing a bandeau-type bikini top, clearly a female. A person stood in the companionway hatch holding the VHF. The voice on the recording of the VHF transmission was that of a male. When asked the vessel's name he replied "*Breezeway*." A helicopter crew member had written it as "Breeze Weigh."

"*Breezeway*," Franklin said. "Pretty much nails it down I'd say."

FLIR cameras captured heat signatures in low resolution. From any distance, a face was just a blob of white, muddied and indistinct. Identifying an individual through facial features was impossible. But that did nothing to lessen the agents' certainty about what they were seeing.

"Yeah," Barrett agreed. "No doubt."

"Damn we're good," Franklin said.

"Really? Good at what? Can't even see the boat name cause of the way they have the dinghy mounted. So far all I see is a carefree couple sailing to paradise."

"But everything tells us that 200 miles north of there they were up to something very heinous."

"We think."

"We believe."

"Where were they headed, I wonder."

"Tape transcript says Virgin Islands."

"That was November," Barrett said. "They still there?"

"Who knows? And what would we charge 'em with?"

"Failure to Report a Serious Marine Incident."

"Gosh, wow. Civil fines. Like Tim Jameson, left for dead, was a fuel leakage."

Franklin shrugged. They were quiet for a time, staring at the images. "Tim's partner in the accounting firm said the wife's mother mentioned something about the French West Indies," Barrett said.

"So she's the only one who's been in touch?"

"Seems so."

"Why don't we find out more about her parents? Talk to them, see what they know."

"Very next item on my to-do list," Barrett said. "I'll call Maya, see if she can get me a number. Meanwhile, maybe you can contact law enforcement in the French West Indies. I did some research. The islands are considered part of France, so I'm thinking maybe their cops take things seriously. And, there's an FBI legat office in Guadeloupe. Might come in handy."

"Send them the boat name, description, crew description?"

"Sure."

"And what?"

"You know, keep an eye out."

Franklin wheeled his chair over to a laptop, tapped at some keys. "Let's see ... there's six islands that make up Guadeloupe, and it looks like Martinique has, like, sixteen anchorages. TB, we're talking a couple hundred boats, at least, from all over the world, spread across 100 miles, with another country, Dominica, in between. You going to ask the French cops to sort through all that for a Failure to Report a Serious Marine Incident?"

"Persons of interest, wanted for questioning in connection with ..."

"What?"

Barrett hesitated. "I'm reaching here: attempted murder?"

"They find the victim with a life vest and a strobe? How's that's attempted murder?"

"Don't know. Said it was a reach."

"Best we can do is ask the French cops to check their customs records, see if a U.S.-flagged boat by that name with our two lovebirds aboard checked through. Hell, that shouldn't take more than a few keystrokes."

Sarah Forsyth felt an unwelcome leap in her heart rate as she listened to this voicemail:

> "Good morning, Ms. Forsyth. My name is Troy Barrett. I'm calling from the U.S. Coast Guard Investigative Service. We're conducting an investigation into an incident at sea involving the rescue of Mr. Tim Jameson, who's your son-in-law I believe? We have reason to believe that your daughter Lauren and another individual were aboard a sailing vessel with Mr. Jameson at the time of the incident, in early

November. We've not been able to contact Lauren and are unaware of her whereabouts. Mr. Jameson nearly lost his life in this incident, so we are treating it with the utmost seriousness. We're anxious to speak with you. We're hopeful that whatever you can share with us will help shed more light on what might have happened. Please call me, Agent Barrett, at your earliest convenience. My number is 904-555-1212, extension 769. We'll look forward to hearing from you soon. Thank you."

Prior to Barrett leaving the voicemail message, when he'd contacted Maya for the phone number and names of Lauren's parents, Maya updated him on Pauline's call to Sarah Forsyth. According to Pauline, Maya said, the phone call was adversarial in nature, and did not end on a good note. When Pauline discovered what Tim had been through, she was stunned that the Forsyths hadn't been in touch, shocked and outraged that Lauren was off on her own somewhere and not by Tim's side. Barrett had wondered the same thing. Maya added that during the call Pauline had mentioned the involvement of CGIS.

Too bad, thought Barrett. The Forsyths would have a heads-up before his call. He'd rather have made it unannounced, but it was unreasonable under the circumstances to think that in-laws wouldn't have been in touch. He probed Google for what there was to learn about the Forsyths. Turned out it was quite a bit. They were fixtures in the firmament of Washington D.C.'s social elite. He was a major-league lawyer who, between stints serving in senior posts in two administrations, had represented major-league clients. Sarah Forsyth, a former congresswoman from North Carolina, recently passed the baton as head of one of the Capital's most powerful lobbying firms.

She was semi-retired but had stayed wired-in to the circuitry of Washington's power brokers.

Sarah called her husband, not on the office line but on a mobile number only she and a few others had. "A man," she said when he answered, "an agent from the Coast Guard Investigative Service called, wanting to talk to me, or us I suppose, about Lauren. Said they were conducting an investigation involving Tim, and what he called an 'incident' at sea. What in God's name has she gotten herself into?" She might have said, What in God's name has she gotten *us* into?

"I don't know," Elliott said, "but let me contact the Coast Guard and find out what this is all about. Meanwhile, it's time to get ahold of Lauren no matter what. No more of her radio silence act. These people want answers. I can stonewall it. But they'll think we're hiding something, or she is, and that'll only whet their appetites. Tell her that. We can't help her unless we talk to her."

What if, Sarah thought as she hung up, she actually *does* have something to hide?

Franklin held up an email to show Barrett. It was from the Commissariat De Police in Basse Terre, Guadeloupe, Antilles Francaises. "Seek and ye shall find," he said. "Turns out our mystery couple did indeed check through French customs on 9 January. Two U.S. Citizens, Lauren Jameson and Blake Wentworth, arriving aboard a 37-foot Island Packet. Nothing to declare, admitted on a standard 90-day tourist visa."

"Amazing," said Barrett. "So here's the first question: assuming the Forsyths call us back, do we tell them we know where they are?"

"I would think not," Franklin said. "First, if they know, let's wait and see if they tell us. Second, if the parents tell the mystery couple that we know, it might only spook them, maybe drive them somewhere more obscure and farther away. I say play it like we're clueless, give it the old 'just trying to gather the facts, get the story straight' routine."

"Yeah, well, her father's a big-time lawyer. Sure he's heard it all."

"Except this time it's his daughter who might be in big-time trouble. That changes your whole perspective. Hell, she might even be a fugitive. I mean, they have to be wondering why she is wherever she is and not by her husband's side." Franklin put the email aside. "You said that was the first question. What's the second?"

Barrett stood and paced. "I've been wondering how long two people in this situation can hold out. How long can they just keep wandering? Anchorage to anchorage? Island to island? Whatever their plan is now wasn't part of the original plan, I know that for sure. They've only got ninety days where they are now. July starts hurricane season. I'm trying to use my intuition to figure when the stress of trying to disappear becomes too much for people like this. Money issues, maybe, too much time on your hands, always looking over your shoulder."

"What's your point?"

"I'm guessing that some combination of those factors might make them think it's better to make a run back to the States, take their chances. A lot easier to blend into the background here."

"And that's when we—"

"Yup. Put out the word, place 'em on the lookout list." What Barrett described was a broadcast to all Coast Guard units operating vessels of every size throughout the Caribbean and the Southeastern U.S. to 'Be On The Lookout' for a sailboat matching *Breezeway's* description. The effect was a maritime all-points bulletin. A central issuing authority would push the BOLO notice out to Intelligence Fusion Centers in Puerto Rico, South Florida and North Florida.

Franklin and Barrett were well aware that between budget cuts and mandated roles in efforts ranging from drug interdiction and immigration enforcement to anti-terrorism, Coast Guard units were stretched thin. A sailboat with two ill-starred adulterers aboard was somewhere down the list. It was just a question of timing, though, and whether they could get inside the heads of two people whose decisions had been inexplicable till now. Still, it was a wide net with extra sets of eyeballs on the open seas and inland waterways. Never know, they agreed, could get lucky.

Sarah tapped out an email to Lauren: "Imperative that you call me immediately. Law enforcement authorities have contacted us and want to speak with us an urgent matter concerning you. We are helpless to respond without talking to you. We must know what is going on. Please—call without further delay. I'll wait to hear from you.
Mom

14

Lauren and Blake had finished the last bites of their croissants and settled back in their chairs, lingering with a second cup of coffee. The seats were on the deck of a boulangerie overlooking the anchorage in Deshaies, a town on the west coast of Basse Terre, the westernmost of the two main islands of Guadeloupe. They'd decided to indulge themselves to breakfast out this one morning, for no particular reason other than they felt they were due.

Indulgences were becoming less frequent. Given that her bank account was funding this idyll, Lauren was the arbiter of when an indulgence was warranted or affordable. The email tone on her phone hummed twice and chimed. Incoming email traffic, like the indulgences, had slowed considerably. The tone startled her. She looked down and flicked her thumb until she came to the message. As she read, her face clouded over.

Blake noticed. "What?" He was alert, his antennae twitching, to the slightest hint of the trouble they'd left behind suddenly tapping them on the shoulder.

"It's from my mother. She's telling me in no uncertain terms to call her. It's not a request, it's a demand."

Blake sensed the inescapability and instinctively scrambled for the exits—any exit, no matter how unlikely or farfetched. "Maybe the email went to your spam folder by mistake," he blurted. "Or there's a glitch in the WiFi."

Lauren shook her head. "No, dude. Sorry. She said they've been contacted by law enforcement."

Blake lowered his forehead to his palm. "Jesus." Now his face mirrored the alarm in hers.

"She wants to hear from me now. I've got to call."

His face tightened. Residual instincts from prison welled up. "What are you going to tell her?"

"About what?"

"Christ, Lauren! About us. About what happened. About where we are."

"I don't know. I haven't—"

"Remember what I said about bread crumb trails? Why do you think the cops are calling? They want to know what the hell happened with Tim. And they can't talk to the only two people who know, so they want to know where the hell we are."

Lauren shook her head. "That's not what I'm worried about. My father's a heavyweight lawyer. He'll know how to deal with that. I'm more worried about how horrified my mother's going to be. And she'll know more about Tim's situation, whatever it is, than I do."

"We decided on a story. Nobody knows any different except you and me."

"So you're saying lie."

"The truth is you and I thought Tim was dead and we dumped his body overboard. Is that what you want to tell her? Besides, you already told her twice that Tim was fine. Was that the truth?"

"Of course not."

"Okay then."

"I've got to make the call." She stood up and walked a short distance away.

Lauren listened to the rings, her innards clenched. Finally, *Hello?*

"Hi, Mom. It's me, Lauren."

"Lauren! Oh my God. I can't believe it's you! What the—? Where—? I don't even know where to start. Oh, oh yes I do. First you. My God. Are you okay?"

"Yes, I'm fine."

"You got my email."

"Just now."

"Then you know."

"Know what?"

"That a man from the Coast Guard Investigative Service called and left a message. They want to know your whereabouts, to talk to you. Something about an incident at sea."

Lauren was quiet.

"Are you there?"

"Yes."

"And then, my God, Tim's mother Pauline called me, absolutely incensed. Here it turns out Tim was rescued out at sea, unconscious, nearly dead. He was in a coma for weeks, but it seems he just came out of it. He's awake, or conscious I guess. She said this agent person had been on the Eastern Shore asking questions."

Lauren felt a stab of horror. Christ! They'd lowered him over the side convinced that the fall from the cabin top had killed him. But my God! He was alive! The thought of dumping a live human being into the ocean, leaving him to the mercy of the elements made her blood run cold. She gulped in air, closed her eyes, fought to maintain composure. She knew if she spoke her voice would waver or crack.

Lauren's silence stoked Sarah's energy. She had more than enough to carry on the conversation for the two of them. "Pauline wondered, naturally, as your father and I have, where you've been during all this? Why did you tell me Tim was fine?"

Lauren's response was muted, hesitant. "I was ... untruthful." It was her spin doctor's way of sugarcoating an outright lie.

"To say the least," Sarah replied. Having spent years in the hallways of congress, both as a lawmaker and later as a lobbyist striving to shape those laws to her clients' benefit, Sarah was no stranger to the seamier side of human nature. She knew how words got twisted and bent until an original meaning was perverted beyond recognition. Lauren was playing rope-a-dope, and Sarah would have none of it—not now, not with an ominous-sounding agent waiting for a return call and Pauline simmering with righteous anger. "I can wait as long as necessary to hear your explanation, Lauren. I'm not going anywhere."

Lauren paced along the waterfront, waiting a few moments before she unveiled the narrative without any preamble. "We had a system of rotating watches, one person on, the other two off. Tim's watch that night was eight to midnight. Usually Blake would go up an hour or so early to sit with whoever was at the wheel. For some reason that night he didn't. When he went on deck for his midnight watch, Tim was gone."

"Gone."

"Yes. Overboard. Blake woke me immediately. We had no idea how it happened, or when. We reversed course, sailed back, tried different courses taking the wind and currents into account. All we could do is guess, sailed this way and that for hours. Until we just gave up."

"Wouldn't there be some procedure," Sarah said, "to report something like this? I don't know, what do they call it? S.O.S or something?"

"Mom, I was out of my mind with panic. We both were. Blake said if we reported that Tim was gone, lost overboard, no one would believe us. They'd think we did something to him. We'd be suspects."

"Why would he think that?"

"I—I don't know."

"Really? You don't know? Why would someone jump to that conclusion?"

Lauren faltered. "I—

"Oh, no," Sarah groaned. "Don't tell me. Please, no. Were you screwing this guy?"

Lauren's silence answered the question.

Sarah sighed, in a plaint sent skyward to nothing other than the fates. "Dear God."

The exhalation signaled profound disappointment and the swipe of a reproach. The tone of it was such that Lauren's voice broke as she stumbled into the rest of the fiction, though oddly enough this part had some element of truth to it. "We made choices—or, I made choices—at an incredibly stressful moment. You can't imagine. It was dark, we were 300 miles at sea, the wind and waves had picked up. I was scared. Scared out of my mind, Mom. Okay? Were they the wrong choices? Yeah, without a doubt. Horrible, disastrous choices looking back." She took a deep breath and gathered herself. "But I can't change it. It's my nightmare now, mine alone. I'm not going to let it become yours."

"Lauren," Sarah said eventually, "can you at least tell me where you are?"

"A place where I can pull the covers over my head, hoping I wake up some morning and this nightmare's over."

As she listened to Lauren's wavering voice and sniffling, Sarah's maternal instincts softened the stoniness of her disapproval. For the moment, Lauren was the little girl she had held in her arms. "You can't hide under the covers forever, darling."

"I know."

"Don't you think you belong by Tim's side?"

"I didn't know where he was or if he was even alive until you just told me. Did Pauline say anything else?"

"No. As I said, only that he'd been in a coma for weeks and just came out of it. Apparently, he'd suffered a severe head injury."

An instant replay of revulsion coursed through her as she was forced to recall the picture of Tim floating astern of the boat. Not dead, as she believed, but clinging to life. "Jesus," she breathed.

Now it was quiet on both ends. The enormity of what had happened placed their understanding of it on two different planes. There was no way for them to have a common context.

"We will have to make our way north," Lauren said finally. "It'll take some time."

"You can't just fly back? We'll send you the money if that's the problem."

Lauren's experience in helping public officials measure the angles of impossible dilemmas, often involving untoward behavior, gave her perspective. If I'm already a villain, she thought, going back now won't make me less of a villain. I'm in this. I can't straddle the consequences of what happened.

"And what will I come back to?" she asked her mother. "A stoning in the village square? Maybe an 'A' on my forehead? I need room, some time to work through this. I told you, I made some disastrous choices. I know I'll have to own up to them. But I'm not ready for that just yet."

Sarah sensed calculations going on, some hedging, Lauren giving herself space as she sifted through the options. "You're running from something, Lauren, or hiding," Sarah said. "Or both."

"Yeah, no kidding. If you only knew. But it's my nightmare, okay? Let it torment me, not you."

She walked back to the small shelf of beach that fronted rows of shops and dwellings along the waterfront. Blake had been idling, ambling along as he waited. When she approached, her face was drained and ashen.

"That bad, huh?"

"My mother thinks I'm a slut."

"Oh. Sorry."

"It gets worse. Tim is alive."

Blake's face sagged. Before he could muster a response, Lauren spoke again.

"He's been in a coma since our fiasco that night. But my mom said he's come out of it. He's conscious."

"Holy shit."

"My sentiments exactly. The law enforcement guy who left a message for my mom is a Coast Guard Investigative Service guy—an agent. She said they've been on the Eastern Shore asking questions"

Blake began to pace, head down, where the water lapped up along the shore. "You know, I could start to panic, but I'm not going to. Not yet. I still say it comes down to who knows what happened on the boat that night, and right now that's only you and me."

"Really? What about Tim?"

"Christ, Lauren, he was in a coma until what, a couple days ago?"

"I don't know. Yeah, I guess."

They sat on a knee wall a few yards from the water's edge, gazing out over the anchorage, looking for something, or past something, each keeping whatever it was private. It was the second time Blake had retreated to what he must have believed was a safety net: that the two of them were the only witnesses. It must not have dawned on him, she thought, that the other side of the mutual dependence he hoped bound them to a common cause was the specter of mutual suspicion. Along with the reassurance that came with sticking to the same story, was the prospect that one of them would abandon it and turn on the other.

It occurred to her that all Blake ever considered were the logistics of dodging the consequences of what they'd done. He never once seemed to burden himself with the sheer amorality of it. And if he was unconcerned with the amorality of what they'd done, how hesitant would he be to give her up to save his own skin?

She stood slowly and walked out onto the nearby dinghy dock, stopping a short way out, putting a distance between them. She was taking an inventory of where her culpability stood in all this. In the story they'd concocted, she figured that what they did—giving up the search and sailing on to paradise—was shameful and despicable, unforgivable in the eyes of almost anyone. But, so far as she knew, not a crime.

If she returned to the Eastern Shore, it would come out, inevitably, that she and Blake were involved. The infamy would amplify the suspicion and heap on the shame in proportions few could withstand. Life there would be untenable.

The wild card was how much Tim might or might not remember. If his memory cleared and he recalled what happened, suddenly their concoction falls apart. The reality of what took place that night on *Breezeway's* deck and cockpit was not only scandalous and heinous but also a serious crime. More than that, there was a line between making an appalling choice believing Tim was dead—and making that choice if there was the slightest chance he was still alive. It was a dimension to which she could not travel, something she could not live alongside.

She would have to replay those hellish moments in the cockpit when Tim lay motionless, inert, no sign of a pulse or respirations. He was dead. Blake said he was. Blake looked like he knew what he was about. Would she have helped Blake lift the body over the side had she known or even suspected Tim was alive? God no. No way in hell.

What about Blake? Did he push them into it, rush their decision because he was worried about spending ten years in jail for manslaughter? She'd almost said it a few minutes before but didn't. In the end, she'd gone along with it. Yet it was Blake who'd wasted no time in broaching the suggestion, and Blake who had the most to lose. If he was that willing, with little hesitation, to dump Tim overboard, how long would he hesitate in giving her up? She hadn't seen what really took place on the cabin top that night. What would happen at crunch time if their story fell apart, as Blake thought it might? Would it then come down to her word against his?

She turned toward him sitting on the knee wall. He looked back at her. "Time to head back to the boat?"

"Sure." My boat, she thought. My money, my everything. Soon the time would come to formulate an end game with Blake.

15

Barrett checked the caller ID on his phone set and turned to Franklin. "It's Elliott Forsyth. This should be interesting." He picked up: "Agent Barrett."

"Good afternoon, Agent Barrett. This is Elliott Forsyth, Lauren's father, returning your call. You left a message that you wished to speak with us."

"Thanks for returning my call, sir. Yes, I did leave a message."

"About what, may I ask?"

Barrett knew he'd made it plain in the voicemail why he called, but there was no point in dicking with a guy like this. "Mr. Forsyth, we're looking into the circumstances surrounding what we're calling an incident at sea. We have reason to believe your daughter, Lauren, and another individual were aboard a southbound sailboat, somewhere around the latitude of the Florida-Georgia border on the night of 12 November 2019. On that night, or I should say early the next morning, Mr. Tim Jameson—Lauren's husband and your son-in-law, who was also aboard that boat at one point—was rescued by a fishing vessel very near that location. He was by himself, floating, wearing a life vest, unconscious, suffering severe hypothermia. He was in very bad shape, Mr. Forsyth, close to breathing his last."

Silence from Forsyth's end.

"I'm sure you can understand, sir, why we would like to clear up what happened that night on that vessel. Somehow, he'd sustained a severe head injury, either through a deliberate act or as the result of an accident. We would like to find out which of those, and how he came to go overboard and wind up in the ocean, near death."

More silence.

Game-playing. Barrett tried not to let it irritate him. "Hello?" It was almost a bark. "Still there, Mr. Forsyth?"

Forsyth, slowly, quietly: "Yes, I'm still here."

"Oh, good. Well, sir, your daughter and this other individual—we believe his name is Blake Wentworth—chose not to report the fact that your son-in-law had gone missing. Instead of reporting it by radio and heading for the nearest port, evidently they chose to keep sailing south. We have high confidence that audio and video recordings from a search and rescue helicopter, roughly thirty hours after Mr. Jameson was rescued, place them on a southern heading, some two-hundred miles south of where the incident took place."

After a pause, Forsyth said, "I'm listening, Agent Barrett."

"Sir, I'm sure you can imagine how your daughter's behavior in all this raises questions in our minds. Why would a wife continue sailing and not report the fact of her husband's disappearance overboard? I've been in the Coast Guard for 14 years and a CGIS agent for 11 of those. I've never seen or heard of anything like this. People are usually frantic when a loved one goes missing."

Barrett was trying to wring some sort of concession out of a man whose clients paid him $700 an hour to rarely, if ever, concede anything. "Agent Barrett," Forsyth said, "has my daughter been charged with a crime?"

"No, sir."

"Is she a fugitive?"

Barrett decided to dispense with the 'sir' stuff. "No."

"In any case, she is under no obligation to get in touch with you, correct?"

"Correct."

"And with all due respect, Agent Barrett, neither are we, my wife or I, under any obligation to communicate with you."

"No, that's true. But to reiterate, for Lauren to have abandoned her husband on the open ocean, and avoided cooperating with us to learn what happened, certainly places her under a cloud of suspicion."

"Suspicion notwithstanding, Agent Barrett, what you describe sounds like a family matter, not a criminal matter."

It was Barrett's turn to stay quiet. Family matters can become criminal matters, he thought. This guy was reaching into the defense lawyer's toolbox.

"So if you don't mind, please, allow us to keep private family matters private."

"Mr. Forsyth, family matters are your business till they become our business. Something happened out there on the ocean that night, and it's our job to find out what. Two people were there and know what took place."

"Correction, Agent Barrett. Three people."

"Tim Jameson was in a coma and unresponsive until a couple days ago," Barrett said. "In our minds he's a victim, not a witness, unless his traumatic brain injury was somehow self-inflicted and he flung himself overboard and manages to recall all that."

Elliot Forsyth's voice went flat. "Agent Barrett, please make a note to your file. For the record, my daughter Lauren is represented by counsel. From this point forward, any communication with her, in any form, is to be directed through me. Are we clear on that?"

"Yes."

"Excellent. Will there be anything else?"

Barrett decided to play their only hole card. "Just this Mr. Forsyth: We know through contacts with an EU law enforcement agency that your daughter and her, um, companion have cleared customs and immigration in Guadeloupe, in the French West Indies. They have not cleared out of French customs, so we believe they're still there. Our hope is that your daughter would come forward. If you or your wife are able to persuade her to do so, maybe we can clear this up and everyone can go on with their lives."

"I've told you, Agent Barrett, this is a private matter."

"And I've told you, Mr. Forsyth, that when we're forced to discover the facts in a case like this, with no cooperation from the principals, by definition it becomes our business. There's an FBI legal attaché office in Point a Pitré. We may avail ourselves of their assistance in following up on this. We're not without resources."

"Nor am I, Agent Barrett. Nor am I."

Barrett slammed the receiver down. "Fuck you." He turned to Franklin, who looked back at him with no expectations.

"Just make a new friend, TB?"

"Arrogant son of bitch." Barrett said. "Copped an attitude with me, playing hardball."

"Sounds like you did too, toward the end there. Thought we weren't going to tell them what we knew. And what was the thing with the FBI?"

"Guy pissed me off, which is always a mistake. And I don't care who you are, you start thinking the FBI's involved, it has to make you at least a little nervous. And maybe if the parents are nervous, they pass that nervousness on to the daughter, who starts thinking about her options. Which may not include lover boy."

Franklin tilted back in his chair. "I don't know. From what you're saying, the daughter's lawyered-up right out of the box, right? And though we think they're somewhere in the French West Indies, we don't know where for sure. Maybe it's time to reassess."

Barrett stood up and walked over to a window. "I keep coming back to the idea that something really, really bad, evil goddammit, happened on the boat that night. I mean nobody, *nobody*, loses a spouse overboard and just keeps going. That's a deliberate choice. So why do you make that choice? Christ, it can't be easy. It's gotta be gut-wrenching."

"You make the choice because you want him gone. But why?" Franklin asked.

"We know the answer to that. When I was up in Maryland, I heard all kinds of ugly rumors that the wife and the boatyard guy, this Blake character, were getting it on."

"So that's a motive. They wanted him out of the way."

Barrett shook his head. "You want to get rid of him, you tie a weight to his ankles before you dump him overboard. You don't put a PFD on him with a flashing strobe."

"How bout this: He's on watch by himself, falls overboard, hits his head somehow. The lovebirds come in deck, see he's gone, and think, problem solved. Sail on."

"Yadda, yadda, yadda. Point is, we don't know. But those two lovebirds know. How the hell do you just let somebody float away like that. Like I said—evil, man, nothing but evil. And they're sitting down there drinking rum punches thinking they're about to get away with it. Bullshit. Not as long as I've got something to say about it. Somehow, some way, I'm going to find them, and one of them is going to tell us. So help me."

Franklin lurched back forward in his chair. "There we go. That's the TB I know and—oh, damn. Almost forgot. We got a call from Doc Nichols. He wants to see us."

"What for?"

"Tim's mother flew down from Maryland yesterday. Turns out she's quite the bundle of determination."

"Putting it mildly. She's a roll of barbed wire when it comes to her in-laws."

Franklin smiled "Between her energy and just having Maya here,

Tim's coming around better than Doc Nichols figured he would. Thought we'd be interested in seeing for ourselves."

"Yeah, yeah. 'Scuse me if I don't get my hopes up."

"Didn't say you should. But TB, man, think positive. Okay? I remember what Doc Nichols said. But I also remember what he didn't say."

"Like what?"

"Chances of Tim coming around and telling us what happened aren't good. We know that. On the other hand, he never said there was no chance at all."

Barrett and Franklin walked in and stood quietly at the margins of the room in which Tim Jameson was recuperating. Pauline beamed and strode toward Barrett, enveloping him in an enthusiastic hug. "How *are* you!" she said. "I'm so glad to see you again." She turned toward Franklin. "And who is this handsome man?"

Both Barrett and Franklin were smitten. "This is my partner, Ms. Jameson, Agent Franklin."

She shook his hand with vigor. "So glad to meet you, sir. Are you going to help us find the cheating adulterers who tried to kill my son?"

Maya charged to her side. "Mom!" she hissed. "No! Stop. Not here. Not now. This is about Tim, okay?"

Dr. Nichols walked over, smiling, and shook their hands. "Come say hi to Tim."

Tim sat in a wheelchair, eyes darting, a faint smile lighting his expression. "Hi, Tim," Barrett said.

Tim slurred a response. "Hi." His smile grew wider.

Franklin leaned in. "Hi, Tim. Good to see you."

"Me too," Tim said.

When Barrett looked over, Maya's eyes were brimming with tears. "Let's take a walk," Dr. Nichols said. "One of you can stay here."

"I will," Franklin said, "Tim and I can shoot the breeze." He pulled a chair over and sat near Tim, smiling. Tim grinned back.

They made their way to a small outdoor courtyard. Nichols addressed his comments to Barrett, updating him on what Pauline and Maya already knew. "I'm pleasantly surprised at the progress Tim has made," he said. "Maya's and Ms. Jameson's presence by his bedside has really made a significant positive difference."

"I'm glad to hear it," Barrett said. "We've all been pulling for him."

"So much so," Nichols continued, "that I'm recommending that Tim be transferred from our facility here to home care."

"That's great," Barrett said. "Where?"

"At Ms. Jameson's home, in Maryland."

Barrett smiled. "Wow. That's fantastic. You two must be thrilled," he said, nodding toward Maya and Pauline, "you'll have him right there with you."

Maya nodded. "It's like a miracle, how far he's come since I got here and first saw him."

Nichols stood and paced a little. "Being a physician and having spent 16 years treating traumatic brain injuries, I tend to discount miracles, but I never rule them out. In this case, I'm leaning on my still-unproven theory that Tim's hypothermic condition helped mitigate the damage, the inflammation, swelling and bleeding. His brain is in better shape than it otherwise might have been, and that's allowing him to make more progress, much more, that we thought initially."

Barrett smiled, keeping his other agenda to himself. As they made their way back to Tim's room, Barrett gently took hold of Dr. Nichols' elbow. "A word?" he said as they slowed behind Pauline and Maya. Pauline looked back, intuiting Barrett's reasons for buttonholing Nichols.

He turned to Nichols and drew close. "So, Dr. Nichols, beyond my best wishes for Tim's recovery, you can imagine what my professional interest is at this point."

"Sure. Will he ever regain enough memory to tell you what happened out at sea that night?"

"That's it."

"It's still a long shot, but not out of the realm of possibility. One of the reasons I want him to go home with his mother and sister has to do with all the really encouraging research done recently on how beneficial it is for recovering TBI patients to be around family in familiar surroundings. The voices, faces, familiar objects and places—they've shown to be enormously valuable in speeding up recovery. There's a former neurologist colleague of mine out of a hospital in Annapolis. I've already talked to her. She's excellent. When they get him into some occupational and speech therapy, get him up on his feet and moving with some physical therapy, you never know. He could surprise us."

They slowly walked toward Tim's room. "I will say I've seen near full recoveries from brain injuries worse than his," Nichols said. "It's rare, but it does happen."

"Is it out of your hands at some point?" Barrett asked.

"Yeah, possibly. God, the fates, luck, or in this case maybe hypothermia."

They were gathered back in Tim's room. Franklin checked his watch. "I'm sorry, we have to get going."

Barrett walked over to Tim. Both he and Franklin had become attached to him and rooted for him for reasons other than just law enforcement expedience. "It was good seeing you again, Tim. We wish you the best."

Tim smiled. "Me too."

As they edged out Pauline followed. She stopped them outside the door and got right to the point. "Have you talked to Lauren's parents yet?"

Franklin and Barrett exchanged a glance. "I have," Barrett said. "Mr. Forsyth called me."

"So? Was he any help? Was he concerned about Lauren or at all worried about what happened?"

Barrett thought for a moment. If what he said to Elliott Forsyth was true, that they considered Tim Jameson the victim, then there was nothing wrong with sharing details of the investigation, up to a point, with the victim's family. "No, he was not," Barrett said. "He was not cooperative and seemed disinclined toward any form of cooperation. In fact, he was adversarial, playing hardball."

"Okay," Pauline said, "that's all I wanted to know."

The two agents exchanged another glance, not connecting with whatever point she was making.

"We'll be in touch, Ms. Jameson," said Barrett. Then he followed up with an unusual helping of personal intensity. "When you go to bed at night up there in Easton, I want you to remember that I am not going to let go of this. It will be on my checklist first thing each morning and last thing each night."

Pauline smiled. "I knew there was a reason I liked you."

Lauren's text message chime sounded. Sprawling in the cockpit with a book, under an awning, she swiped the screen to check it. It was from her mother. "You didn't want to tell me where you were. That's OK because now it doesn't matter. Coast Guard investigators told us they believe you're in the French West Indies. They said there's an FBI office there??? FYI."

TOM HITCHCOCK

16

Lauren turned to Blake as he came up the companionway steps with yet another beer in his hand. "Um, we're getting low on Heinekens. Just saying."

Something about his timing and the oblivious beer announcement, as if all he had to do was announce the fact of a diminishing beer supply and it would somehow replenish itself, sparked a flash of irritation.

"They know we're here," she said with a cold abruptness meant to jerk him back to some sense of urgency.

"Who knows?"

"The Coast Guard—whatever."

"Who told you that?"

She held up her phone. "My mother, in a text."

Blake took a swig of beer. "How does she know?"

She wanted to slap the beer out of his hand. "Goddammit! The fuckin' Coast Guard people told her. That's how!"

"Shit."

"Yeah, that's helpful. What's the next part of your plan?" The tone of her remark suggested the ground had shifted under the relationship. There was a new, pungent edge to this conversation. Blake could sense the ground rules changing. "And you ready for this? My mother said something about an FBI office here somewhere. I don't know, Point-a-Pitre? Who knows?"

The commercial center of Guadeloupe, Point-a-Pitre offered extensive services for both visiting yachts and commercial vessels. They had taken *Breezeway* there for some deck hardware, fuel, and to restock staple items for the galley. Lauren's mother's text was an unnerving dose of reality. Here they were, trying to stay far off the beaten path a thousand miles from home, and they'd ventured practically to the doorstep of an FBI office.

"Nowhere to run, nowhere to hide," she said.

"Yeah, well, I don't know about that. But we can't stay here."

"We should head back, back up north."

"How do you figure?"

"Because we can't just keep wandering around forever like a Flying Dutchman."

"A what?"

"God. Never mind." She stood, went down the companionway steps, and reemerged with a Heineken. She held it up. "See this? There's not an endless supply of this. A limit. I'm not an ATM. That's the other reason we have to—or I have to—figure out how this ends, and where."

They took sips from their respective beers. "Okay," Blake said, "why north? Why not, like, Mexico?"

Lauren looked at him. "Got a job waiting in Mexico? Otherwise, you can't afford Mexico. What I'm saying is, head back in a direction no one expects. They got us located here? Go back where they might not look. Called hiding in plain sight."

Blake sensed, not unreasonably, that he was coming closer to being offloaded. It was probably overdue, he thought, but still—a blow to male pride. In the end, though, she was right. There was no future in the two of them playing Bonnie and Clyde aboard a sailboat, which, despite its thirty-seven foot length, seemed to grow smaller as time went on.

"Okay," he said, "you want a plan, here's a plan. We head back to Vieques but go around to the north to a smaller island called Culebra. Only a little bit farther from here. It's very laid back, not a lot of activity. A good place to reenter U.S. territory without being noticed. We hang out there for a couple days, then head for Key West. That's where we go our separate ways. You okay with that?"

"I think it's best. Not happy we've come to that and I wish it didn't have to be. But I don't see another choice. Do you?"

He sighed and looked at her. "I don't. Got to be grownups. If they're looking for two of us, it's better if we split up."

"Oh, yeah? Where am I going?"

"This is the best part of the plan. You take the boat from Key West to Marco Island, then on to Fort Myers. Two short trips, day sails, in protected water. For you, no sweat at this point. At Fort Myers you cut across the state, west to east on the Okeechobee Waterway, till you come to Stuart. At Stuart you turn north on the Intracoastal Waterway, travel up the coast till you come to this really cool little town in Florida, right near the Georgia border."

"Are you kidding? The Georgia border? My God, Blake, that's right where—"

"I know. But it's like you said, right? Last place they'd look? You'll be inland all the way, marinas, places to anchor if you want. We're talking maybe seven, eight days. Depends on how far you want to go each day—or hang out an extra day somewhere."

She smiled. Maybe Blake wasn't so obtuse after all. "So what's this cool little town you're talking about?"

"It's called Fernandina Beach."

"Never heard of it."

"That's kind of the point. Been a while since I was there, but back then it was known as kind of a hippie, surfer-type place. Chilled out. Live and let live. You could just blend in, nobody asked too many questions. Nobody cared all that much. Do your own thing. There's three routes to get there by boat, from the north or south on the ICW, or through a river inlet from the ocean. Lots of coming and going, no way to keep track. Perfect place to be as anonymous as you want."

"So, okay. Fernandina Beach."

"Yup."

"A beach?"

"Yeah, nice beach. Lots of nice beaches."

"What about you?"

"I know people in Key West. I can always hook up with something there. Working on boats, maybe some deliveries."

There it was, suddenly. The exit strategy Lauren had been looking for, planned, ironically, by Blake. To her surprise, it sounded as though Blake had been thinking about it too. It was a pretty good plan, she decided. She had to give Blake credit. It actually made sense, more carefully thought out than she might have imagined. As a bonus, it gybed with what she'd told her mother about heading north. She'd decide on the next phase from Fernandina Beach.

They sat in the cockpit, finishing their beers, looking out over the water, not letting their eyes meet at this crossroads moment. It was odd, she thought, how the physical attraction to him had ebbed as they spent more time together. But in its place a bond had developed, a strange brand of camaraderie. They'd been through a lot, the baggage of an emotional voyage always draped over their shoulders as they dealt with winds and currents. He'd toughened her in a way, taught her how to manage the hard work of skippering a sailing vessel of considerable size and displacement. She was stronger, less intimidated by waves that rolled by like small liquid hilltops. He'd allowed her to grow, pushed her to grow in fact. She owed that to him.

"When do we leave?" she asked.

"Day after tomorrow. Lots to do to get ready. But you already know that."

"Okay. Tell you what. Let's get cleaned up. We'll take the dinghy in to pick up some more Heinekens. And we'll have dinner. I'm buying."

He laughed and shook his head. She smiled, but behind the smile she wondered what it would be like to have Blake Wentworth untethered, a repository of information that could send her to prison. The same held true from his perspective, of course. They would circle in their respective orbits, without the telescope of one seeing the other or knowing whether or when an insistent, loud knock would come at their door. It would be an uncertain way to live. No way to live, she thought, with your fate resting in the hands of someone whose judgment or day-to-day existence featured trap doors that could either take you down with him—or you in his place.

Mark O'Reilly, a reporter with the Washington Post's metro section, sat at a table with a clear view of the restaurant's door and entranceway. He'd let the hostess know he was expecting another party. He and Pauline had agreed on a Kent Island location. Situated at the eastern edge of the Bay Bridge, Kent Island was a good halfway point between Washington, D.C. and Easton.

O'Reilly willingly agreed to meet Pauline at an Eastern Shore restaurant, irrespective of whether the story idea she'd described to him panned out. Oysters were still in season at this time of year, and he loved Chesapeake Bay oysters. He could get them in Washington, albeit marked up to reflect the fixed and variable costs of the restaurant featuring them on the menu, not to mention supply and demand, which was to say, unreasonably expensive. Here, across the bridge, oysters came directly from workboats tied up at the docks adjacent to the restaurant.

A fit, striking woman with short, salt-and-pepper gray hair walked in. She was smiling and had an air about her. Had to be Pauline. As the hostess gestured back toward his table, he stood. She walked toward him, extending her hand, gripping his with a pronounced enthusiasm.

"Mark."

"Yes."

"I'm Pauline. So nice to meet you. Thanks for agreeing to see me."

O'Reilly shook her hand warmly. "Any time I get a chance to come over this way, it's a treat, believe me."

They sat down and worked their way through the rituals of small talk and ordering food. Pauline allowed that she loved crabs but had never acquired a taste for oysters.

O'Reilly had run the outlines of Pauline's story idea past his editor. She was as intrigued as he was. It was the kind of story that might have a slow fuse, but those were the narratives that had legs, kept readers waiting and watching as pieces of it dribbled out. The catch, as always, would be getting corroboration. He'd have to look for sources beneath the surface. Dig deep. See what turns up.

After finishing his appetizer of raw oysters on the half shell, O'Reilly pulled out a small recorder and a notebook. "Okay," he said, "let's take a step back. Start from the beginning, but you don't need to go into too much detail. Just the broad outlines for now. Sound alright?"

"Perfect," she said, pulling out a yellow legal pad filled with notes. "Okay, in early November of last year, my son Tim and his wife Lauren set out from Tilghman Island with the intention of sailing to the Caribbean. They took a guy with them, this guy Blake, who was supposed to show them the ropes, you know, be sort of a teacher or coach."

"Where did they know Blake from?"

"He worked in a boatyard on Tilghman Island where they kept their boat over the winter."

"So if I go to Tilghman Island, people there can verify this?"

"Absolutely. I mean, Tim and Lauren have a house on the island. My daughter, Maya, went down to Tilghman and talked to people. So did the CGIS agent."

"What's CGIS?"

"Coast Guard Investigative Service."

"They're involved?"

"Sure."

O'Reilly scribbled. "So, if I remember right, the Coast Guard rescued your son out at sea."

"That's right. A fishing vessel picked him up out of the water. He was unconscious, near dead."

"When was this?"

"November 12th, ten days after they left Tilghman."

"And then what?"

"Well, the Coast Guard was naturally curious how a guy, my son, winds up in the water like that. No abandoned boat, no distress call, nothing."

"So CGIS starts looking into it."

"Right, but the other thing is, Tim had sustained a really severe head injury. He was in a coma. They also wanted to know how that happened."

"Jeez."

"Yeah, jeez is right. Weeks go by and we didn't hear anything. Maya goes to Tilghman Island, asks around. A guy there suggests she file a missing person report with the Coast Guard, which she does. Somehow the report finds its way to a CGIS office in Jacksonville, Florida. The people down there contact us, an agent flies up and starts asking questions."

"Asking questions about what? To whom?"

"Started with us, wanted to know all we knew. Then on to Tilghman, and who knows where else? But meanwhile no one on our side of the family has heard from Tim's wife. The guy who Blake worked for hasn't heard from him either."

"Who's the other side of the family?"

"Her name is Lauren Jameson. That's her married name, used to be Forsyth."

O'Reilly jerked back in his chair. "You sure?"

"Of course I'm sure. Her parents are—"

"I know who her parents are. I know who she is too. Believe me, a lot of people in Washington know those names."

Pauline looked down at her notes. "My son Tim was lying in a coma in an ICU in a Jacksonville trauma center, and yet no one, that I know of, has heard from his wife or the, um, what do I call him? The other guy."

O'Reilly's entrée arrived: oyster fritters. Pauline chose crab cakes. "Do you have a number for the CGIS agent?" She tore off a piece from her legal pad and handed it to him. "What about the doctor in Jacksonville?"

"Dr. Nichols. I'll get it for you."

"I'll need you to sign a release."

"No problem." She was encouraged. It was sounding like Mark was going to run with this.

"Have you spoken to her parents?" he asked. To him it seemed only natural that in-laws would have reached out to share information.

"I didn't hear from Sarah Forsyth until I called her, well after Tim had been rescued."

"Had she heard from her daughter?"

"Only a few times, she claimed. A couple calls from Lauren, an email. Said she was disappointed at not hearing from her more often."

"Did you believe her?"

"What choice did I have? But I did ask her how she could reconcile the fact that my son, her son-in-law, was lying in a coma while her daughter was nowhere to be seen."

"What did she say?"

"Not much. Tap dancing."

"Where is your son now?"

"He's home with us, here on the Eastern Shore. The doctors think the familiar surroundings will help his recovery."

"I'm sorry for asking this, but I assume he has no recollection of what happened?"

"No. He's awake, aware, starting to form thoughts, a few basic phrases like 'I'm hungry.' It's day to day."

O'Reilly put down his pen. "Pauline—I'm sorry, may I call you Pauline?"

She smiled. "Yes, of course."

"Tap dancing is a way of life in Washington. People who are skilled at it make a lot of money. People like Lauren's mother, and Lauren. But I can tell you this—just between you and me, okay?—if I can stitch together the pieces of what you've told me, it will test the skills of Washington's foremost tap dancers. And after having done this for more years than I care to remember, somehow I wonder if they'll equal to this."

17

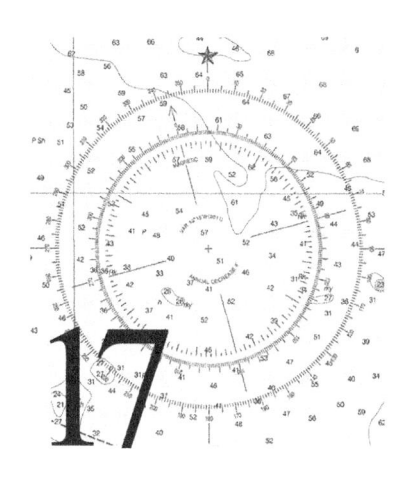

O'Reilly was arranging and rearranging squares of colored post-it notes on a corkboard panel in his cubicle. There were apps that did this, but he was still old school enough to cling to the tactile, hands-on method. The story Pauline outlined to him had intersections, and layers, like stairs that led between floors of a structure. The challenge would be to tell it in such a way that readers had an inkling of where the stairs led, without giving away whether up or down was the right direction. Some conclusions they'd have to reach on their own.

At first glance, it seemed like a time-worn account of an adulterous couple doing away with a spouse who was the third wheel. Scandalous in its own right but nothing new or even provable. But the part about the wife having vanished along with her paramour, interlaced with her parents' place in the firmament of Washington's A-list couples, was one of those stairways almost sure to heighten reader interest.

As O'Reilly examined the layout of his squares of colored paper, he jotted notes on a yellow legal pad, prioritizing tasks. Tomorrow morning, he would travel to Tilghman Island to talk to people from the list Pauline and Maya gave him. Next, he'd call Agent Barrett of the Coast Guard Investigative Service. Barrett had given Pauline his email. She'd be more than happy, she said, to pave the way for his call with an introductory note.

When he'd filled in some of the blanks from Pauline's account, he'd call and leave messages with the Forsyths. He had no illusions that either of them would answer his cold call or return it. But his message would put them on notice that a *Washington Post* reporter was sniffing around some unpleasantness involving their daughter.

O'Reilly had been to Tilghman Island once before. Some years ago, he and his wife spent a long weekend at a lovely B&B overlooking a cove with the lyrical name of Dogwood Harbor. He recalled consuming oysters in an array of varieties, riding bikes down quiet lanes, sipping beers alongside a waterway with boats gliding by. By and large, having a very nice time in a place where life seemed decompressed. It was a world away from the non-stop channel surfing of meetings, emails, traffic, texts, deadlines, and phone calls—the maelstrom of everyday life in the megalopolis he called home, which was not all that far over the western horizon from the Bay.

He recalled thinking during the previous visit that he might like to move to Tilghman someday. That is, as soon as he was no longer writing checks for his two daughters, one a senior in college and the youngest just entering. Until then, he and his wife could spend time thumbing through real estate listings, laughing as they ruled out the ones in the seven figures.

The next afternoon, having coaxed all he could from sources of information on Tilghman, some of whom commented that he was the latest in a line of people asking questions about the Jamesons and Blake Wentworth, he drove back north across the drawbridge. As he followed the ribbon of road that would take him back through the Eastern Shore landscape toward Route 50 and home, he was sure of one thing and wrestled with the implications of another. First, there was no doubt that the three principals, Tim and Lauren Jameson plus Blake Wentworth, had left Tilghman Island together on the Jameson's boat headed down the Bay bound for destinations somewhere in the southern latitudes.

Second, though their suspicions were based on rumors and hearsay, more than one of the people he talked to strongly suggested something of an illicit nature had been going on between Blake and Lauren. None of them had direct knowledge of an affair, however, and no one wanted their name used. Without any way to confirm the speculation, he couldn't include it. On the other hand, he was sure the basics of the story—husband abandoned at sea, wife and other man keep going—would lead people to obvious conclusions. And, once the story got picked up by other news outlets, as he believed it would, it was likely that some online journalists would not feel constrained by the same ethical standards in sourcing. Some iteration of the extra-marital affair would emerge. Another staircase, another layer.

Pauline had cc'd O'Reilly in her email to Troy Barrett, so when he called, Barrett was expecting it. Pauline had given O'Reilly her stamp of approval and that was all he needed to know. And though he'd never let O'Reilly know, privately he was delighted that a reporter from a big-time paper was interested in this story. He suspected Pauline's hand in this, her way of tilting the playing field in her favor. That was fine with him. Although the contact was not something he could have initiated, he was hopeful the publicity might somehow break the investigative logjam.

"This is Agent Barrett," he answered when O'Reilly called.

"Yes, sir, Agent Barrett. My name is Mark O'Reilly. I'm a reporter with the *Washington Post*. Pauline Jameson may have given you a heads-up that I'd be calling?"

"She did, Mr. O'Reilly. In the office here we've developed a certain fondness for her. She's a special lady."

"Yes, sir. I agree. And please, call me Mark."

"I will, if you stop calling me 'sir'."

They both laughed and settled on 'Mark' and 'Agent Barrett' as a happy medium. "How can I help you this morning, Mark?"

"Well, I'm calling to follow up on a story Pauline related to me concerning the rescue of her son at sea."

"Okay..."

"Are you able to confirm that your service is investigating the circumstances surrounding that rescue?"

"Yes."

"Yes, you're investigating?"

"Correct."

"Do you suspect wrongdoing?"

"When you ask me like that, Mark, I can't comment."

"Okay, let me ask you this. Was your investigation prompted in any way by Tim Jameson's rescue at sea?"

"Any time a person is found in Mr. Jameson's condition, the Coast Guard's mission is to do everything possible to find out what may have happened. Our service becomes involved if the circumstances are such that too many unanswered questions compel us to consider all the possible scenarios."

"Like foul play?"

"All the possible scenarios."

O'Reilly was quiet for a few seconds. "Agent Barrett," he began again, "when Tim Jameson was rescued, it was discovered that he'd sustained a severe head injury. Was that a factor in launching your investigation?"

Is this guy trying to trap me? Barrett wondered. "I didn't say we'd launched an investigation. I confirmed your phrasing of 'investigating the circumstances surrounding the rescue.' Mr. Jameson's head injury falls into the category of unanswered questions and all the possible scenarios."

Barrett could have just said "no comment" and ended the conversation. O'Reilly got the sense instead that Barrett was trying to guide him to the right line of questioning.

"Mark," Barrett said, "let's do this. Let's take what I'm going to tell you next and call it background. Is that okay?"

"Sources close to the investigation?"

"Yeah. That works."

"Good."

"So, this guy, Tim, is rescued 300 miles off the coast, in the middle of the night. A fishing boat pulls him out of the water."

"Pauline told me he was in really bad shape."

"That's right. But here's the bizarre part of this whole thing. He's wearing a life vest, and it's outfitted with a flashing strobe that can be seen a long way off. In the meantime, there are no distress calls, no man overboard calls from any boats, the Coast Guard doesn't hear anything from frantic family members telling us he's overdue somewhere, nothing. We theorized that possibly he was a single-hander who somehow fell overboard, hitting his head really hard on the way over the side. The strobe is water-activated so that explains that."

"In all the possible scenarios, how much stock did you put in that one?"

"Deep, deep background, okay? Not much."

"What happens to the boat then? Did it sink, maybe?"

"Probably not. It's actually harder than it seems to sink a modern boat. We've rescued people off boats in severe storms that looked all set to sink. Go back a day or two later and they're still floating. No reason why this guy's boat, John Doe we were calling him, couldn't have stayed afloat for who knows how long. The Coast Guard sent out notices, alerts, bulletins, press releases to papers up and down the coast, asking people to keep an eye out for an abandoned boat. Of course, we had no idea what kind of boat. They even sent out two search helicopters, which is incredibly expensive."

"Did the helicopters find anything?"

"Um, that would have to be off the record or a no comment."

"Okay." Barrett's response told O'Reilly that the helicopters found something relevant, impossible to guess what.

"By the way, Mark," Barrett said, "you can find the records and texts of all those bulletins and notices online, if you need to." O'Reilly thought they might provide context for what the Coast Guard thought they were looking for at first.

"Thanks." He'd never run across an investigator on the federal level who was so helpful. "So, Agent Barrett, I think somewhere along here I can pick up the threads of the story. According to Pauline, her daughter, Maya, wondering where her brother is, registered a missing boater or missing person report with the Coast Guard in Maryland. Next thing they know they're being contacted by you."

"Sounds about right."

"Can we go back on the record?"

"We don't comment on the substance of ongoing investigations."

"Maya and Pauline find out that Tim's lying in a coma in Jacksonville."

"Sorry, no comment. But you already know that answer."

"You find out from them who else was on the boat with him, and the story behind that."

There was a smile in Barrett's voice. "Sorry, no comment."

"Meanwhile, no one's heard from the wife or her companion since the night of the incident."

"Mark, I'm sorry. No comment. And you already know that too."

"Are they suspects?"

"No."

"Are they persons of interest?"

"We don't use that term."

"Do you know where they are?"

Silence from Barrett's end. O'Reilly could take that as a no comment, or a tacit admission that they did know but weren't saying. O'Reilly would write, 'When asked if they knew the whereabouts of the presumptive crew members, CGIS officials declined comment.'

"Are you looking for them?"

"We would very much like to talk with the individuals involved, to hear what they have to say."

"That's for the record?"

"Yes."

"Anything else, Agent Barrett, for the record?"

"Yes. Like any investigation, this is a quest for the facts, for the truth. We are simply looking for answers to whatever took place that night, 12 November, 2018, aboard that boat, some 300 miles at sea. We would strongly encourage anyone with any information to contact the Coast Guard Investigative Service, to come forward. We owe a duty to the victim and his family to find that truth."

Those last two for-the-record quotes, he felt sure, were intended as broadcasts, signals to the Forsyths and, if they were in contact with their daughter, indirectly to her. And when the story broke, a wide swath of the Forsyths' contemporaries, the higher strata of Washington's power elite, would read about a strange and troubling narrative: Tim Jameson, the man married to the Forsyths' daughter Lauren, went overboard off a sailboat, offshore, in the dark of night. Lauren Jameson, nee Forsyth, kept going, leaving him behind—sailing off into the night with another man. And hasn't been seen since.

The Forsyths got a foretaste of the cold front of awkwardness about to descend into their lives when they listened to voicemail later that day. "Hi, my name is Mark O'Reilly. I'm a reporter for the *Washington Post*. I'm working on a story involving your daughter, Lauren Jameson, her husband Tim, and events alleged to have occurred aboard their sailboat in November of last year. I've spoken to

Coast Guard investigators, who confirmed that they're looking into what they call an incident at sea, and to members of the Jameson family, as well as numerous other sources on the Eastern Shore. I'm hoping we can arrange a conversation so I can ensure that the voices of the principals are presented objectively, with the proper context, and that the story includes your perspectives. Please text or call at your convenience. Thank you."

He left his number at the Post and his mobile number. He'd be shocked if they responded. People like the Forsyths didn't dirty their hands with reporters like O'Reilly. That's okay, he thought. You don't have to answer my questions. But when details of the story emerge, like how your son-in-law was pulled from the ocean, barely clinging to life, for sure you'll encounter some painfully uncomfortable questions at the next Kennedy Center gala, or at a champagne reception at the National Gallery.

18

"Morning, Tim. "How are you today?" Andrea Gibson approached him in Pauline's living room. He was seated in a chair, smiling. Andrea's presence brought out an animated warmth in him.

"Good," he said.

"Good?" she asked. "Just good? What happened to fine?"

"I'm fine," he answered.

"Fine? or Good?"

"Both."

Andrea clapped her hands and grinned broadly. "Perfect answer, Tim! That's wonderful." She was Tim's occupational therapist. In weekly sessions at Pauline's home, she, along with other therapists, coached him in the restoration of a hundred small things Tim had done every day without conscious effort. "Did you have breakfast this morning?"

"Yes."

"How was it?"

"Fine."

She smiled. "What did you have?"

"Um, cereal."

"Nice. What else?"

"Juice."

"Okay. What kind of juice?"

Tim hesitated. "The ... yellow kind."
"Yellow? You mean orange juice?"
"Yes!"

Andrea beamed and cast a sidelong glance at Pauline and Maya, who stood apart in a doorway leading to another room. "So, cereal and orange juice. Anything else?"

Tim knitted his brow in effort. "Yes."

"What else besides cereal and juice?"

He looked at her intently. "Um ..."

"Was it—?"

"Wait!" he said. "I know." His mouth moved as he tried to form the word, concentrating intently. "Uhh, bread ... that was ... toast!" he blurted finally. It was a triumphant exclamation.

"Yay, Tim!" She clapped again. "That is amazing." She turned to Maya and Pauline as they walked in. Pauline wiped away the tears commingling with her smile. "He is really doing incredibly," Andrea said, turning toward Tim and taking his hand. They were sensitive not to talk past him anymore, in the third person. He was aware, cognizant to a degree, and tuned in to at least some of what was being said, which was a victory in and of itself.

"I think," Andrea said, "that since it's such a beautiful day and Tim is doing so well, that maybe we should take another walk out along the water."

Tim sat up and brightened. "Can we go fishing?"

Andrea tried to avoid a gasp. She clapped her hand to her mouth. The last time they'd gone walking along the property's shoreline, a man had been fishing off the end of a neighbor's dock. She recalled Tim staring intensely, mesmerized, as the figure drew back the rod over his shoulder and whipped it forward, flinging the hook and bait out into the water. Fishing was an all-consuming passion across the breadth of the Eastern Shore. Tim was no different than any kid who'd grown up here, carrying the passion with him into adulthood.

Today, two weeks later, he'd dredged up the memory of the man on the dock and connected it with an innate longing to get out on a dock and try his luck.

Memory, both short- and-long term, was among the casualties of traumatic brain injury. The fact that Tim was able to recollect the details of his breakfast and recreate the image of a man fishing at the neighbor's dock meant that the extent of Tim's recovery at this stage, within four months of the injury, was leapfrogging expectations. Andrea made a note to email Tim's neurologist in Annapolis with an update on Tim's interaction this morning.

The neurologist's name was Dr. Xiang Wen. Dr. Nichols had handed her the reins when Tim moved north to live with his mother and sister. She'd trained at Johns Hopkins but opted for the lifestyle amenities available to a family living away from the urban grit of Baltimore and nearer to one of the many creeks, rivers or coves that comprised the circulatory system of the Chesapeake Bay.

Maya and Pauline had traveled across the Bay to see Dr. Wen. She was an advocate of an active rather than passive therapy regimen for brain injuries. From her phone conversations with Dr. Nichols and the records he'd sent along, she could tell that Tim was benefitting from the embrace of his home turf and family. His verbal, motor and cognitive skills had accelerated. She noted too that the acceleration wasn't linear, but multi-level. He was building a scaffolding of skills, gaining proficiency in speech, memory, reasoning, and seemingly simple things like brushing his teeth.

Maya, Pauline and Tim sat in Dr. Wen's office. When she'd seen Andrea's email, she suggested a stepped-up schedule of appointments. After conducting a series of exercises and evaluations, she pronounced: "Tim's progress is excellent. While there is no set schedule for recovering from traumatic brain injury, he is way ahead of any expectations, whether Dr. Nichols' or mine." She looked at Tim, who was smiling, proudly. He seemed to take credit for the prognosis, which, oddly, was not entirely unjustified. Tim seemed motivated by something, eager to be pushed in each of the therapy modalities—speech, physical and occupational. Whereas the therapy regimen of many brain injury patients was limited by issues of stamina or an incapacity to move forward, Tim welcomed the physical and mental challenges. He was impatient between sessions and shrugged off the frustration of small failures or setbacks.

When the right word wouldn't come to him, he adapted, substituting a work-around word with a similar meaning, unashamed if it wasn't right, willing to try and fail rather than give up. Pauline and Maya had invited Dennis Cox, his accounting firm partner, to visit. When Tim saw him, his face brightened. He smiled what had become his trademark beaming grin.

"Do you know who this is?" Maya said.

"Sure, yes." Tim said. As Dennis moved to shake his hand, Tim said, "Douglas." He had the first consonant and the number of syllables right. "He's my friend."

Maya smiled. "Pretty good, Tim. Really close. How about ... Dennis?"

"Dennis!" Tim said. "Yes! I'm glad to see you, my friend." 'Friend' could be taken a couple ways. Though the two had a close working relationship over the last few years, they weren't friends in the truest sense of the word. Maya figured that Tim meant partner, and for now friend was close enough.

"Hi, Tim," Dennis said. "It's good to see you too. You look great. Ready to come back to work soon?"

Tim smiled, hesitated. "Um, I don't know. I don't..."

"Well, I hope so. It's just not the same without you. We need you there."

"Okay," Tim said. "I'll try real hard."

Dennis reached out and shook his hand. "I know you will, partner, I know you will."

Dr. Wen took all this into account when she urged Pauline and Maya to take Tim to the next level of rebuilding memory. She recommended a trip to Tilghman Island. Take Tim to his house, she said, and to the marinas. Let him reabsorb the elements of his life there, see what the effect was on his awareness, what else could be unlocked.

Franklin sat forward and tapped his mouse a few times. "What do we have here? Okay, according to this, our lovebirds have cleared out of French customs. Thank you, mes amis."

Barrett pulled out a large-scale paper chart of the Caribbean, which included the Windward and Leeward islands, Jamaica, the Turks and Caicos, the Cayman Islands, Cuba, the Bahamas, Puerto Rico, the Spanish, U.S. and British Virgin Islands, the Florida Keys and Southern Florida.

"Headed where, do we think?"

Franklin covered his eyes, moved his forefinger in wide circles, dropped it to the chart and said, "I think right—here." His finger came down in the middle of the ocean, far from any land. "Christ, TB, could be anywhere."

Barrett bent over the chart. "I don't know why, but my scientific wild-ass guess is that they're coming back here somewhere." He drew a circle around Florida and the Keys. "No reason to think that, other than I'm guessing their world may be collapsing around them more than it was."

"You mean the reporter guy from Washington?"

"Yeah, that's part of it. For the woman at least, I have to wonder what it's like to be cruising around, knowing that everyone you or your parents know thinks you're a scumbag who left your husband behind to drown. Or worse, tried to murder him. On top of that, they have to be looking over their shoulders constantly. That's a ton of emotional baggage. I imagine it's a helluva strain. And sailing from place to place won't get you out from under it."

"So ..."

"So it's like I keep saying, maybe they come back here, stay put, lay low, figuring it's easier to blend into the woodwork."

Franklin looked at the chart. "I don't know."

"I said it was a scientific wild-ass guess. Maybe not even that scientific. And there's this too: I talked to Pauline yesterday. She told me Tim is making amazing progress. 'Amazing' is the word the docs and therapists are using."

"That's great. But our couple on the boat doesn't know that."

"No, not yet."

"What's that mean?"

"Pauline and I wondered if Tim's progress might make O'Reilly's story even more interesting."

Franklin smiled. "And?"

"She said she'd call him and find out."

Maya and Pauline walked slowly up to the front steps of Tim's house on Tilghman Island. The lawn and shrubbery were overgrown and unkempt, having been neglected for months. Tim's face was a slideshow of emotions. Bewildered one moment, nostalgic the next, disconsolate when he noticed the ragged state of the landscaping. He was quiet, his sister and mother could only guess how his compromised brain was processing the moment.

Custody of the house key had been entrusted to Dennis Cox. He'd dropped it off the evening before. "Would you like to go inside, Tim?" Pauline said.

He looked at her absently. "Sure. I guess."

Maya asked, "Do you know where this is? Why we came here?"

"Yes." He was noncommittal. Often during his therapy sessions, he was reluctant to admit he was uncertain of something. His default response was to hedge, answering "yes"—affirmative but ambiguous.

Pauline eased the door open. Inside it was dark and musty. Maya was afraid of how depressing it might seem to Tim, not knowing how or whether he could or would connect any memories to the surroundings. She went around and turned on a few lights.

Tim stood in the center of the room, looking around and up, his eyes following the bannister rail leading up the stairs to a large loft area. He moved to a side table that had photos of him and Lauren in various settings. He picked them up and studied them, first one, then another, then a third. He mumbled quietly, forming a word somewhere known only to him. Finally, he breathed it: "Laur...en," letting the last syllable fade.

Maya edged closer. Tim looked at her. "Lauren," he said, with more volume and force.

"Who is she?" Maya's tone was gentle.

"Married," he said. He looked down at his left hand and touched his wedding ring. Unlike times past when Tim's rediscovery of a word or skill prompted a wide smile, now he was contemplative, almost somber. There was a concern that thrusting Tim back into the recent chapters of his life might cause a relapse, a retreat from unwelcome recollections, those causing pain or heartache.

After a time, though, he breathed deeply, stood straighter. "Our house," he said. "Yes?"

"Yes," Pauline said, "it's your house. It's lovely." They looked out through the wide bay window that opened on an expanse of water. A late afternoon cold front had kicked up the chop, white caps rolling in advance of the wind. A workboat made its way toward the entrance to the Narrows off to the right. It was tossed, pitching and yawing until it gained the quieter water inside the day markers. Tim watched, in the same way he'd watched the man fishing off the dock next to Pauline's house.

"Lauren," he said. "She could steer."

Maya and Pauline looked at each other. "What do you mean, Tim?" Pauline said.

He looked out at the workboat sliding through the Narrows. "Lauren."

19

It was on a Sunday in April, a day when many in Washington, D.C. looked forward to spending more time with their newspaper. An extra cup of coffee, a leisurely breakfast, less skimming, more deep dives into the content. Though she wasn't a political or news junkie like so many in Washington, on this morning, across the Bay on the Eastern Shore, there was another reader as avid as any: Pauline Jameson.

On the front page of Sunday's *Washington Post* Metro Section, above the fold, this headline appeared:

QUESTIONS SWIRL AROUND GOP OPERATIVE'S ROLE IN MYSTERIOUS "INCIDENT" AT SEA

Spin Doctor Lauren Jameson's whereabouts unknown since husband's dramatic rescue

by Mark O'Reilly

That something went seriously wrong aboard a sailboat named *Breezeway* on the night of November 12, 2018 is no longer in doubt. Whatever the uncertainties about what happened that night, 300 miles off the Atlantic coast, this much is known: It led, first, to a life-and-death helicopter rescue of one of the crew. The remaining two crew members, a male and female, presumed to be still aboard the vessel somewhere, have not been seen since. Their disappearance has raised eyebrows, suspicions, and a host of unanswered questions.

Of the three people said to be aboard the boat that night—those holding the keys to the answers—one, the rescued crew member, is currently undergoing therapy at the family home in Easton, Md., recovering from the effects of a brain injury. The whereabouts of the other two are unknown.

From Coast Guard documents, interviews with Coast Guard officials, family members and other sources, pieces of the story—some facts, some conjecture—point to this basic narrative. In early November, three people left the Chesapeake Bay aboard the sailboat, bound for the Caribbean: A couple, Tim and Lauren Jameson, *Breezeway's* owners, and a third person, Blake Wentworth, who was to act as an advisor or instructor, sources said, schooling the couple in the demands of blue water sailing.

On the night of the 12th, ten days after setting off from the Chesapeake, a Coast Guard helicopter lifted Tim Jameson from the deck of a fishing vessel, whose crew had pulled him from the ocean. He was comatose, having sustained what turned out to be a serious head injury, and suffering from hypothermia. His condition was critical, according to Coast Guard records and the accounts of medical personnel whom the family has authorized to divulge details of his care.

Jameson was flown to a trauma center in Jacksonville, Fla., where physicians described him as "clinging to life."

The circumstances surrounding Jameson's rescue drew the attention of the Coast Guard Investigative Service. Said Lt. Cdr. Troy Barrett, a CGIS agent, "Any time a person is found in the condition of that victim, whose identity we couldn't determine, the Coast Guard's mission is to do everything possible to find out what may have happened. Our service becomes involved if the circumstances are such that too many unanswered questions compel us to consider all the possible scenarios."

Sources close to the investigation added that in such cases the absence of a distress call from a boat in trouble, or inquiries from friends or relatives seeking information about a missing or overdue boater, is almost unheard of. Asked if that was reason to suspect foul play, Agent Barrett only reiterated the latter part of his statement: "to consider all the possible scenarios."

From there the Post story went on to recount how CGIS, seeking to identify the victim, broadcast bulletins and press releases up and down the Atlantic coast in an attempt to locate anyone with information. And how it wasn't till Maya's filing of a missing person report with the Coast Guard that officials matched her description with that of the victim. And, finally, how that link led to knowing who the original crew members were, and that those crew members sailed on without stopping or reporting the incident. Neither Lauren Jameson nor the other man, Blake Wentworth, as far as anyone knew, had been seen since.

The reporter included a capsule bio of Lauren Jameson, her reputation as a top-flight shaper of opinions, most of which was already known among the Washington elite. Her parentage, that of Elliott and Sarah Forsyth, was also widely known among a certain caste of Washingtonians.

O'Reilly also included the obligatory and not unexpected disclaimer: "Repeated calls and emails to the Forsyths went unanswered."

When O'Reilly was crafting the story, he was concerned that its storylines led off a cliff. The suggestion was that something dreadful must have occurred aboard the *Breezeway* that night. Three people knew the story. Two had obviously chosen to stay underground.

Originally, Tim Jameson's injury was judged so severe that the odds of him recalling anything were beyond remote. That left O'Reilly with a buildup: intrigue, mystery, the daughter of Washington brahmins possibly involved in something tawdry, a string of questions he'd planted in readers' minds—but no answers.

That is, until Tim's recovery shifted to a fast track. Two neurologists, his therapists and his family were all marveling at how quickly he was regaining his faculties. O'Reilly quoted Pauline, Maya, Drs. Nichols and Wen, plus Andrea, the occupational therapist. As one, they cited a startling, even extraordinary, rate of progress.

This wrinkle planted a stay-tuned element. It was just how he and his editor had figured it: a story with a slow fuse, the prospect of a to-be-continued essence that could give it staying power.

O'Reilly capped it off with his final exchange with Barrett.

"When asked if they knew the whereabouts of the presumptive crew members," he wrote, "or if they were being sought, CGIS officials deflected the question."

"We would very much like to talk with the individuals involved, to hear what they have to say," Agent Barrett said. "Like any investigation this is a quest for the facts, the truth. We are simply looking for answers to whatever took place that night, 12 November, 2018, aboard that boat, some 300 miles at sea. We would strongly encourage anyone with any information to contact the Coast Guard Investigative Service, to come forward. We owe a duty to the victim and his family to find that truth."

Barrett's innocuous pronouncement was really a form of summons, cloaked in official blandness. The subtext of these statements was always, "We want the people involved to submit willingly to an interview with us and just tell us the truth. If there's nothing to hide, there's nothing to fear from the truth." They suggested, too, that "You're on our radar, we're interested, not going away, only waiting for more evidence."

In effect, Barrett's implied summons also applied indirectly to Lauren's parents. They, not unlike Lauren, had pulled the blinds shut, though in a different context.

The fallout from the Post article, however, was such that for Sarah and Elliott Forsyth, shuttered blinds were insufficient. Shock, and in some cases revulsion, coursed through their widespread but selective network of movers and shakers. This was an ugly story. The severe brain injury part of it left disturbing implications open to interpretation—scenarios too awful to contemplate. Taken as a whole, it wasn't that much of a leap to imagine that Lauren and the other man, one or the other, had tried to murder her husband, braining him with a heavy object and dumping him overboard. That wasn't true, of course, but there was no one to refute it. And even if weren't true, what was known was bad enough: Lauren and the other man—whoever he was, put two and two together—and sailed off into the night, abandoning her gravely injured husband to the cold waves and water.

The boundaries of Washington, D.C. and its environs were too cramped to shield the Forsyths from the flood of doubts, speculation, and yes, shame. Their email inboxes and cell phones were overloaded with messages, most from well-meaning friends, others from members of the press who knew them, circling in a pack, trying to wedge their way to the front of the line, angling for a comment or quote they knew full well would never happen.

For the first time, a few neighbors in their gracious Georgetown neighborhood avoided their glances. Twitter pages with a range of viewpoints blossomed. One had a hashtag of #wheresLauren? inviting users to post theories on Lauren's whereabouts. Another focused on a theme of how Lauren was so adept at putting a smiley face on the most blatant and venal forms of influence peddling, or tamping down repercussions from some especially noxious episode of sexual misbehavior. Yet now, when the facts didn't lend themselves to being twisted or spun, she was missing in action.

The onslaught was too much for the Forsyths. They decamped and fled to what they hoped would be a sanctuary, their home in Oxford, Maryland. Oxford was within the orbit of Eastern Shore tourist destinations, but off by itself, separate somehow. The moneyed end of Talbot County: dignified, quiet. Stuffy and boring some said, but it was how the townsfolk preferred it. The Forsyths' home, an estate really, was well outside the town proper, a stately federal-style mansion on its own six-acre point of land jutting out into the Tred Avon River. It was sequestered at the end of a long gravel lane, which was at the end of yet another narrow, twisting road, along which no houses were visible, only the occasional gated entrance to a lane leading back to an isolated estate very much like the Forsyths'.

20

On a warm April afternoon a few days later, Sarah and Elliott Forsyth sat side by side in a pair of Adirondack chairs, placed on the downslope of the lawn as it led to the water. Angled sunlight from the west glittered across the river's wavelets. On a small table between them was a bottle of excellent Sauvignon Blanc, chilling in an earthenware cooler.

For any other couple in their position, under almost any circumstance, an idyll. A time to wind down, take deep breaths, close your eyes and lean back. Yet for the Forsyths, the physical isolation of their Eastern Shore home did nothing to dampen the effects of the disgrace Lauren had shoveled onto their family. Even here, it plagued them, intruding, casting a pall over what should have been a delightful afternoon.

The irony, Elliott thought, was that Lauren understood better than most how the feeding frenzy worked in Washington. She'd helped powerful people tap dance out of harm's way. A story flared up, flames burning brightly for a time, then dying down to embers and forgotten as the next outrage took its place. But only to a point. There was a difference between classes of outrage as well. For standard-issue corruption or perjury, malfeasance of the unlawful variety, the feeding frenzy was usually contained inside the beltway. What's more, the scale of corruption in recent years had grown to a point where it barely qualified as news.

Offenses that broke other kinds of rules, however—extramarital affairs, dalliances with interns, child pornography found on a smart phone, or in Lauren's case, sailing off with another man while leaving your husband behind to drown—had a universal appeal. People of influence caught in some variant of flagrante delicto feeds the guilty pleasure of tabloid voyeurism, secretly or openly relished by consumers of news everywhere—from Washington's corridors of power to main streets across the heartland.

The Forsyths were guilty of none of that, of course. But their daughter was—or certainly seemed to be. And staying out of sight or out of reach only stoked the flames, prolonging the stage in which the flames burned brightly. Worse, the story's tabloid appeal meant it was just a matter of time until it spilled out across websites whose standards for restraint or objectivity were less than rigorous.

Elliot knew this, and he knew Lauren was fully aware of it too. Yet she remained cut off from him and Sarah, cut off from those whom she knew could navigate the most turbulent and dangerous rapids of career-ending scandals. Why? Was it that her jeopardy endangered more than a career or reputation? He felt a distinctly unpleasant heaviness, like an elevator counterweight that sunk slowly down through his core. What if? God no. Please.

He took a generous sip of wine and turned slightly to Sarah. "I know you told me this before, but I wonder if you could tell me again what you recall of your conversation with Lauren a few weeks ago."

It sounded to Sarah like an interrogatory during a deposition. But their relationship had reached the point where an economy of language was the norm. And Elliot was merely signaling that he was in serious business mode.

Sarah paused as she tried to reconstruct as closely as possible what she'd told Elliott a few weeks ago. "She told me that Tim had been alone on deck, steering, during his watch." She grimaced as she spoke this name next: "When Blake went up on deck at midnight to take his turn, Tim was gone—overboard. They had no idea what might have happened to him, according to Lauren. They turned back, sailed all around looking for him, for hours she said."

Elliott looked out at the water as she spoke. "Do we buy that?" he said.

Sarah turned to him. "It's what she's told us. And if we don't believe it, it means we've crossed some divide: that we assume the worst about our daughter's word."

"Well, that's sort of not the point."

"Meaning what?"

"I'll explain. But in the meantime, she maintained that the reason they didn't report what happened was because this Blake guy said they wouldn't be believed, they'd be suspects."

"Right."

"And that was because …"

"You know why."

"Because they thought it would come out that they're romantically involved and that would place them under suspicion. So after they gave up searching, they kept going."

"That's it. She said she made horrible, disastrous choices."

Elliot shook his head. "In one way she's right. The disappearing act makes any suspicion worse." They were quiet for a time. Elliott freshened their wine. "I did some checking with a woman at the firm who specializes in maritime law. As far as she could tell, from what's known at this point, the worst legal liability Lauren and this guy might be open to is failure to report a marine incident at sea. It would be a civil matter, not criminal. A big fine, nothing else. And maybe not even that. The party responsible for the reporting is the captain of the vessel. That might not apply to either one of them."

"So she's not in as much trouble as she thinks."

"Possibly. Assuming their story—her story—holds up."

"Why wouldn't it?"

"Two reasons: First, think about Tim: what if somehow he remembers he didn't fall overboard and didn't suffer a self-inflicted head injury? His memory may not recover fully, but what if it does to the point where he could refute their story about him going overboard while he was all alone during his watch? I mean, that whole fairy tale doesn't pass the smell test. C'mon."

Sarah felt ice water wash through her nervous system.

"Second, if they reappear within a jurisdiction of the United States, a U.S. Attorney can subpoena Lauren—both of them—to testify before a grand jury, even if they're not subject to arrest."

"They can do that? Just—"

"They can."

"I don't understand. Why? How?"

"There'll be a lot of public pressure to get to the bottom of this—partly because of who Lauren is, partly because of who we are. The average Joe probably believes something scandalous happened out there that night. The longer Lauren and her friend stay out of sight, the worse it looks. And the media won't let it go away either. Assuming these two eventually resurface, I could see a U.S. Attorney being under pressure to bring the case before a grand jury."

"Just drag somebody in and force them to testify?"

"Well, no. Grand juries can be accusatory or investigative—fact finding. It's possible a crime took place. It's the grand jury's job to find out. But they can't force a person to self-incriminate. Lauren can try to claim Fifth Amendment protection. So can the other deadbeat she's hooked up with."

Sarah cradled her forehead between her forefinger and thumb. "Jesus. Is there a short version of all this?"

"No. There never is when you've made, what did she call them—disastrous choices?"

Sarah flinched at the rebuke. "Ell," she said, "is that a little harsh?"

"That's what I'm getting at. In a grand jury room, no one gives a damn. She won't be able to claim the fifth amendment for all her disastrous choices. A prosecutor will pepper her with questions. Each one may have a land mine in it she can't see. There's no blanket Fifth Amendment exemption for every question. They all stand on their own. And she can't have a defense attorney in the room with her. Neither she nor this horse's ass Blake guy are ready for what it's like."

Elliott stood, picked up his wine glass and carried it. He paced slowly. "I had some people I know do a little checking on Blake Wentworth." Sarah's smile faded. "Turns out he's got a criminal record. He was arrested as part of a decent-size cocaine bust. Drugs were on a sailboat he and some other guys delivered to Annapolis."

"Just keeps getting worse, doesn't it?"

"Yeah. I don't know how it could, but it does. The reason I bring it up is that this guy, being an ex-con, has a lot more at stake, and I bet he knows it. He won't know that so far their only liability is the 'failure to report' violation. He'll believe, they both will, that they're in a much worse jam than that. And they may be right. The difference is he's got survival instincts. It's what they learn during a federal prison stretch. Somebody gives up somebody else, they get a better deal."

"My God, I'm confused. Better deal?"

Elliot sat back down. "If they get subpoenaed, they'd go into the grand jury room separately, at different times, maybe different days. They'd have different lawyers prepping them before they go in—remember no lawyers inside the room. Neither one would have any idea what the other did or did not testify to, what questions were asked, how they were answered. Whether the other person had pleaded the Fifth or not. It leaves people feeling incredibly vulnerable.

Sarah sat all the way back in her chair, running her hand through her hair.

"The prosecutors might even have put an offer of immunity on the table," Elliot said. "Tell us everything, you'll be immune from prosecution. I've seen them do it, play one off against the other when they don't have quite enough against either suspect. Make it a race to the finish line. Whoever crosses first, helps us make a solid case on the other one, gets the get-out-of-jail-free card: immunity. You'd be surprised how many people cave to an appeal like that."

"Then we need to make sure Lauren's first across the line," Sarah said. "How do we do that?"

"Well, that may be a little premature. Everything I've said assumes they'd even show their faces back here."

"When I questioned Lauren on that, about coming back, she said all she'd be coming back to was a stoning in the public square."

Elliott sat back down. "She's got a point. Be lucky if she gets away with just that." He shaded his eyes as he looked out over the water. "I think we need to contact her, tell her about the article in the Post, that people are asking some very difficult questions. The longer she stays underground, or whatever, the worse it looks. Make sure she knows she's in a bad spot. If things start to close in on her, she has to look out for her own interests. This Blake guy's not in her best interests; we are. Just like she'd tell a client, your only friend is you."

"And us."

"Right, us of course," Elliot said. But it came out with a slight hitch, an unintentional beat. The elevator counterweight sensation sunk down on him. Those asking the difficult questions included him. His daughter, yes, their daughter. Fine. But how to compartmentalize the questions, simply put them on a shelf. Say it's okay. No. It wasn't. It wasn't okay.

He knew Lauren well enough to know her antennae for disrepute were more attuned than most. She had to be imagining the reception she'd get: "Oh, hi, nice to meet you," they'd say. "Aren't you the one who left your husband to drown and sailed off to the Caribbean? And then hid out for months while he was recovering from a severe head injury?"

How could she ever live down that sort of notoriety? And how would she ever face Tim and his family? No, Elliot thought, hard to believe she'd come back anywhere near her old haunts. Not any time soon that's for sure. He looked over at Sarah. Had they lost a daughter? Hard to know exactly. But coming from Lauren, the assessment that she'd made horrible choices that night could only mean that nothing would ever be the same.

TOM HITCHCOCK

21

A day out of Guadeloupe, Blake was steering *Breezeway* on a close reach, headed northwest. With a fresh breeze veering out of the northeast, it was the balance of wind and sail that *Breezeway* was made for. She heeled moderately to port but kept her feet, gliding with the wind and carving through waves to plunge forward on a steady track.

Lauren sat with her legs stretched out, facing aft with her back resting against the bulkhead alongside the companionway. *Breezeway's* wake foamed astern, reassuring in the sense that it represented a plan, a straight line away from indeterminate wandering and drifting, toward ... something. Toward what was not exactly clear, she realized, but at least it would close the current chapter. What lay in store in the next one was open to question. The difference was it would play out with a direction, in a defined arena whose familiar culture and language offered a degree of comfort. They both recognized, though, that it was filled with trap doors. Unseen or unanticipated contingencies could mean stepping through any one of them. At any stage, they knew, the next chapter could be the last one. But the alternative was running away, running from, running—a directionless, meandering journey that would never end.

As she followed the wake's trail astern, her eye caught the bow wave of a boat coming up from far off at a high rate of speed. It bounced and bucked as it came on. "Blake," she said, pointing, "what the hell's this?"

Blake turned, took a long look, and turned back to her. "Take the wheel."

"What? Why?"

"C'mon. Just do what I ask, okay? Take the wheel."

She moved aft, sliding behind the wheel, casting anxious glances back over her shoulder. Blake went below, made his way to one of the less accessible storage lockers and reached deep into a seldom-used cranny. From within a protective cloth container he retrieved a Glock 9mm handgun and one of two magazines. Each magazine could hold up to fifteen bullets. He did a brief inspection of the Glock, working the slide a few times before inserting the magazine up into the cavity in the gun's grip. He placed the gun, barrel down, in the waistband of his shorts, between his spine and hip. With the chamber empty, he rehearsed pulling the gun out quickly and pointing it. After four or five repetitions, he seemed satisfied. Racking the slide one more time to chamber a round, he tucked the pistol back into his waistband. He shook his hands and forearms a few times to loosen them, closed his eyes and took three short exhaled breaths. He climbed back up into the cockpit.

The approaching boat was now a hundred yards astern and beginning to slow. Its occupants could never be totally sure who or what was aboard a boat they were about to accost. Though the odds were slim to none that anyone or anything would be a threat, a visual inspection as they drew near was prudent.

"Blake," Lauren said, her voice tight, "who are they?"

"They're pirates," he said. "Hijackers. Very bad news. These things don't end well."

"What are we going to do?"

"I would like you to go up and stand near the mast. Don't hide behind it, that'll piss 'em off. Just stay near it, keep your hands visible, shoulder height. You can grab onto a shroud if you have to but just stay quiet, calm if you can. Nothing sudden. Okay?"

"What about you?"

"I have a plan. We'll just take this thing moment to moment. Breathe deep, be calm."

The pirates eased up alongside. They were three black guys in a good-sized center console boat, no doubt seized from another set of victims somewhere. Mounted on the transom were three powerful and expensive outboards. Blake liked the idea that the center console layout, everything above the deck open, meant all three hijackers were visible.

One guy carried a short, nasty-looking assault rifle. He appeared to be the leader. A few feet away from him, another crew member held a semi-automatic pistol similar to the one Blake carried concealed behind him. The guy at the controls, the wheel and throttle behind the console, had a pistol stuck down the side of his waist band.

Blake raised his hands slightly as a sign of submission. The pirates glared from their boat, eyeing Blake and Lauren warily. They bobbed closer. "Heave to, mon!" shouted the putative leader. He motioned with the barrel of his assault rifle. "Stop your fuckin' boat! Stop it! Now!"

Blake steered up into the wind, letting the sails luff. He centered and sheeted in the mainsail to steady the boom, keeping it from swinging back and forth. *Breezeway* slowed gradually. As it did, it lost steerage way and began to rock from side to side in the waves. When the hijackers' boat edged closer, the sides of the boats formed a resonant chamber, causing the waves between them to get bigger and choppier. The deck of the sailboat and the gunwale of the hijackers' boat bobbed and rolled back and forth, lurching up and down out of sync, making the gap between them treacherous. The crew members were yelling at each other, the boss man calling out instructions to the man at the helm, who goosed the throttles and spun the steering wheel in response. Their efforts had no effect.

Finally, the boss man ordered the other pirate to get a line on one of *Breezeway's* cleats in order to draw the boats together. The man tried to throw a loop on a cleat with one hand while holding his gun in the other—impractical from the outset. He shoved his pistol into the holster strapped to his waist and tried again.

Blake was standing in a cavity at the aft end of the lazarette bench and the seat behind the steering wheel. He was able to brace his calves and knees against *Breezeway's* motion. The pirate crewman was still not equal to the task of securing the two boats. *Breezeway's* bulk and weight were too much for one man to handle in the heaving waves. The pirate boss had no choice but to lend a hand. He cast a menacing glance at Blake, shook his assault rife in a threatening gesture. Blake responded with wide eyes, raising his hands higher, the left grasping a stay behind him. With no more than ten feet separating him from any of the three assailants, the range was nearly point blank.

His glare lingering on Blake, the pirate boss evidently decided that their prey aboard the sailboat was sufficiently cowed. He slung his assault rifle over his right shoulder and leaned in to help his mate control the pitching boats. Blake lowered his hands slightly, braced his feet and lower legs, and snatched the Glock from his waistband. The pirate boss caught the motion and raised up. Blake aimed at center of mass, the bulk of the human body between the shoulders and the diaphragm, and squeezed off two shots in half a second. A sudden dipping of the boat threw off his aim just a bit. One bullet entered the pirate's neck in the space between the two clavicle bones, the second just beneath his chin, shattering his larynx and glancing off his cervical spine.

In a flash, Blake jerked his arms a foot to the left and fired again. The second pirate was struck in the chest as he was reaching for his pistol. The third crewman, behind the wheel, gawked in shock and surprise for a precious second before trying to retrieve his sidearm.

Blake pivoted again and fired three times in a second. The first shot struck the helmsman high in the left chest, staggering him. The second two, fired half a heartbeat later, hit home twice, both times in the thorax. The helmsman lurched backward and fell heavily against the interior cockpit wall.

Blake leaped up on to *Breezeway's* gunwale to look down into the other boat. The boss man pirate was gurgling and choking on a fountain of blood coming from his neck. The second pirate was crawling, groping for the pistol still in its holster. Blake fired two more rounds into his back. The crawling stopped.

Lauren had watched in stunned silence as the five seconds of bloodshed exploded. When Blake's delivered the coup de grace to the crawling pirate, its abrupt, cold-blooded brutality triggered a shock that overloaded her circuits.

"Oh my God, Blake!" she screamed. "What the f—?" I can't believe you—" He glanced at her briefly before moving aft to check on the helmsman. The pirate boat was drifting away. The helmsman fell where only his legs were visible. They were still. The outboards idled, rumbling as the wind and waves pushed the boats apart. Blake kept watch on the hijackers' boat, guarding against the possibility that one of them had enough strength left to rise up and take a parting shot. When it had drifted a hundred yards off, he felt sure none of them could hit anything at that range and neither could he. He turned back to Lauren, who was quaking, her system flooded with adrenaline. He moved nearer to her, clicked the Glock's safety on and tucked it back behind his waist. She stared at him with wide eyes. "Sorry you had to see that," he said. "It was them or us."

Lauren groped for words. "I— I just ... don't know what to say. My God. Where did that ... ?"

"Long story. No time now. We've gotta put some distance between us and that boat."

"Once again, run for the hills, right?"

He flared for an instant. "No. Not *again*. Bullshit. Nothing like that. Let me tell you something. If those guys'd made it aboard this boat, by now I would probably be dead, and you'd be wishing you were. They would have made you a plaything, the same way people kick around a soccer ball as a plaything. Nothing gentle. They would have passed you back and forth between them, slapped you around a little just for fun, and then maybe shared you with some of their buddies ashore, wherever that is. Then, after a while, when they were tired of you, they'd have killed you. Now, what's it gonna be? You want the wheel or the sails? We gotta get going."

Lauren sagged, moving toward the wheel in a daze as she eased behind it and coaxed *Breezeway* off the wind. Sheeted and trimmed, the sails filled and *Breezeway* was once again galloping toward the northwest. She saw Blake staring aft and turned to follow his eyes. The outlaw boat was but a fading white dot back on the horizon.

Sailing in silence was not an uncommon state of affairs between them but this was different. The residual trauma and shock of having been up close and personal with sudden violence and death sunk down on them. And yet the natural urge of many people following episodes of violence was talkativeness, a therapeutic replay of sorts, thoughts spilling out in an adrenaline-fueled catharsis. That, and the weight of too many unanswered questions made them acutely aware of the silence. Its weight seemed unnatural and forced—more uncomfortable the longer it hung between them. Lauren had never been one to let unresolved issues linger. She broke the silence. "What happens when they find that boat?"

Blake looked out over the water. "Depends who finds it."

His answer seemed evasive. "I know that," she said. "Assume whoever finds it sees the three dead bodies and reports it."

"That's the problem. Report it to who? These islands all have their own cops. They don't care too much about anything that happens outside their territory. They claim they do, but they don't. If the bad guys' boat happens to drift close enough to one of the islands, it'll get someone's attention. DEA's got some branch offices here and there. Maybe them."

"Then what?"

"They'll figure it's a drug deal or a hijacking gone bad. Nobody'll shed any tears for the guys on the boat. And sure as hell the boat they were on was hijacked or stolen. There's tons of cocaine coming out of South America. And a big market for it in the States. One of the favorite routes is through the Caribbean. Everyone thinks it's such a paradise but there's definitely some bad dudes and some bad neighborhoods around. You saw that."

She shuddered. "My God, I won't ever forget it. I've never seen anybody get shot ... or killed."

"Makes two of us." Blake said.

"What? How? How did you do all that? With the ... ?

"I don't know. I knew what the stakes were. Adrenaline's a powerful thing. It just took over. I was on automatic pilot. Don't feel real good about it right now. It'll hit me later, I guess. But they didn't leave us a choice, did they?"

"No."

"Want a beer?"

"Um, seems a little weird. But sure, I guess. What are we celebrating?"

"Not being dead."

When Blake came back up, they sat for a time, sipping, gazing across the expanse of sea and sky. "You know," Lauren said after a while, "reading you is like reading a book. Turn a page, learn something new."

"Like what?"

"Like, what you did with the gun. Where's that come from? And don't tell me it's just adrenaline."

Blake waited a few moments, seeming to chew over exactly how he'd answer. "You know how I was in the boat delivery business, right?"

"Yeah."

"Well sometimes, not all the time, the boat might have had extra cargo on it."

"Drugs."

"Let me tell the story. That cargo was worth a lot of money."

"Drugs."

"Whatever. That meant a lot of people wanted to get their hands on it. If the wrong people found out about the cargo, they might want to take it. Kind of like a hostile takeover, I guess. The people who were in charge of running the drugs started using boats you might not suspect of carrying drugs."

"Like a sailboat."

"Sometimes."

"So ..."

"So to the people who wanted to steal the cargo, we were expendable. Witnesses. A guy I knew told me, get a gun, learn how to use it. Said he'd teach me. The other thing he told me was, get good at it. Practice. Train. Train like your fuckin' life depends on it, he said, cause it does. I never really knew what he meant till today."

Blake had been absently examining the shape of the sails. Lauren's followed his gaze up as she considered the next unanswered question. "When you shot that guy," she said, "the second time, the guy lying on the deck, was that part of your training?" She was still recoiling at what she perceived as the calmness of it, Blake's businesslike administering of the second round of shots. Much more like an execution, really, than self defense.

He looked at her. "The guy was reaching for his gun. And yes, it was part of the training. If you're outnumbered, knock them down first, then go back and make sure they're no longer a threat. What I was taught was, there's no such thing as second place. If it's you or the other guy, never hesitate: always, *always* make sure you're the one who comes in first."

He sat back against the coaming to finish his beer. Lauren's head swam with the contradictions. In all likelihood she owed her life to him. But he'd exercised his proficiency as much to save his life as hers. What would happen if it ever came down to the two of them in the ring, pitted against each other in a contest to escape the consequences of what they'd done to Tim? She'd just seen what Blake was capable of. Possibly it wasn't the same, but she couldn't ignore what she'd witnessed. She'd store away her own version of what Blake's lesson had taught him: Train, train like your life depends on it—because someday, who knows, it very well might.

TOM HITCHCOCK

22

The colors of the water in Ensenada Honda ranged from azure, to cerulean, to light turquoise, to clear as gin. Lauren sat out on the foredeck of *Breezeway*, absorbing the many ways in which this anchorage in Culebra checked most of her boxes for what she envisioned as the haven—one of the ideal places on earth to become like a snail curled inside its shell. She could follow the anchor rode down more than fifteen feet, just past the point where it met the length of chain that created a comfortably safe angle to anchor in thirty feet of water.

The anchorage was protected from almost any wind direction, yet large enough to allow someone to mind one's own business. Ashore, a smattering of necessities provided a sufficient level of sustenance: a few bars, a restaurant, small stores and stalls that carried enough in the way of staples to make cooking meals aboard both affordable and practical.

As Blake stowed items in the lazarette and dried things off, he saw Lauren up forward thumbing a text on her phone. He climbed up and walked forward to sit alongside her on the crown of the cabin top. "Nice spot, eh? What'd I tell you?"

She brushed the hair out of her eyes and took a moment. "Yeah, it is. Definitely."

He nodded toward her phone. "That to your mom?"

It flashed briefly through Lauren's mind to ask him what business it was of his. But she didn't. It was a reasonable question. "Finally got some coverage here. I wanted to let her know we're okay."

What Lauren texted was this:

"Have worked our way north, back in U.S. territory. Everything fine. Not really. Will feel my way, a little at a time. Love you."

Blake wondered what it would be like to have someone to text, to let them know you're okay. His mother had passed away some years ago; his father thought him a wastrel, a vagabond sailor who would never amount to anything worthwhile. Sitting here on the foredeck of the *Breezeway*, with the uncertain prospect of getting by on his wits in Key West in less than a week, it was hard to dispute his father's assessment.

Yet Blake had a unique capacity to live in the moment. The next few weeks were about as far as his horizon went. He put his hand on her shoulder. "Thing is, though, hate to say it, it's spectacular for sure, but we can't get too comfortable here. A couple-three days, then on to Key West. That's the plan. Agreed?"

"God, what a shame. Come across a place like this but we have to scurry and run, like cockroaches. What a wonderful way to live. Fucking paradise." Her expression was bleak. "Joke's on me I guess."

Blake had little to offer in response. "Hey, don't think of it like that," he said. "Just make up your mind you'll come back some day."

"Oh, don't worry. I already have. Sooner rather than later if I can figure out a way."

Blake took note of her first-person singular phrasing, not so surprising given that they'd decided to go their separate ways when they reached Key West. Still, her tone had a distinct lone wolf quality to it: Not much doubt that her vision for the future didn't include him. "Tell you what," he said, trying to brighten the mood, "let's take the dinghy in, stretch our legs, scope out whatever we need for provisions, then plunk out butts down on some stools at a great little local bar I know. Cuba Libre with lime. Killer."

His choice of adjective for the drinks was unfortunate. It slipped out, hung in the air for a few moments. And just then, Lauren's phone buzzed with an incoming text. She stood, walked to the bow reading it. "It's my mother. She wants me to call. I'll call her when we get ashore." She thumbed a response. "Let's get cleaned up and go."

Again, the tone was abrupt, clipped, with an authoritative certainty. She was in charge, which made sense since it was her boat and she was paying all the bills. He was used to it, but also tired of it. Neither of them harbored any illusions about the endpoint of this relationship. Blake had never been dependent on anyone to put food on the table or keep a roof over his head. The fact that it was a woman whose credit and debit cards seemed to have few limits made it all the more emasculating. Another week, probably less, they could cast each other adrift.

Blake and Lauren took a brief tour of the shops and restaurants clustered within a few blocks of the public dinghy dock. Finding that necessities for the next leg of the trip were readily available and sufficient, they happened on a small, open-air bar with a distinctly local flavor. It was tucked off by itself, just as Blake recalled it, and they were the only customers, which was their preference. It was early, though, by the standards of Culebra. The bartender, stirred from his lassitude, served them two rum and cokes, after which he returned to a small room behind the bar, for reasons that were unclear. A radio could be heard; a man's voice, fulminating in Spanish, presumably voicing some political grievance.

They looked around at the chaotic, brightly colored decorative motif, which had been assembled over time with no apparent thought given to how, or if, one element tied into a mélange of others.

Lauren smiled. "I like this," she said. "It's not trying to be anything. It just … is." She imagined the bar as a place to keep things at arms-length, to blend into the background. A place where the bartender wouldn't pester you with questions, and fellow cruising yachtsmen wouldn't crowd you with the clingy, intrusive bonhomie typical of the waterfront bars they frequented. She raised her glass. "A toast."

"To what?"

"To a shell, inside of which a mollusk may be safe, secure, and barely visible."

The allusion was just a shade too obscure for Blake. And it was past the point where it would be worth having it spelled out. He raised his glass and smiled. "Whatever."

His response was vapid, incurious, she thought. But so what? His intellect was not what she'd been attracted to. Why was it that one rarely seemed to go with the other? You interest me in one way, but you can't hold my interest for any length of time in the other. She theorized that as he taught her to be strong, to manage an increasing share of the boat's power and complexity on her own, that his skill set was not as much of a mystery, not quite so compelling. She could never hope to match what he'd mastered over the course of multiple blue-water voyages, but that was never the point. Now she was a little less in awe of it. And as the mystique of it waned, so did his.

More corrosive than any of that, however, was the part each of them had played in committing a vile and shameful act. Lauren was unable to escape the involuntary instant replays that cycled through her mind, grating at her conscience and invading her dreams. They'd done something shocking and contemptible—together. How could two people sustain an attraction knowing what each had been capable of in the dead of that night, with no one watching?

Blake had stuck with her until now, she thought, pushing her and instructing her. For that he deserved some credit. But beyond that, together they had been little more than a bright-burning sparkler that familiarity and an enduring torment had snuffed out.

The first round of rum and cokes was bottoming out when she pulled out her phone. "I've gotta call my mother. I'm just going to walk down here a ways," she said, pointing. "Get us another round if you can. I'll be right back."

She forced herself to dial, dreading the conversation to come. She paced, listening to the first few rings, hoping on one hand for the reprieve of leaving a message, but on the other, to hear the comforting embrace of her mother's voice. She was startled by how quickly her mother answered. "Lauren!" her mother breathed. "My God, I can't believe I'm hearing from you. Do you have time to talk?"

Lauren stuttered, caught off guard by the urgency of her mother's tone. "Y–yeah. Yes, I do of course. Why? What—?"

"Sorry. I'm sorry. Are you okay?"

"It's all relative, mom. Physically? Yes. Emotionally, I'm a train wreck. As you might imagine."

"My God, Lauren. Where are you? You said U.S. territory."

"Closer than last time we spoke," Lauren said, and then was quiet.

"I don't understand why you can't tell me." Sarah's voice was strained, with a slight edge.

"I said I'd have to feel my way, a little at a time."

"Okay, well, your father says the longer you stay out of sight, the worse it looks."

"The worse what looks?"

"There was a story in the Post about a week ago—about you, about an incident at sea, how they found Tim alive, and how you and this Blake person kept sailing on without your husband. You can imagine the reverberations it set off. Your father and I had to retreat to the house in Oxford."

Lauren listened, her face burning, picturing the opprobrium

coursing through the salons of Washington: the shaking of heads, the texts, the Twitter feeds, the wonderment over glasses of Merlot. Lauren? Good lord. How tawdry. What a shame for her parents. What was she thinking?

The humiliation silenced her, drained the phone conversation of words.

"You still there?" Sarah said.

"Yeah." Her voice was muted, beaten down.

"Your father said to tell you you're in a bad spot. His words. He talked about how a U.S. Attorney could pull you in front of a grand jury. And your friend too. But not together, separately."

Lauren's patience with the hectoring wore thin. "I'm familiar with how it works, okay?" Lauren did know about grand juries. She'd crafted many a statement on behalf of clients caught in their investigative machinery. You either testify, truthfully, and face an indictment; perjure yourself and face an indictment; or plead the Fifth, which in the minds of many is the same as an admission of guilt. Or the prosecutor dangles immunity agreements in front of one or both subjects, waiting for someone to cooperate.

"I'm only passing on what your father wanted to make clear. We're worried sick. You know how he is."

"Sure."

"The only other thing he said was that you need to look out for your own interests. He found out this Blake person has a criminal record. Did you know that?"

Lauren's tone was flat. "Yes."

"Well, he said the reason that matters is an ex-convict has more to lose, and therefore more to gain in cooperating."

"You mean, if it comes to that."

"The story in the Post makes it more likely it will come to that. Your incident at sea—that's what they're calling it—is in the headlines. High profile. You know how it goes. A few online news outlets have already picked it up. Your father says it's the kind of case any ambitious U.S. Attorney would love to go after."

Lauren looked up and down the quiet, narrow street that wound through the town of Culebra. There were few signs of activity. A couple of kids rode by on bicycles. Down the street an old man sat in a chair on a tiny front porch. That was it. How was it possible in a place like this to feel the walls closing in on you? The incongruence was such that harsh realities like U.S. Attorneys or grand juries might well have been from another planet.

Sarah moved the conversation forward with what she hoped would be the clinching pitch. "Lauren," she said, "I would really like you to come home. *We* want you to come home. Your father's already arranged for a top lawyer in his firm to represent you. She's a former U.S. Attorney. Dad raves about her. They'd operate as a team, of course, your father behind the scenes. He believes they could preempt any move by a U.S. Attorney if you agree to cooperate, get your side of the story in front of them."

"How does he know what my side of the story is? How do you?"

"Well, we don't, obviously. But what we're imploring you to do is look out for your own interests."

"Mom, think about it. How is it my interest to come home to shark-infested waters? You know what it's like—a pack of wolves. Can you imagine the frenzy? It'd be out of control."

"You can stay at the house in Oxford."

"Forever?"

"No, just until your lawyer—and Dad—convince the prosecutor to drop the charges."

"By me flipping on Blake."

"Well, yeah. I—"

"Oh, that would be just great. First, I'm the slut who abandoned her husband out at sea. Then I'm the slut who throws her adulterous partner under the bus so she can skate free of the whole mess. Christ!

I'd be a modern-day Bonnie Parker. The only thing missing would be a lynch mob."

Sarah's voice broke. "Oh, God, Lauren."

Lauren could hear the sobs through her mother's voice. "Mom, please. I told you this was my nightmare. I didn't want it to become yours."

"How did you think that was possible? How does a missing daughter, who you desperately want to help, won't even tell you where she is—how did you think that wouldn't be a nightmare that plagues your father and me every hour of every day?"

Now Lauren broke down. Sniffles and sighs punctuated the intermission. Lauren looked back at Blake a block away and waved, indicating she was trying to sign off. "This isn't helping either one of us," she said. "I'm sorry. I don't know how this nightmare ends, but I do know I won't be controlled by it forever. As best I can, I will manage what happens to me. Does that make sense?"

"No."

"That's okay. Listen, I have to get going. I don't know when, but I'll call you again. Soon as I can, I promise. I love you."

"I love you too, darling. Okay? No matter what. With all my heart."

She walked back toward the bar, wiping her eyes. As she sat, Blake could see her state. "How do you order a double in Spanish?" she said.

He shook his head. "These calls," he said, "seems like they put you though the wringer. Just saying."

She sighed deeply, looked off in the middle distance.

"I'll get us two more," Blake said.

Roused from his perch in the back room, the bartender brought two more rum and cokes. Blake was hard pressed to know how to react to Lauren's anguish, so they sipped their drinks in silence. Finally, he said, "Guess we got ourselves in a helluva mess."

Lauren smiled and shook her head at the depth of his understatement, the vacancy of his unintended irony. "Putting it mildly."

"I'd ask what upset you so much in your phone call," he said, "but I figure it's none of my business. And there's probably nothing I can say that'd make any difference." He was hoping the backhanded tone of his observation might prompt Lauren to open up about the call.

She stared down into her drink. "It's like you said, we got ourselves in a helluva mess. Beyond that, you're right. There's nothing to say. That's it ... one helluva mess."

Her despondency was what concerned Blake. He was having a hard time tamping down a queasy sensation he'd first experienced at McKean Federal Correctional Institution. Where was she on the barometer of abdicating? As he watched her expression he wondered where the "we" might give way to "you."

At McKean, jailhouse informants were a prime source of leads and evidence for cops and prosecutors. Inmates knew that of course, and as a result trod very lightly in conversations with other inmates about the specifics of their crimes. Asking another inmate about details was more than a major faux pas; it was dangerous.

Blake well understood the transactional nature of information and testimony. For inmates it remained largely unspoken but was always just beneath the surface.

The jeopardy was magnified for two individuals involved in the same act and grew from the same dynamic. I didn't just hear it; I was there, I saw it. Still, for Blake and Lauren, over the next few days that's where it would stay—unspoken. But by now they both had to guess it had crossed the other's mind.

TOM HITCHCOCK

23

Troy Barrett and Neal Franklin sat comfortably on a sofa in the U.S. Attorney's office in Jacksonville. Seated opposite, around a coffee table, were an Assistant U.S. Attorney from the Middle District of Florida, Steven Alvarez; the Middle District's very own U.S. Attorney, Amy Sellers; and an official from the Department of Justice's Criminal Division in Washington, Warren Davis. The presence of the latter two was an indication of the meeting's status in the hierarchy of priorities. Barrett and Franklin welcomed the meeting. They and the DOJ lawyers were of one mind in pursuing the investigation, though for slightly different reasons.

After pleasantries and abbreviated small talk, Sellers got down to business. "So, let's review where we are at this point," she said, looking at Barrett.

Barrett ticked off the points on his fingers. "We know the three principals were aboard when they left the Chesapeake; one of them, the husband, was rescued at sea, near death; the other two, the wife and … whatever the guy is, abandoned the husband to his fate and continued sailing south without him; we're nearly 100 percent certain that one of our SAR choppers had contact with the boat and the couple, on a southbound heading, roughly 30 hours after the rescue."

Alvarez looked down at his notes. "And the husband had suffered a severe head injury, correct? Sorry if we're covering old ground."

"No problem," said Franklin. "So severe that the neurologist at the trauma center, who has some experience with forensics, couldn't piece together how someone could deliver a blow, from that angle, with enough leverage to inflict the kind of impact this guy had suffered."

Sellers spoke, looking at Davis first, then at the agents. "This case is generating some interest from Washington," she said. "You guys know there was a story in the *Washington Post*, right?" Both agents nodded, Barrett stifling a smile.

Davis spoke up. "The article was pretty seismic in Washington. But at first it was mostly the titillation and scandal factor. Now it's mutating, evolving into another kind of story. It's morphed into a social justice theme and being picked up by other news outlets. How are these privileged people not held to the same standard as others? She's white, the daughter of prominent parents. The privileged, the elite. She and her white-guy lover are yachtsmen. What would happen to a minority suspect in the same situation? See where it's going? So there's more than just some interest. It has political overtones."

"From what you've told us, I think we have enough to empanel a grand jury," Sellers said.

"That's great," Barrett said, "except it's hard to serve a subpoena on a target if you don't know where they are."

"Well, that's not always necessary," Davis said, "but that's part of the perception problem as well."

"Perception," Franklin said, his voice flat.

"That the couple becomes viral cult heroes, living high in the Caribbean, thumbing their noses at law enforcement."

"They might be," Barrett said, "for all we know. Though I very much doubt it."

"We any closer on that score?" Alvarez asked.

"They checked in through French customs in Guadeloupe, stayed there for twenty-one days, then cleared back out. That was nineteen days ago. After that, it's a big ocean. They could have gone anywhere on any point on the compass. If they'd have checked back into the U.S. through CBP, we'd know that."

"Credit card or phone records?" Sellers asked.

"Need a warrant," Barrett said. "Not quite enough probable cause to pass muster with a judge."

"What about a way to track or trace the boat somehow?" Alvarez said.

"There is," Franklin said. "It's called AIS. But they're way too smart to leave that activated. Anyway, Troy has a theory about where they might head."

The government lawyers turned to Barrett. "This is from my gut, no way to substantiate it other than my years of doing this job." He paused. "What I said before about it being a big ocean is what makes it intimidating. In theory you can go wherever you want, but in practice there are limitations. Most countries have restrictions on how long you can stay as a cruiser. There's food, maintenance and parts for the boat. Money. People who embark on these cruising adventures plan them out, sometimes for years. It's a long-term goal. They may have family members join them. For these two, people fleeing the scene of a crime, if that's what they did, it's reactive, spur of the moment. They're on the run, figuratively anyway. All alone, probably cut off from whatever they left behind. That's stressful. Not carefree or idyllic, not living out some dream."

"You think," Sellers said.

Barrett said, "I believe. How's that?"

Davis sat forward in his chair, looking at Barrett. He didn't come here for speculation or theorizing. "Agent Franklin said you had an idea about where they're headed?"

"I think they'll come back to the States, dodge CBP, and try to blend into the woodwork. Might be back here, somewhere, already."

"If your instincts are right," Davis said, "how do we tighten the noose?"

"We can issue what's known as a Be-On-The-Lookout notice," Barrett said. "It goes out to all Coast Guard units in the Caribbean and Southeastern U.S. There's a central issuing authority that disseminates the BOLO notice to Intelligence Fusion Centers in Puerto Rico, South and North Florida."

"Is that as impressive as it sounds?" Sellers asked.

"Um, not really. You have to remember that the Caribbean, South America, Central America, the Keys, the whole coastline of Florida, the panhandle, all of it—it's a rat's nest of smuggling routes and bad people: drugs, human trafficking, illegal immigration. All that's on the Coast Guard's plate. Plus, pursuing and prosecuting polluters, inspecting the piece-of-shit foreign merchant ships that come into our ports every day. Let see, what else? Oh, maintaining the buoy systems, issuing notices to mariners, boating safety for all the yahoos with an extra hundred and fifty grand who buy their Clorox bottles without the slightest notion of how to operate them safely, Search and Rescue when those yahoos get in a jam, or the commercial fisherman yahoos who never met a safety regulation they couldn't ignore. And in the most recent federal budget, they want to cut the Coast Guard budget by 1.3 billion. We're in DHS, not DoD. We don't have a whole roster of patron saints in Congress. Am I whining? No. Or yeah, maybe I am, dammit. But I sure as hell don't hold out much hope that our BOLO bulletin will rivet the attention of the average overworked Coast Guard unit: Be on the Lookout for a pair of lovers on a sailboat, one of whom may have broken her marital vows."

The law enforcement cadre went quiet. Davis's face was grim. He had come down from Washington to infuse a sense of urgency. Now it was time to reach into the toolbox for some prosecutorial tools with more teeth.

"Before we forget," Franklin said, "there's also the factor of what the woman's father said to Troy."

Davis sat up. He was keenly aware of who Lauren Jameson's father was. They had locked horns in some of Washington's epic legal skirmishes. "You mean Elliot Forsyth? You spoke to him?"

Barrett nodded. "We contacted him to see if he and his wife might help in persuading the daughter to come forward to help us, as the saying goes, clear things up, find out what happened."

"Let me guess what he told you," Davis said.

"Yeah, he stiff-armed us in polite but no uncertain terms. Said his daughter was 'represented by counsel.' Any communications to her were to be directed through him. So even if some eagle-eyed Coastie happened to spot them, I don't know what we could do. Neither one of them's charged with a crime, and she's lawyered-up. They could do a safety inspection, but so what?"

Davis stood and paced, head down. "We're caught in the middle of all this," he said. "We got word the other day that a Washington TV station had approached the Jameson family with the idea of interviewing Tim. Can you imagine what a spectacle that would be? How that would make the mob even more restless? The victim, the poor guy whose cognitive ability is obviously impaired, struggling to respond to an interviewer's questions?"

"We'd heard about that from Tim's mother," Barrett said. "I got the impression she wanted no part of it."

"You're in touch with her? With the family?" Sellers asked.

"Sure," Barrett said. "Fairly often in fact. We like her, don't we Neal?"

"We do. A lot. Straight shooter. With Pauline, you always know where you stand."

"We keep in contact with her, her daughter Maya, Tim's neurologist and therapists," Barrett said. "He's the only other one who was out there that night. We cling to the hope that someday he'll be able to tell us what happened."

"Someday?" Sellers asked. "How far away is someday?"

"Closer than we ever thought it might have been four months ago," Franklin said. "They've taken him on a tour of the island where he and Lauren lived. Their house, photographs of the two of them together, the marina where they docked the boat, the boatyard where they worked on it. He remembers her, the boat, sort of remembers Blake, the guy they took with them. He remembers leaving on a 'trip' he calls it, and remembers being in the water, vaguely."

"Who's encouraging all that?" Davis asked.

"Pauline, his mother," Barrett said. "To say she wants justice done on Tim's behalf is an understatement. If you could have seen him in the trauma center in Jacksonville, hanging on by a thread, what Neal describes is nothing short of a miracle. Sometimes I wonder if it's due to sheer persistence of will on Pauline's part."

Sellers looked at Davis. "Are you thinking what I'm thinking?"

"Damn right," Davis said.

Barrett and Franklin exchanged looks. "Oh, c'mon," Barrett said, "You're not thinking..."

"Not just thinking," Davis said. "Doing. If Tim could recall a few more details, it's a start."

"A start how?" Franklin said.

"In a grand jury proceeding," Davis said, "the prosecutor controls everything. No defense lawyer to object, no judge to overrule questions. And Tim would be a cooperative witness. The prosecutor could be as patient as he or she had to be, asking questions in different ways, or as often as necessary."

"Till they get the right answers?"

"No, not to that extent," Davis said. "Not quite. But we could also bring in the folks you referred to from where they lived—where was it—something island?"

"Tilghman Island," Barrett said.

"Right. Bring in those people to testify to the widespread belief that this Lauren woman and—I'm sorry, Blake? Right?—were having an affair."

"We never proved that for sure," Franklin said.

"That's not the point," Davis said. "You don't have to. The burden of proof's not the same as in a trial. We know at least one of them, the wife—Lauren?—won't testify in front of the grand jury anyway. Her father won't allow it. No lawyer would. That makes serving a subpoena pointless, moot, so we don't need to waste time trying to find these people just for that. If Tim ever reaches the point where he can reconstruct a little more of what actually took place, with the testimony of those other people, we'd probably have enough for indictments. Hearsay and rumors are good enough as long as the weight of them, along with enough other evidence, convinces twelve grand jurors out of twenty-three to vote for a true bill of indictment. All we need is probable cause, a reasonable suspicion, that a crime may have been committed."

Davis continued pacing. "All that, plus the fact that the couple sailed off—you're almost sure you have them on the boat—leaving Tim behind, a sympathetic figure in front of the grand jurors. The adulterous couple is in hiding. Why? Why haven't they surfaced? We have motive, opportunity and means, classic elements of a crime." He stopped and moved his thumb and forefinger close together. "We're close, *this* close to indictments. We issue arrest warrants, the warrants go to NCIC. Then it's no longer just your Coast Guard people playing hide-and-seek with this pair: It's them, plus FBI, Federal Marshals, state and local cops—armed with warrants."

"I like the sound of that," Barrett said. "What's the charge?"

"Conspiracy to commit murder," Davis said.

Barrett turned to Franklin. "I like the sound of that too."

24

Blake and Lauren stood on the public dinghy dock in Garrison's Bight in Key West. Blake's packed duffel was at his feet. The awkwardness of the moment, though unspoken, was suffocating. Neither of them could sort through exactly what the nature of their bond had become, what their parting meant at this juncture, or what words were appropriate. They'd been through a nightmarish ordeal together, certainly, which typically forged the intimacy of having weathered a dreadful experience only through one another's support and steadfastness.

Blake had stuck by her, bolstering her morale when necessary, and tutoring her in the operation and handling of the boat. She owed him for that. From Blake's perspective, Lauren's forbearance on monetary issues was something he appreciated. She never really lorded it over him—picking up checks in restaurant and bars, handing a debit card to cashiers at grocery stores with little discernable change in her expression.

But beyond the crucible of their shared experience, the gratitude they owed each other for the gentle handling of their day-to-day relationship, what were they? Were they lovers? No longer. Were they friends? Maybe, but not in the true sense of selflessness and loyalty the term implies. Were they survivors? Yes, for the time being, until, in a few minutes hence, they went their separate ways.

Blake put his hands on her shoulders. "Got your route all set? First night in Marco Island? Should be nine hours or so. Then Fort Myers. You can stay close to shore most of the way. Two easy legs, then across the state and north."

Lauren smiled gently. "I've got it. We've been over it. Anyway, I'm a blue-water sailor now, thanks to you." She thought his plan was sound, the splitting up. Assuming people were looking for them, they'd be looking for two. She'd change her look when she got to Marco Island.

He looked in her eyes. "I worry about you."

"I know you do. I worry about you too." It got oddly tender for a few moments. She reached in her pocket and pulled out a small pack of folded twenties—five of them. "Here, you'll need some money, right?"

Blake pushed her hand back. "No, it's okay. I appreciate it, but you keep it. Besides, I've got just a little left over from your fee. I know a guy lives a few blocks from here. He'll stake me till I get my feet under me with some deliveries."

"Okay," she said, and then it was quiet. "Guess I better get going." Her eyes filled with tears.

"Yeah." They embraced, and hugged, which grew tighter and more genuine as they held on to each other.

He leaned back. "Remember what I told you: Take care of the boat, she'll take care of you. And you take care of yourself, okay?"

"You too," she said.

"I'll miss you."

"And I'll miss you."

Their eyes met and the awkward silence returned. "All right," he said after a time, "let's see you start the dinghy motor." She climbed down in and yanked the starter rope. On the second pull the engine purred to life.

He knelt down. "There you go. Nothin' to it." She untied the painter and shoved the dinghy's nose away from the dock. "Good luck, Lauren. Take care."

She twisted the throttle handle slightly and eased away from the dock, heading back out to where *Breezeway* was moored. She looked back at Blake. He smiled, took one hand out of his pocket and waved. She waved one last time, turned away and goosed the throttle.

When she'd managed to unmount the engine from the dinghy, wrestle it up into the aft end of the cockpit, and mount it on the bracket meant to secure it to the stern pulpit rail, she then turned to the task of maneuvering the dinghy up on the transom and lashing it athwartships. She double- and triple-checked every knot.

The sun was getting lower in the west. She judged herself deserving of a glass of wine. Pouring one in the salon, she climbed back up into the cockpit and looked toward the dock off in the distance. Blake was gone. She was alone. She and *Breezeway*. She felt an inrush of cold dread. Its onset was sudden, and it struck her as odd that it had taken till now for her to feel it. This moment had been coming for some time. She looked around the anchorage and wondered whether a set of eyes might be scrutinizing her boat, or her. Suddenly she felt vulnerable and exposed. Blake could lose himself in a crowd, her identity was tied to *Breezeway*. It would be part of her signature wherever she went. Did Blake get the better end of their exit plan?

Among her strengths, in addition to a nimble intellect, was the force of her will. Now she summoned that force to consciously battle her trepidation and self-doubt. She had readily agreed to the plan, believing it sound when Blake outlined it. And Blake had taught her thoroughly and well when it came to managing the boat. She had many hundreds of miles and several weeks of seafaring under her belt. The short jaunts from Key West to Marco Island and Fort Myers were easy sails, inshore most of the way. Then two days across Florida and four, maybe five, days more on the ICW headed north.

Yet it was the first time she'd be piloting *Breezeway* with no other presence, no other voice, no other set of eyes and ears to help weigh judgments and decisions. She sat on the lazarette hatch cover in the cockpit and sipped her wine as she balanced whatever disquiet there was in piloting the boat alone versus the alternative: flying home to Dulles only to encounter a hornet's nest of brickbats, scorn and condemnation, and who knows what else—a feedback loop that would force her to endure it again and again until the mob tired of it. No, whatever lay ahead in her series of short day trips till she reached Fernandina Beach was vastly preferable to being chewed up, spit out and ground under the heels of a media frenzy and a malign Greek chorus in Washington.

She'd decided that tomorrow night for a change she'd tie up in a marina in Marco Island instead of anchoring out. She had need of certain shoreside amenities for the makeover she planned, an attempt on her part to alter her appearance enough to create a modicum of uncertainty about her identity. She had doubts whether it would do any good, but beyond that mission she was also overdue for a meal ashore and some solid ground under her feet for a few hours.

Swiping her I-Pad, she rechecked the details of navigating the waterways leading to the marina. Study it and study it some more, Blake had told her. When you're entering an unfamiliar harbor it never looks like it does on the chart. The more you've committed to memory, the better off you'll be. She would set a waypoint on the chart plotter for the outermost buoy leading into the channel, and another for the coordinates of the marina. The GPS really did make things less challenging.

The sun eased toward the horizon. Sunset was a big deal among tourists and a mindless cult in Key West. She cared not at all. At 7 a.m. tomorrow she'd be underway, making landfall in Marco Island by late afternoon. For now, a freshened glass of wine perhaps, some munchies, some music—and then to bed. By herself.

Lauren spied a young man in a blue t-shirt waving at her from the end of a dock in the Gulf Haven Marina on Marco Island. He was a dockhand, signaling and motioning to her that she should pull alongside the T-dock he was standing on. She breathed a sigh of relief. A T-dock formed the top of a T as it crossed perpendicular to the main dock. Tying up at one meant no maneuvering in tight quarters, trying to back in between pilings into a normal slip. Instead, she could ease *Breezeway* up to the dock broadside, like pulling up to a curb. Another plus was no talkative or curious neighbors in adjacent slips thrusting their unwanted camaraderie on her.

The dockhand entered Lauren's credit card information on a tablet. She used an older credit card that was still in her maiden name, unsure if it was necessary to cover her tracks but a safer choice nonetheless. Signed with her finger on the tablet, her signature was all but illegible. She hosed the salt off the boat, plugged in the shore power cord, and, as Blake had instructed her, did a deliberate once-over visual of all the fittings and hardware. That chore done, she settled back with a glass of wine.

She had missions in mind. First, dinner out. This being Marco Island, there were any number of well-recommended choices nearby. After dinner, she'd make her way to a CVS store within easy walking distance. There she would buy a pair of barbering scissors and a hair-coloring product. When she emerged from the marina's showers later that evening, the physical Lauren who existed just hours before would look very different. A baseball cap and sunglasses would complete the transformation.

When she left Marco Island and made her way across the state, then north along the waterways in the coming days, the frequency of shoreside encounters would become a fact of life. She couldn't dodge all human contact indefinitely. When she reached Fernandina Beach, she'd need a legend. She'd heard it called that in the espionage game—a cover story that bore up under minimal scrutiny, consistent in its telling. But Lauren's agile mind concocted one that not only sounded credible but would preempt further questions or intrusions. One that would let her retreat into her own private world while gaining the sympathy of those who heard even a small part of it.

25

Lauren swung *Breezeway* wide around a point of land that jutted into the Amelia River from her right. As she came around the bend, the Fernandina Beach waterfront opened in front of her. Along the length of it was a series of commercial and industrial structures, including smokestacks from a papermill, warehouses, and towering cranes designed to load containers on and off merchant ships that docked along a bulkhead farther ahead. A string of freight cars stood on railroad tracks to her right. Not the most picturesque setting, she thought. But Blake had extolled the town's virtues as a destination to get lost in the shuffle. It was a crossroads where the north and southbound ICW routes intersected with the St. Mary's river, which led directly to the ocean. The comings and goings in three directions meant an ever-changing cast of characters among the types and sizes of boats that stopped in Fernandina Beach on their way to somewhere else.

She could see the municipal marina up ahead. The pleasure craft tied up along two long piers identified it as such. Rows of mooring balls stood off a short distance from the piers. Lauren knew from her cruising guide that the daily or weekly fees for hooking on to one—more private and affordable than tying up at the dock—could be handled over the phone by calling the marina office, which she did.

The downtown retail district led away from the water to the

east. Since this was to be her home, ostensibly, for the foreseeable future, she elected to forego the usual rigors of cleaning, checking and straightening. Instead, she released the dinghy from the transom and mounted the engine. She was anxious to get the lay of the land, a feel for the ambiance of this town.

The foot of the main street leading up through town was less than a hundred yards from the dinghy dock. She walked past a tourism office and up one side of the street, past an assortment of shops featuring apparel and gifts, art galleries, coffee shops and restaurants, some with sidewalk tables, a book store, real estate offices, a bank, a church—a more or less typical assortment of the offerings found in most tourist destinations, all nestled along a tree-lined, cobblestone street in an agreeably welcoming setting.

Side streets branched off to each side. More restaurants, galleries and bars were sprinkled along them. Here and there a scattering of couples and families strolled, unhurried, scanning, their interest occasionally stirred by something in a store window.

Like the unexpected surge of dread that hit her a week ago in Key West, just now she felt something different—a wave of loneliness from out of nowhere. Stranger in a strange land, she thought. But both sensations were out of character for her. And just as she'd done that evening in Key West, she steeled herself against it, refusing to let it take hold. Down one of the side streets was a place called the Flying Fish Café. Live music spilled out into the street from a porch facing the sidewalk. As she walked closer, she could see outdoor tables lining both sides of a porch that bent back alongside the building. There were a few open seats, any one of which would be the ideal antidote for what ailed her.

She walked back, comfortably distant from the volume of the music and took a seat. Two women sat at a table across the short breadth of the porch. The conversation did not seem to be going well. There was some animation, gesturing with hands; one looked at the other with something just short of a glare. After Lauren had sat for a while, their conversation reached an impasse. They were quiet. One of them, noticing Lauren waiting, leaned toward her. "It's kind of self-serve here," she said. "If you want something, you need to go into the bar." She smiled and shrugged.

Lauren smiled back. "Thanks." She stood, walked into the bar and ordered a rum and coke. When she came back out to her table, the woman who'd spoken to her was alone, slumped back in her chair. She was late 30s, maybe edging 40, medium-length brown hair with subtle highlights of dirty blonde, done well, subtly, for a purpose it seemed to Lauren.

When Lauren happened to catch her eye, she smiled and raised her glass. "Thank you ... again."

The other woman sat up straight, smiled back and raised her own glass. "I take it you haven't been here before," she said. "I hate to watch people sit and wait for somebody who's not coming."

"No, I haven't," Lauren said. "Anyway, I sure appreciate it."

"No problem," the woman said, standing up with her empty wineglass. "Speaking of which, I think I need another one of these." She walked back into the bar area. When she came back out, she looked at Lauren and smiled in a resigned sort of way.

"I saved your seat," Lauren said.

"Oh, thank you."

"It's fine. It was two guys. I couldn't deal with it."

"I hear you." As she started to sit down, she hesitated. "I'm sorry, stop me if I'm butting in, but are you waiting for someone?"

"Nope. Just me." Lauren felt her radar picking up an encroaching person, but for some reason she was less wary about the incursion. Instinct, maybe. Still, she let the other woman take the next step.

"Could you use some company?" the woman asked.

"Um, sure. Please." Lauren gestured.

"Thanks. What a day it's been."

Lauren wondered if that had anything to do with the tone of the interplay she'd seen a few minutes ago.

"So, you live here in Fernandina Beach?" the woman asked.

"I don't, no. I just got here today."

"Today? Oh, well welcome." The woman raised her glass in a toast. "I'm Rachel."

"Hi, Rachel. Lauren. Nice to meet you."

"Didn't take you long to find the coolest bar in town. Where are you staying?"

"Actually, I'm on a boat. Just walked up the main street till I heard the music. Here I am."

"A boat," Rachel said. "How cool. What kind of boat?"

"Sailboat, 37 feet. She's moored out in the river."

"Awesome. Where's the rest of your crew?"

Lauren met her eyes. "I'm it. You're looking at her."

"Whoa. I'm impressed."

Lauren allowed a shy smile, the first spontaneous smile of any kind for some time. Rachel's energy and warmth were infectious. "So, you hang out here for what, a while? Then move on. Next stop, somewhere? That how life aboard a boat works?"

Lauren hesitated. "Well, not actually. I was thinking of maybe settling in here, getting off the boat for a time and living on dry land. I've heard good things about this town, this island. Seems nice just from what I've seen so far."

"Yeah, it is," Rachel said. "Attracts a certain kind of person, in a good way. I mean, I'm here. Can't imagine anywhere else as a place to get grounded, breathe in, smile and say hello."

Lauren dipped her head. She was wearing her baseball cap and sunglasses cover-up. It seemed overly mysterious given the circumstances. She took off her sunglasses.

"What happens to the boat?" Rachel asked.

"I'll put it up in a cradle, on dry land. She needs some work, some

TLC, some rest."

"Sounds like you're talking about a person, a she."

"In one way I am." Lauren said. "She's taken care of me, now I'll take care of her."

"Then you need to find a place to live."

"I do."

"Not that easy here. Just saying. Any ideas?"

"No. I just got here."

"Course, sorry."

"It's okay."

They were quiet for a time. Rachel looked over at Lauren's glass.

"Want another one?"

"Sure, I guess."

"Be right back."

Lauren's attention was drawn to the music while Rachel was gone. Two guys, one with a bass, another with an amplified acoustic guitar, and a young woman who sang with them. The music washed out from the porch onto the street, a pleasurable narcotic touching people for a block in either direction—a festive, almost celebratory effect. Lauren allowed the feeling to seep in just so far, soothing nerve endings worn thin by weeks of running from the spectre of real and imagined pursuers.

Rachel came back out and sat down.

"This is nice here," Lauren said. "I like the music."

"Yeah, they get decent groups in here sometimes." They turned to listen till the song ended. When it had, Rachel turned back to Lauren, whose tanned arms and slightly weathered face gave her the authenticity of someone who'd spent time on the water. "So, Lauren," she asked, "when you're not sailing hither and yon, what else do you do?"

Lauren paused a beat. "I was a ... communications consultant." Without waiting, she flipped the question back on Rachel. "What about you?"

"I'm a flight attendant. For Delta. Going on 16 years now."

"Wow."

"Wow what?"

"I don't know, flight attendant. Always sounds sort of—"

"But it's not. At least not most of it."

"Do you fly anywhere exciting?"

"My usual trips are from Jacksonville to Atlanta, then connecting flights to Europe, sometimes Japan, South America. Lately I've done some flights to India."

"Do you get to see much of the places you fly to?"

"Depends. We may get a 24 hour layover, or possibly 48. So yeah, we get to see some stuff. But most of the time you're just bone tired or jet-lagged."

Another pause. "You married?" Rachel asked.

Lauren was surprised by the directness of it, but prepared. "Um, it's complicated. Long story. What about you?"

"I've been married twice. First time I discovered that infatuation doesn't last. Second one? I thought it was working, he didn't. After a while, I agreed. Now I've just given up on the whole idea. So where were you a communications consultant?"

Lauren's eyes flickered. "Up north."

Rachel could sense a shade being drawn. "Sorry, I'm prying. Don't mean to. It's just that—"

"Just what?"

"Oh, man. That woman I was talking to when you sat down?"

"Yeah."

"She was my roommate. I find out she's moving, Monday."

"Moving ..."

"Out. Like gone."

"Oh."

"Yeah."

Lauren wondered whether she was a bystander to this drama or figured into it somehow. Rachel answered the question. "Here's the thing. I'm away a lot as you can imagine. But it's not like me to be totally footloose. I try to have it both ways, one foot here, one foot in Hamburg or Buenos Aires, or whatever. There are pieces of my life I want to keep here. And I need someone here to help me keep a handle on those things, the pieces I care about here. Am I making any sense?"

Lauren smiled. "A roommate."

"Yes."

"Me?"

"Yes."

"You're kidding."

"No."

"I don't even know you. You don't know me."

"Well, you haven't exactly spilled your guts."

"Why would I? We just met. And besides, I have my reasons."

The familiarity of the back and forth hit them at the same time—jawing like old friends. They smiled at each other. "I don't know," Rachel said. "I get a good feeling about you. I trust my gut on these things."

Lauren cringed at the yawning gap between Rachel's judgment and the ugly reality of what she'd done—and had become in the meantime. Rachel continued with the pitch. "The thing is, Lauren, Fernandina Beach is a tourist and vacation destination. People who own rental units make a lot more renting them out by the week to vacationers. There aren't that many normal rental units around. Even if you can find one, it'll be expensive. You seem to be a pretty private person, but a landlord's gonna want a credit check and a background check."

Lauren shook her head. "I'm just not in a position to go through a background check right now."

"I gathered. So if you want to stay in Fernandina Beach," Rachel said, "that pretty much leaves me. I've got my own background check, right here." She patted her stomach.

Lauren gave her a long look. If only Rachel knew how badly her radar was misreading the character of the person sitting across from her. And yet, it seemed Rachel was close to offering a near perfect hole in the wall. No sense letting the weight of her guilt displace practicality.

"And," Rachel said, "if you, um, feel like sharing even a tiny hint of what you meant by your 'reasons'—you know, help me understand—I want to be a good listener. If not, that's fine too."

Lauren drew upon her skills as a manipulator of language, how to sound like you were saying something while saying almost nothing. She had a prepared spiell, carefully rehearsed. Let just enough of it dribble out, then stop. "Um, I'm trying to get out from under an abusive relationship," she said.

"Oh, God. I'm sorry."

"No, no. It's okay. Please. I'm handling it. I got a protective order. Then we underwent counseling, got back together. I was so naïve. Stupid. It got worse. He threatened me, said he'd kill me. Got another protective order, but they're not bulletproof. He's not supposed to call, or email or text—but he does. Or come within 500 feet or something. But I'd see him drive by. I mean, you can't have a 24-hour armed bodyguard, right? So, I ..."

Rachel tilted her head. "What?"

"I decided to take our sailboat and head out. I was desperate. It was the only way I could think of that he couldn't follow me."

"By yourself?"

"Yeah."

"Where did you go?"

Lauren went dead-air for a few moments. She reasoned that because Rachel was abroad so much of the time, she was less likely to have seen the media accounts of the whole sordid business involving Blake and Tim. It was the only reason she'd gone into as much detail as she had. But then her voice went flat: "I wound up here."

Rachel nodded. "Okay."

"I can't leave a trail," Lauren said. "I don't know what he's capable of." Her inner moral compass, what was left of it, lurched and twisted, contorting her insides with the malignance of her fabrications. Tim was the furthest thing from abusive. If anything, his agreeable passivity used to irritate her from time to time. Now she was casting him as a predator, when it was she who had dumped his inert form into the cold waves. "If you're worried about money," Lauren said, "I took what I believed was my share from our bank account. I'd done really well with my consulting, so a lot of it was mine anyway."

"Quite a story," Rachel said.

"That's where it ends," Lauren said, "for me." She sat back. "But I guess I'm wondering why you're leaning so hard into this. What's in it for you?"

"I have a cat. She's low maintenance but I don't like leaving her alone for days at a time. I have house plants. They don't survive my schedule. I like coming home to a stocked refrigerator, having the lights on, a glass of wine, someone to say glad to see you, welcome home. It's important."

"Makes sense," Lauren said.

"Here's the other part of it, maybe a deal-breaker, maybe not."

"Sounds like time for another one of these," Lauren said, raising her empty glass. "My turn." When she came back to the table, Rachel raised her glass and took a sip of wine. "I have an online business I run out of the apartment. It's not a big money-maker, but it's something I got into with a few other crew members on a flight to Mumbai last year. We came across a collective of women, artisans, who make these crafts by hand—bracelets, necklaces. They make the jewelry, ship it here, and we sell it online. I need someone to manage the details of that when I'm gone."

"A job," Lauren said.

"More like a way to occupy your time," Rachel said, "and it comes with a salary."

"Nice. How much?"

"You live at my place, rent free. How's that?"

"I told you I had money. I can pay my share."

"The rent's not the issue," Rachel said. "I've got that covered many times over. It's all the other stuff."

The goddess of good fortune was smiling, Lauren thought. I walk into a bar to listen to some music and this falls in my lap. Unreal. She wanted to ask why the other woman would walk away from such a great arrangement but decided it was none of her business.

"Oh, I almost forgot," Rachel said. "One other thing. You can use my car while I'm gone. Just for local stuff, though—errands, whatever. No road trips, please."

"I—um, sure. Of course." Lauren was speechless. The goddess of good fortune had just broken into a broad grin. But she was a believer in karma. She'd done nothing to deserve this. In fact, the karmic opposite was true. It would come back to bite her. Wouldn't it? Maybe not. After all, she recalled vividly how any number of scoundrels and villains, with her help, had skated out from under the consequences of wrongdoing and despicable behavior and landed on their feet. All she could do now is enjoy the moment and keep looking over her shoulder.

26

Tim, Maya and Pauline Jameson strolled slowly around the boatyard on Tilghman Island. It was the second such trip to the yard, spurred mostly by Pauline's insistence that they should come one more time.

Maya wasn't so sure. She wondered if Pauline had become a metaphorical Ahab, a thirst for retribution playing itself out through Tim. It seemed he'd become not just a victim but an instrument of Pauline's festering bitterness. When she'd raised the issue with Pauline, Pauline's eyes became steely and cold, like the color of a darkening sky at sea when the weather is turning worse, like the night Tim was set adrift. And left for dead.

"All I can think of is my son fighting for his life," she said, "alone, at night, bobbing among the waves, believing he was about to die. That image makes my blood run cold and fills me with a sadness and anger I can't begin to quantify. He can't seek justice on his own. He can't hold those two cowardly criminals to account for what they did to him, unless we help him, unless we help him remember what happened. Each time we've been here he salvages a little bit more, a scrap here and there. And our two agent heroes told us every little scrap helps."

Maya had no reply to the intensity of Pauline's jihad. She felt it, understood it, but hoped Tim could bear the cost emotionally.

As they walked among the boats braced with jack stands, Tim

gazed up along the hulls. His eyes were bright, a faint smile graced his features. "*Breezeway*," he said after a time. "*Breezeway* ... where is she? Sailed away. Sailed away." When they'd walked a bit farther, Tim blurted out, "Blake!" Then, "Blake. Where'd he go?"

Just then, Darryl Cummings, the boatyard owner, came striding out through the office door. He saw the two women and Tim walking slowly along a row of boats and edged toward them. He called out. "Well, hello there, folks. Mr. Jameson, right? How've you been?"

Tim grinned. "Good. Yes."

Cummings looked at Maya. "And I know you, you're—"

"I'm Maya, Tim's—"

"Sister. Sure. I recall. How are you?'

"Fine, thank you. This is my mom, Pauline."

"I recognize you too," Cummings said. "You were here a while back."

Pauline nodded and smiled. "Yes, hi. We're just trying to help Tim refresh his memory a little. Okay if we walk around?"

"Sure, sure," Cummings said. "No problem."

Tim looked at Cummings and suddenly blurted out: "Blake! Where's Blake?"

"Well, I wish I knew, Mr. Jameson, but I haven't seen him in quite some time."

Tim's face clouded over. "Angry. Blake. He pushed me."

Pauline looked at him. "What do you mean, Tim?"

"Pushed me." His face darkened. "Angry. Really angry." He looked off in the distance.

"Where, Honey? Where did he push you?"

"Out there."

Cummings thought it best to take his leave. "Well, I gotta be goin'," he said as he eased away. "Nice seein' you folks again."

Maya and Pauline smiled and waved. Tim was lost in contemplation of some sort. They walked slowly. Tim looked at the ground as he walked, focused on something. "Lauren," he said after a time.

Maya said, "What about her?"

"Where is she?"

"We don't know," Pauline said.

Tim looked up and off into the distance again. "I wonder."

"Wonder what?" Maya asked

"Lauren, she ..." Tim said.

Pauline was straining at the leash. Tim was clearly making an effort to sift through what fragments he could piece together. Maya put a hand on Pauline's arm. Pump the brakes. At some stage, among those fragments might well be Tim's original discovery—and subsequent rediscovery—that Blake and Lauren were involved. In his fragile state, there was no telling how quickly or how well he could absorb a sudden recollection of unpleasant or painful realities.

Maya had urged Pauline to temper her eagerness to coax out Tim's story. But Pauline couldn't help putting herself alongside Tim in the water that night, her firstborn, her boy, floundering, gulping, shivering, barely conscious. She ached with the horror of it, seethed with the cruelty of the act that put him there.

In Pauline's last conversation with Agent Barrett, he suggested, but never came right out and said, that the prosecutors were mildly optimistic about the chances of securing indictments. And how indictments would generate arrest warrants, a serious ratcheting up from simply being sought for questioning to names registered in an FBI database as having outstanding warrants. For Pauline, that couldn't happen soon enough.

The extent of Tim's recollections was the key, of course, and his utterances today were like the early letters being turned in a game of Wheel of Fortune, tantalizing hints of a story slowly coming back to him.

They walked slowly alongside a boat raised up on stands. Tim ran his hand along the curvature of the hull, at the point where the antifouling paint on the bottom met the gelcoat along the sides. "Waves," he said. "Big waves." He climbed up a few rungs on a ladder propped against the boat. "Up to here." He raised his hand to a foot below the place where the side of the hull joined the flat section of the deck. "Big waves. Wind." He climbed down and gazed off in the distance.

Pauline put her hand on his shoulder. "When, Tim? When did you see the big waves?"

"Night. Getting dark. Big waves." He turned to Pauline, eyes widening. He sucked in a deep breath, abruptly. He was haunted, or spooked by something, his face contorted with the effort to verbalize it.

Running her hand up and down his arm, she asked, "What, darling? What is it?"

Tim shook his head. "I couldn't ... breathe. Swallowed water." He gulped. "Big waves." When their eyes met again, his were filled with tears. Pauline looked at Maya. Her eyes had that same stormcloud caste to them: icy, brittle, vengeful.

Lauren watched as *Breezeway* rose up out of the lift well, the travel lift's two massive straps under her belly. The machinery would lift her clear of the well, move her forward on four oversize tires to a point where the yard crew could direct the concentrated streams of a pressure washer to scour the bottom clean of accumulated marine growth.

From there, the travel lift would trundle slowly across the yard to *Breezeway's* appointed space, a cradle—aptly named and designed, nestling the boat upright for however long it was destined to spend stored on dry land.

For Lauren the occasion was a crossroads. The new living arrangements she'd stumbled across not only made cradle storage more affordable, but more practical as well. By water, the marina was a short, right-hand jog off the river to a creek, an artery that wound back along the elbow of a protected canal just north of the town of Fernandina Beach. By bicycle, it was fifteen minutes from Rachel's, much less by car. For the moment, she was relieved of any pressing need to plot out how *Breezeway* would fit into her life, or how it might shape her existence according to the protocols of living life afloat: Waking each day on a body of water, somewhere, in the confines of a cramped living space that rocks ever so slightly, with the sound of water lapping at the hull. To many, it was a sublime way of life, sought after, an end in itself.

Lauren recalled the irony of her own idealized version of that life. She'd lived it vicariously through cruising publications, forums and blogs. Yet the version she'd been forced to endure was far from anything she'd pictured. Instead of an idyllic adventure, it was a headlong flight, running from the horror she and Blake had committed. No leisurely drift through tranquil anchorages, but scuttling from one to the other, fleeing from the shadows of ever-present guilt and the fear of discovery. The shadows had chased her here to Fernandina Beach, forcing her to adopt a disguise, shrinking from normal social contacts, lying low even as she looked over her shoulder.

Breezeway was in need of some repairs and routine maintenance. Most were within Lauren's capability; others would require the tools and skills of the yard crew. The serendipity of the Rachel connection reduced the urgency of having *Breezeway* ready to go at a moment's notice. She could spread those tasks out over weeks instead of compressing them into days.

For the first time in months, the pressure had eased just enough to allow her rib cage to expand, room to inhale slowly and let out a deep breath. The vibe of Fernandina Beach seemed to agree with her. Blake was accurate in his labeling of the town as a live-and-let-live niche where many people were from somewhere else. Where you'd been or where you came from were of little consequence. What mattered was the present moment. Her easy synergy with Rachel was a case in point. She felt the weight of the shadows easing, letting her up off the floor. In time, she and *Breezeway* might resume their voyage. For now, she had the leeway to think about when or in which direction. Nothing she could sense through the telescope loomed on the horizon. Today, tomorrow, next week, she could live for the moment.

Agents Barrett and Franklin, and AUSA Alvarez sat before a computer monitor watching a video Pauline Jameson had sent them from her iPhone. It was an interview with Tim Jameson, conducted by Pauline and Maya. Tim was centered in the frame, Pauline and Maya were off camera.

Pauline was asking Tim questions about the sailing trip he'd embarked on with Lauren and Blake. He remembered some parts about getting ready for the trip and the departure. What riveted the agents' and Alvarez's attention was when Tim repeated the fragments of what might have happened on board the boat that night. He used the word "angry" in reference to how he felt about Blake. "Blake pushed me," he said. "Blake, Lauren ... they ... why?" He shook his head.

"Why what, Tim?" Pauline asked.

"They were ... bad. Things. Bad things. I was angry. Me. Blake pushed me."

Barrett, Franklin and Alvarez lurched forward in the chairs. "What happened when he pushed you?" Pauline asked.

"I don't know. I fell. I think." Tim recalled being in the water. "Cold, sleepy. Really tired. My arms ... so tired."

Pauline asked him a few more questions. He couldn't recall anything else. Then this last one: "Tim," she asked, "what was the name of the boat you and Lauren were on?"

Tim brightened and sat up. "*Breezeway*!" Where is she?"

"Who?"

"*Breezeway.*"

"We don't know," Maya said.

"Did Blake and Lauren take her?" he asked, "Where? Where did they go?"

"Sorry, Tim. We don't know," Maya said again. Tim slumped and hung his head. The video ended.

"Man-oh-man," Alvarez said. "Definitely fourth and inches."

"Who makes the call to go for it?" Franklin asked.

"I gotta send this to Amy. She'll kick it up to wherever. But with all the other pieces—think about it. Coast Guard IDs the boat headed south, this guy Blake tells 'em the boat's name is *Breezeway*, the poor husband's been fished out of the ocean. Meanwhile the other two vanish. All you need's probable cause. You're a grand juror. How do you vote?"

Barrett and Franklin both gestured with an emphatic thumbs-down. "But then again," Franklin said, "we're biased."

TOM HITCHCOCK

27

Three months later
May 2019

Blake sat at a table back in the corner of a McDonald's. Part of his seating choice was a legacy of sixteen months in a federal penitentiary, the rest was an instinct to keep the traffic flow of customers in a 90-degree arc to his front. He could see everyone who came through the door.

As he ate, between the scans of people coming and going, he perused the headlines on a newly purchased iPad. The iPad and other recent discretionary purchases had been made possible through a sudden and dramatic jump in his income.

On his arrival in Key West some ninety days prior, he'd sought out a close friend and former boat mate hoping to join him as an experienced hand in boat delivery assignments. At the outset of their conversation that day, Blake noticed that his friend, Ken, known also as K-dog, was unusually circumspect. Distant, he thought, given that the two had spent many hours together aboard boats, most of them on the open ocean, dependent on each other's skill, judgment, and seafaring acumen.

"Been a while since we worked together," K-dog said. "What've you been doin' with yourself?"

Blake sensed a purposeful tone to the question, beyond casual catching up. He made a point of meeting K-dog's gaze. "Last year or so I worked as a yard foreman at a marina on the Chesapeake."

"Didn't work out?"

"Ah, you know. Lotta hard work for not enough money. I guess it was okay, just not where I wanted to spend the rest of my life. Time to move on."

"So here you are." K-dog said.

"Here I am. Lookin' to pick up where we left off."

"Well, thing is, business has changed a little."

"Changed how?" Blake said. "Takin' a boat from point A to point B. How can it be much more than that?"

"I wish," K-dog said. "Difference is, these days more of the boats are carryin' cargo. That's all I'm gonna say." Blake understood immediately, and K-dog's eyes telegraphed that he knew Blake recognized all the ramifications of what he'd just said, and the way he said it. There was a great deal being communicated without the exchange of words. It was transmitted through a common set of understandings, most of which Blake had acquired in prison and K-dog through the hard truths of the business sideline he'd taken on. For all K-dog knew, Blake's approach could be the opening gambit in an undercover operation. They hadn't been in touch for well over a year.

"Well, K-dog, I was hoping I could do the trips without the cargo. I don't need to know about the rest of it."

"Not that simple. Like I said, more and more of the trips involve cargo. The ones without it, the straight trips, are getting scarce. You'll have a long wait between gigs." K-dog looked down at a sheet. "Next one I got is coming up in a few weeks, Miami to Norfolk."

"How much?"

"Your end of it's 700 bucks."

Blake's shoulders drooped. "K-dog, man, I'm in a bad spot. I need some cash flow."

"I hear you. But you see my problem with this conversation. I've already told you more than I should."

"Course. But you I did a few cargo trips in the past. Not like I'm a greenhorn when it comes to this stuff."

"These guys I deal with, the paranoia level is intense. I gotta be very careful."

"Okay."

"Like, for instance, I recall you did some time for cargo you took along on a trip to Annapolis."

"That's true, I made a mistake and signed on with guys I hardly knew. The money was too good for the trip. I should have known."

"And?"

"And somebody ratted 'em out."

"You did sixteen months."

"Yeah."

"Pretty light."

"I had a good lawyer. He convinced the prosecutor I didn't know about the coke."

K-dog tilted his head. "You have to sing for your supper?"

"Nothing to sing about. Like I said, I barely knew these jokers. Didn't know they'd brought a load of product." Blake felt pathetic, being grilled by old shipmate, like a job interview or something. Between the two of them, the vacuum of not knowing what to say next led to an awkward stretch of dead air.

"Listen, Blake, dude," K-dog said finally, "this is so uncomfortable. I hate this."

"No, no," Blake said. "It's me who put you in an awkward spot." He stood to leave.

"Wait a minute. Hang on." K-Dog took a long look at Blake, who could sense where this was heading. K-dog was about to make an exception. Blake's hat-in-hand manner and willingness to get up and leave were convincing. K-dog figured a real confidential informant trying to make inroads would have been more persistent. But Blake clearly knew the rules about boundaries, how certain kinds of questions posed in a certain way were more than just unwelcome. And what the hell, he knew the guy. They had done some good paying trips in the past.

"Listen," K-dog said, "normally I wouldn't do this. But I figure you and I put a lot of miles under the keel together, so I'm takin' a chance, okay? And it just so happens there's a backup in the pipeline. Got the customers, got the product, need a bigger pipeline. That's where you come in. One more way to get the product to the market. Understand? Logistics. If you want in, I can start you with a trial run."

Blake stuck his hands in his pocket, dropped his head and walked in small circles, thinking. The question was whether he wanted to be drawn in that direction. An internal weighing of choices and risks: between a more or less steady inflow of fifteen or eighteen-thousand dollars a month, maybe more, versus the calamity of a ten-year prison term, and a life consigned to the dumpster thereafter if it all went wrong. "How much?" he asked.

"Seven grand."

"No shit."

"Nope. And that's just to start."

Blake stopped pacing and folded his arms. "K-dog, when I got pinched before, I got away light. If I go down again, Christ, it's serious time, man. Serious. I gotta know how leakproof this setup is."

"It's leakproof. Dude, these are no-bullshit hombres. I mean it. No-kidding scary. I don't even know real names. I only know they're all business, no smiles, no small talk, no chit-chat. Face time kept to a minimum, which is fine with me because the look in their eyes puts the fear of God in you. You won't know anybody else's name, either, except mine. And they won't know yours. But you'll never tie me to any product, or any money. It's all kept separate."

When Blake set sail from Tilghman Island with Lauren and Tim, he had a job, an apartment, a pickup, and a minimal set of belongings. Standing on K-dog's porch on Key West, he had less than

200 dollars left from the portion of the fee Lauren and Tim had paid up front. He was regretting his nobility in turning away Lauren's offer of a hundred dollars just before they parted.

He was past the point where his dignity would allow him to wallow in the role of leech or supplicant. The moment K-dog offered him a chance to get out from under that, to stand up and pay his own way, he realized he had no choice. To turn the offer down meant living at the margins in Key West, one step removed from a street person. "You know," he said, "if I had a choice, I'd say let's turn back the clock to the way it used to be. But I don't. So, yeah, okay," he said. "I'm in."

That was three months ago. Today, picking french fries out of a cardboard container and munching a Big Mac, his eyes froze on the iPad screen as he locked in on a headline from *The Miami Herald*.

U.S. Attorney: Indictments imminent in mysterious incident-at-sea case

JACKSONVILLE—U.S. Attorney Amy Sellers announced that a Grand Jury in the Middle District of Florida was readying indictments of two individuals under investigation for their role in a near-fatal man-overboard incident 300 miles off the coast of Florida.

Federal law enforcement officials allege that of three people aboard a sailboat on the night of November 12, 2018, one, a male victim, was pulled from the water and airlifted to the UF Health Trauma Center in Jacksonville. Officials further allege that the other two individuals, a male and female, abandoned the victim and continued on their way south.

Sources close to the investigation said the two alleged perpetrators are known to have fled the country at one point and their current whereabouts are unknown—bolstering an already strong prima facie presumption of foul play.

Identities of the grand jury targets will be released upon issuance of the indictments and subsequent arrest warrants, prosecutors said.

Blake's face flushed hot as he struggled to contain a surge of panic. Arrest warrants! Jesus! The panic was close to winning out as scenarios careened through his head, each with its own tangle of threats, each with its own portent of doom.

His immediate urge was to call Lauren—on his new smart phone—to learn if she'd seen the news or was somehow aware of the pending indictments, the pending cataclysm. He got as far as pressing six of the ten digits when he stopped short, an alarm in his brain mashing the brakes. Think, Blake! If she knew, it was possible he was already at some risk. If she didn't, and he told her, he'd be placing himself in the crosshairs. Wouldn't she find out soon enough one way or another? He knew her father was a high-powered lawyer. How long would it take him to approach prosecutors and negotiate a deal for her—a hard bargain made possible at Blake's expense. He'd be lucky to be represented by a halfway competent public defender. Good luck with that matchup, assuming he was even in the game to begin with.

As he sorted through the no-win implications in each of those dead ends, another dimension gripped him with a deep-seated dread. Given what was at stake in the drug-running enterprise, might these indictments, when they came, put him in real danger? More than a mere prison sentence; a bullet in the brain. To the kinds of people running the operation, perception mattered far more than reality. The ruthless, law-of-the-jungle logic of gansters left no margin for error. Even the perception that Blake represented a potential problem would be enough reason to eliminate the problem, without a second thought.

K-dog claimed that the people on the rung above them wouldn't know his name, nor Blake theirs. But K-dog would know his name. In theory, keeping identities in separate brackets insulated the ring's layers against incrimination from above or below. But if it came to light somehow that what's-his-name's girlfriend was about to give him up, would the people K-dog worked for rely on that theoretical protection? Of course not. By the cold-blooded reasoning of people who evolved in the most cutthroat of environments, it flowed naturally that if what's-his-name's girlfriend gave him up, the possibility existed that what's-his-name might in turn try to trade what little he knew about their operation. It was enough for them to cancel his check. And Blake knew that a federal prison wasn't a fail-safe refuge against the long reach of serious cocaine dealers. All it did was confine him and allow them to strike at their leisure.

During Blake's many idle hours in prison, he gravitated to the facility's law library, for no reason other than the topics interested him. Every prison has its jailhouse lawyers, those who devote their spare time to educating themselves in the law, brainstorming with fellow inmates, contributing to a surprisingly sophisticated grasp of criminal law intricacies. Blake had not taken his involvement that far, but he had come to enjoy the welcome distraction of sifting through the language of the federal criminal code.

The french fries had grown soggy, the Big Mac mushy and unappetizing. He wondered what part of that code he and Lauren would be accused of in an indictment. Tim was still alive; couldn't be murder. When Tim was rescued, he had a life vest on and maybe a flashing strobe; couldn't be attempted murder, could it? Blake swiped through the results of his Google search until he came to this:

> **18 U.S. Code § 1117. Conspiracy to murder**
> **If two or more persons conspire to violate section 1111, 1114, 1116, or 1119** of this title, and one or more of such persons do any overt act to effect the object of the conspiracy, each shall be punished by imprisonment for any term of years or for life.

Section 1111 defined the parameters of first and second degree murder. The language of 1117 made it clear that it wasn't necessary to have actually carried out the murder, only that one or more of the conspirators commit an overt act in furtherance of the conspiracy.

He thought back to the frantic horror of those few moments at sea. The spastic, confused, irrational bumbling that took place between them could hardly be called a conspiracy. My God, he recalled how at the time he was convinced Tim was already dead. No murder took place.

Tim was the one who'd put his hands on him in the confrontation on the cabin top. All he did was fend Tim off, knocking his arms away. What happened next was unintentional, a pure and simple accident in the eyes of anyone who might have seen it. The problem was, no one else did—and given the circumstances between Lauren and him, no one would believe it.

Blake knew enough of federal law to think that, despite the accidental nature of Tim's fall, he was probably guilty of involuntary manslaughter, a sentence of up to eight years, more for someone with a record. In the fog of their panicked terror, he and Lauren made an irredeemably cold-blooded decision. Now, as he looked down at the iPad screen, he saw the phrase describing the consequences of that decision: *Imprisonment for any term of years or for life.*

He left McDonald's, crossed North Roosevelt Boulevard and walked along the Heritage Trail, a broad, palm-lined promenade overlooking the expanse of the Salt Ponds. The traffic whizzing past on U.S 1 to his left and the water to his right amplified his sense of no exit, unwillingly shunted onto an express lane toward nothing but bad endings.

Best case, Lauren rolls on him, fills in the blanks in a conspiracy to commit murder case. If he copped to that charge, trying to catch a sentencing break, it might raise red flags within the hard-case drug smuggler community, who were hyper aware when the length of a sentence didn't correlate with their assessment of a given crime. The immediate assumption was that wherever the new inmate landed, he must have snitched—or could at any time in order to reduce his sentence.

Blake had served his previous stretch at FCI McKean, a medium-security facility housing low-level drug offenders, corrupt politicians, and white-collar criminals. If he took this conspiracy fall, he'd end up somewhere more violent and dangerous, with the suspicions of his previous employers stalking him every step of the way in the exercise yard or in the showers.

"If two or more persons…," he thought, recalling the wording of the statute. A realization wedged its way into his reasoning. It made him almost physically ill to contemplate this horrible reality, but there it was: Without Lauren, there's no conspiracy. Without Lauren, there's no deal, none of the testimony that would consign him to a shark tank of predators and a shortened life expectancy.

He wondered if she was still in Fernandina Beach, until it struck him that wondering was not among his options. He made his way home, packed some things, including four fat rolls of currency, and stowed it all in his newly acquired Jeep Wrangler. Sending K-dog a vaguely worded text explaining in code that he'd be gone for a time to take care of some business, he pointed his vehicle north on U.S. 1, setting a course for Amelia Island, Florida.

He had no plan, in the same way a drowning man has no plan, in the same way a drowning man's survival imperative will drive him to clamber on top of a fellow victim, fighting to stay above water, fighting to stay alive.

28

Lauren wondered whether, if she just pretended not to notice the two voice mail messages from her mother, would they somehow cease to exist? It was possible, after all, to miss two, even if it was a stretch. She'd have to answer the next one, though, no matter what. Or respond in some way. As she was juggling just how she'd answer, or what form a response would take, an incoming email set off the phone's chime.

An arm's length communication from her mother, she thought, always preferable to the verbal and emotional gymnastics, the painful cul-de-sacs of a phone call. An email would give her time and space, a chance to tap dance, equivocate. She was off the hook for the moment, until she saw the content of the email. It was a link to a Washington Post news story, preceded by Sarah's insistent ringing of an alarm bell.

"Seems you are avoiding phone calls," she wrote, "but your father and I felt this couldn't wait." The link led to this Post headline:

Prosecutors Close in On Pair Sought in Near-Fatal Boating Incident

By Mark O'Reilly

As Lauren scanned through the copy, she saw quotes from prosecutors in Florida reporting that indictments in the case were "imminent" and that arrest warrants would follow their issuance. The rest of the story followed the same basic thread as the one Blake had seen two days earlier in *The Miami Herald*, with "sources close to the investigation" dropping broad hints as to the compelling nature of evidence supporting a prima facie case.

Elliott Forsyth had already seen the story and recognized it for what it was: a way of beating the bushes in order to flush game. An indictment was a long way from a guilty verdict. Elliott Forsyth knew that; some suspects didn't. By using terms like "evidence" and "arrest warrants," prosecutors hoped to spook grand jury targets into preemptive offers of cooperation, most notably testimony against other suspects in exchange for a favorable plea bargain deal.

Despite having seen the game played out in Washington, occasionally with her father as a principal, the stratagem still had the desired effect on Lauren. She felt the clench, fully aware that she was one half of the pair being sought. Her compass turned instinctively toward Blake at the other end of Florida, wondering whether the other half of the pair knew of the heightened stakes. Had to assume he did; reckless to think otherwise.

They hadn't been tethered in over three months. He could be anywhere, off on a boat someplace. She knew enough about arrest warrants to know that the issuance of one didn't trigger a nationwide manhunt. More often than not, for someone keeping a low profile, leading a normal life and not raising flags as to her whereabouts, a warrant might only catch up to her in the event of a chance encounter with the police, like a traffic stop.

Still, an arrest warrant would be another wall closing in on her. Uncertainty about Blake was yet one more. Which one of us might they find first, she wondered. She knew perfectly well that if she were arrested, her father would work quickly to protect her interests, securing the best deal he could for her—at Blake's expense if necessary.

Why should she assume Blake would do anything less to protect his interests?

The permutations darted through her head. The more they reverberated between the encroaching walls, the more unsettling it became. She fought to control her imagination. Exactly how far would Blake go to ensure his survival? What if flipping on her left too much to chance? Might he simply kill her, preemptively, to close off every avenue of risk? Six months ago, she would have dismissed that idea out of hand. Nah, not Blake. But since then she'd seen him shoot and kill three men without any hesitation. Granted, he'd done it to save both their lives. But she'd seen what he would do in the name of survival. She couldn't just ignore the premise that the capability was there.

With that, she decided to pull the plug on the rest of the movie playing in her head. Assume the worst, yes, but within reason. She was getting ahead of herself, letting the possible narratives spin out of control. That would lead to panic, and she was already paying a steep price for one horrendous decision made under the duress of panic.

Just as she was clearing her mind, taking deep breaths, the incoming email alert sounded on her smart phone. She flinched, startled by the tone. The name and subject line were visible:

E. Forsyth
What you need to know

She swiped, opening the email. Her father had carefully soft-pedaled its opening lines: "Please, I just want to clue you in on a few things. No browbeating, no arm-twisting. Only some items that a very good lawyer and a father who loves you very much thinks you need to know. Please call me. Please."

Her eyes misted at the unusual expression of affection from a normally taciturn and businesslike father. He'd spent so much time excelling in an arena where only objective facts and intellect counted, whatever reserves of intimacy and warmth he'd had in the past had been blunted over the years. As Lauren's career progressed further into a realm in which cynical manipulation of the truth was the standard currency, she found herself becoming more jaundiced when it came to most things genuine or heartfelt. She had come to admire her father's mastery of legal jousting, arm-wrestling prosecutors or committee chairmen to a standstill. He had watched her use of language and engineering of perceptions change the course toward a re-election effort or senate confirmation for individuals whose misdeeds might have otherwise disqualified them. Lauren and her father respected each other as hyper-competent professionals who had evolved in a demanding ecosystem. Over the years, that abiding respect, unspoken, had taken the place of overt expressions of love. Until just now, until he reached out to her and told her he loved her.

She emailed back, "You call me, promise I'll answer." It was an extra precaution on her part: better that a call originated from another phone. Her phone rang a few minutes later.

"Hi, Dad."

"Hi."

"I'm glad you called."

"Glad you answered," he said, chuckling. "Seriously, it's wonderful to hear your voice." His voice caught. "We're worried sick about you."

"Makes three of us. I'm worried about me too. And you promised no arm-twisting."

"I did, didn't I. All right, here it is then. I think the indictments will be handed down late today, maybe tomorrow. Then they issue arrest warrants for you and this Blake guy."

"Okay …"

"And I don't have to tell you it's always better in these situations to surrender voluntarily rather than make them come looking for you."

She didn't respond. Dead air.

"The reason I raise it with you is this," he said. "If you surrender voluntarily, it's likely we'd get a better arrangement for bail. Both the court and the U.S. Attorney look favorably on it."

More silence.

"If they have to come looking for you, when they find you, they make it tougher. You could be sitting in a holding cell for a long time. Or they might deny bail altogether."

After a few moments, she said, "What's the charge?"

Now it was Elliot's turn to hesitate. "Conspiracy to commit murder."

"That's a joke. There was no conspiracy. We were scared shit—" She stopped abruptly.

"Anything you tell me is protected."

"I know."

"If there's an explanation, you can sit right alongside me and tell them your side of the story."

"We both know what's going on here," she said. "They don't have a case unless one of us caves. Even then I'm not sure—"

"There's a difference."

"Blake and I are the only ones who know what happened. And I'm telling you there was no conspiracy. We're guilty of appalling judgment. That's it."

"But the difference is," Elliot said, "people who are guilty of appalling judgment don't run and hide—and stay hidden. People who are guilty of conspiring to murder do that—go underground. That's what everyone believes."

"That's right, and that's exactly what they'll always believe. If I resurface, throw myself on the mercy of the court of public opinion, I'll get crucified: tried, convicted, sentenced. It'll follow me everywhere, for who knows how long? Forever? I don't know. But I'm not strong enough to withstand it. It'll crush me."

Elliott gathered himself for a final summation. "I don't agree. I think you're exaggerating. You spoke of appalling judgment that night. I don't think you're using good judgment now. What *will* follow you is an arrest warrant, and the fact that you ran and hid from it. That's what people will remember."

"Sorry, counselor. I love you, but I disagree. I did this for a living. I dealt with perceptions and I was good at it. The woman who sailed off into the night leaving her husband for dead. Then, when she was caught, threw her lover under the bus to save herself. Are you kidding? There's not enough bandwidth to carry all the Twitter feeds and scandal sheet posts, all the fodder for a digital lynch mob. It'll never run out of energy. So it's either that or out of sight, out of mind—now, instead of later, when I'd have to take off to Nepal or someplace. I don't have much of a choice. A rock and a hard place. I'll take my chances with now."

"What if they find your friend Blake first?"

"Same thing. Rock and a hard place. I'm not even sure where he is. We went our separate ways three months ago. Besides, he's got a lot more to lose than I do. He's the one who got into a tussle with Tim. He's worried about a manslaughter charge. And he's an ex-con. Told me what happens to rats in prison. Anyway, he doesn't have you, and I do— I think. Don't I?"

"Of course, Lauren. No matter what."

Her father was throwing her a lifeline and she knew he couldn't connect with why she was refusing it. The thought pulled her to pieces inside. Her lower lip trembled before she began to speak. Voice quavering, she said, "Dad, my God, I am so sorry I've done this to you and mom. I can't" and then she broke down, sobbing.

Her anguish cracked Elliot's emotional armor plating. His normal reserve gave way. Choking on the words as he spoke, he stumbled, gasping as he tried to make them coherent. "I wish there were a way to turn back the clock on all this, pull you back into our lives, to shelter you and protect you, to have you be my little girl again. We all got so caught up in ... I don't know, things that don't seem to matter now."

They paused, and as they did, Lauren pulled herself together enough to offer her father an off ramp. Neither he nor her mother deserved to be pulled into the gears of her torment. "It's done, Dad. Done. I don't think it's reversible, or redeemable. Sometimes I think what I did is beyond redemption. I have to retreat into my shell, make myself small, and hope that someday the world will forget about me. Maybe then I can crawl back, slink in the back door and pull it shut behind me. I don't know. But that's all I've got for now."

"It's not all you've got."

"Yes, it is. It's all I deserve."

It was quiet again. She was due to meet Rachel soon. "Dad, listen," she said at length. "Let's not do this to each other, please? I put myself in a place where I'm out of options and that's just the way it is. I have to do what I think is best." She paused: "Um, I've got to go soon. Sorry."

He sighed deeply. "Okay. But please, don't just drop off the face of the earth. Your mother is a wreck. Don't make it worse for her."

"I won't. Thanks for being you. I love you."

"I love you too, Lauren. Take care of yourself. Bye."

"Bye Dad."

TOM HITCHCOCK

29

Before walking the few blocks to meet Rachel for drinks, Lauren used cold compresses and eye drops to disguise the evidence of a flood of tears during and after the call with her father. Peering into the mirror and judging it partially successful, she started off for the Flying Fish Café.

Rachel had arrived earlier and with a big smile waved enthusiastically at Lauren from her table. Even at a distance Lauren could feel the positive energy. Between that and the music from the live band, her mood brightened. She edged into a seat across from Rachel, her back to the band. Her smile was wide but seemed forced in an odd way, just slightly unnatural.

Rachel picked up on the dissonance. "Hey there. How are you? Everything okay?"

"Um, yeah. Sure. Why?"

"I don't know. You seem a little, what? Stressed?"

"I need a cocktail, that's all. You good?"

"Yeah."

"Be right back." When she came back and sat down, she raised a glass to Rachel. "Here's to mollusks."

"What? Mollusks?"

"Yeah, a shell in which an otherwise vulnerable organism can retreat, curl up, and shield itself from the world."

Rachel reciprocated with her glass. "Like a snail you mean?"

"Yeah"

"Nice. Okay, to mollusks."

Lauren took a healthy gulp from her drink. "C'mon, drink up. It's happy hour for mollusks"

Rachel laughed and took a generous sip. Her attention was drawn sharply past Lauren's shoulder. "Whoa. Check out this dude."

Lauren turned back to look. When she followed Rachel's glance and saw who she meant, the circuits in her nervous system tripped. Her vision blurred for a moment. A certain place inside her contracted, in one sense pleasurably, in another a pulse of alarm. "Holy shit," she breathed. Standing in a small open space among the tables and people, sipping a beer, taking in the band's music and the people around him, was Blake Wentworth. He walked slowly among the tables on the outside porch, scanning the faces.

Lauren watched, waited. He was here looking for her, she knew, no other reason. When his eyes finally settled on her face, she was staring back. The exchange had a dreamlike quality to it, gauzy at first, slightly unreal. Blake smiled and seemed to drift toward their table.

"You know this guy?" Rachel said.

"Yeah," Lauren replied without looking back.

"Sheesh."

Blake stopped in front of her. "Hi, there."

She flashed a smile. "Hi yourself. Couldn't stay away, eh?"

"Something like that. Missed my sailing soul mate."

Lauren turned and motioned to Rachel. "This is my good friend Rachel. Rachel, Blake. Blake and I spent some time sailing together."

Rachel's smile edged toward flirtatiousness. "Nice to meet you. Want to join us?"

"Sure," he said. "Thanks."

Lauren darted a glance at Rachel. She wasn't at all sure that's what she wanted, but now there was no choice. Blake sat. His smile had turned to a grin. It was attractive, magnetic. Lauren thought back to their first encounters back on Tilghman Island. Blake had a way about him, no question about it.

"Did you come here on a boat, Blake, like Lauren?" Rachel said.

"No, no. Drove up."

What? thought Lauren. Drove? Like in a car? Blake?

Rachel said, "Up from where?"

"Um, the Keys." He looked around the table. "Hey, looks like we need another round." Then at Lauren, "I'm buying. Want to help me bring 'em back?"

Lauren stood and they walked inside to the bar. They were in the second rank of customers awaiting a busy bartender. She had time to notice Blake wearing decent shorts and a nice t-shirt, a marked change from times past. "Nice duds," she said, looking him up and down. "You get all dressed up just for me?"

Blake's smile this time was shy. "Didn't want to show up looking like some bum, that's all."

"You don't, you look great."

"And you look wonderful, like you always do."

His compliment rekindled sensations from stolen afternoons in the days before their lives collapsed. The bartender arrived, looking harried. "Three rum and cokes with lime," Blake said. When she came back, Blake took out a folded sheaf of currency and peeled off a fifty-dollar bill. When the bartender brought change, he left ten dollars as a tip.

Lauren tried not to notice the profligacy. Was Blake being deliberately ostentatious? Or was he too clueless to know that flashing money around was not only in poor taste but possibly hazardous? At the time of their parting a little over three months ago, Blake was virtually penniless. Now he had new clothes, a wad of cash, and as far as she could gather, a car. After the gun play confrontation at sea, Blake had been forced to fill in some of the blanks in his drug trafficking history. The connections between that history and what she was seeing now seemed obvious. Was she jumping to conclusions? Or was it dangerously naïve to pretend otherwise?

They carried the drinks back to the table. "So, Blake," Rachel said when they'd sat, "you look like Lauren did when she first showed up here: weathered just so, in a good way I mean, a certain look. Does that fit you?"

Blake lifted his glass. "Yes, ma'am, I guess."

Rachel recoiled slightly at being called "ma'am." "Please, Blake. It's Rachel."

"Okay, Rachel it is."

"And you're a sailor like Lauren?" Rachel asked.

"No, not like me," Lauren said, looking at Blake. "He's kind of a professional, right?"

"Professional?" Rachel said.

"I deliver boats for a living," Blake said.

And you deliver quantities of drugs along with those boats don't you, Lauren wanted to say.

"Deliver, how? I don't understand," Rachel said.

"I take the boats from one destination to another, usually over a long distance, when the owners don't have the time or can't be bothered, for whatever reason."

"They're rich people," Lauren added, "who can afford to pay other people to do things for them."

"Oh." She looked at Blake. "Is that what brings you to Fernandina Beach? A delivery?" Lauren waited to hear the answer. She had her own suspicions about why he showed up and wanted a read on how he'd handle this.

"No, nothing like that. I was through here a few years ago. I always liked it. Just thought I'd stop back, look up a few friends."

Rachel smiled, "You mean like Lauren?"

Blake shrugged. "Um, yeah. I guess. I heard the music coming from this place and I figured, like, if she's still here in Fernandina, she's probably in there. And sure enough ..."

Sure enough, right, Lauren thought. You were looking for me. The question is, why? For old time's sake? You missed me? Or something else. Looking into his eyes and scanning, his face offered no clues. She used to think that Blake's opacity was due to his lack of depth, a simplistic view of the world and an absence of curiosity about anything outside the universe of boats and sailing. But the clinical, calculated way in which he eliminated the threat posed by the hijackers changed all that. His awareness and survival instincts were as finely tuned as circumstances dictated, which made him unpredictable.

"So where did you two do your sailing together?" Rachel asked.

Lauren and Blake exchanged a quick glance. "Oh, around," Lauren said. "The Caribbean mostly."

"Sounds wonderful."

"Yeah," Lauren said. "It really was." The small talk lapsed.

"Another round?" Blake said. "Who's ready?"

Lauren put her hand up. "I am."

"I'm good," Rachel said. "Got an early flight in the morning."

"Wow, really?" Blake said. "That's too bad. I was gonna take us all to dinner."

"Sorry," Rachel said. "Another time maybe. You two keep the party going. My day starts at five a.m. tomorrow."

"You getting a room at the Hilton tonight?" Lauren asked.

"Yeah," Rachel said. "Just so much easier." On mornings when she had an early flight, Rachel booked a room at a Jacksonville airport hotel. It saved the drive, parking, waiting for the shuttle, all the time wasters that cost her an hour's sleep if she left from Fernandina Beach. "Anyway, three's a crowd, right?"

"Oh please, Rachel," Lauren said. "That's not the way it is. C'mon. Sure you won't join us?"

"Positive," she said, smiling. "You two go ahead." As she sipped her cocktail she looked at the pair over the rim of her glass, first at Lauren, then Blake. What the hell's going on here? she wondered. Why are these two so mysterious and vague about everything? She'd asked some simple questions as conversation starters and they pulled back into their shells like turtles. What's up with that? It was disquieting. Lauren's explanation for her initial reticence when she first arrived was the ostensible escape from an abusive relationship. What was Blake's excuse now? Where did you drive up from? The Keys. Where did you two sail? Around. It would be hard to shut most people up about a trip like that. When Blake arrived at the Flying Fish Café, Lauren's surprise was obvious. Old friends? No text, no phone call?

Lauren noticed the sweep of Rachel's eyeballing. From the way her eyes flickered, it was hard not to imagine Rachel struggling to piece things together and wondering how they fit. What's wrong with this picture? Who was this guy? How does he just show up out of nowhere? How come Lauren never mentioned him? The way her eyes swept back and forth was a warning light to Lauren, glowing faintly at first, a low amber.

Rachel stood to leave after she'd drained the last of her cocktail. Smiling at Blake, she said, "I've got to run. So nice to meet you."

"Likewise," Blake said. "Sorry you couldn't hang out a little longer."

Turning to Lauren, she said, "See you in four days."

"Okay, see you then. Stay safe." They watched as Rachel walked off.

"She seems really nice," Blake said. "I have to say you two seem pretty tight. Maybe it's none of my business but does she play some special role in your life?"

"We're roommates."

"Are you kidding? Roommates?"

"Nope. She's gone a lot and needs someone to take care of her place while she's away—her cat, plants, that kind of stuff. Plus, I help her with a little business she runs. She was a life preserver when I showed up here, recruited me right from this bar. We hit it off. It's really a great situation—or should I say, was."

"What's that mean?"

"It probably wasn't a good idea for you to come here, just show up like you did."

"Why?"

"Didn't you see her checking us out?"

"No."

"My God, Blake. She was, like, what's the story with these two?" Blake didn't know the subtext, and never being one to pick up on subtleties, shook his head. "When Rachel and I first met," Lauren said, "I told her I couldn't tell her much about my background because my ex-husband was after me. I was staying out of sight. Now you show up out of nowhere, tell her we're sailing buddies, she has to wonder if my story's a crock. She's entrusted me with all this stuff, her condo, her car, her business—now she's not even sure who I am."

"Just cause a friend shows up from out of town?"

"God. Don't you get it? Please. Go order us another drink." When Blake came back and sat down, she looked across the table at him. "Nobody was supposed to know I was here. I had this whole legend created around laying low, being invisible. She asks us a few innocent questions; we stonewall the answers. Blake, listen, all she's got to do is a quick Google search. I'm surprised she hasn't already. She'll find out I'm not hiding out from an abusive husband. Instead, she'll find out you and I left my husband for dead out at sea and sailed off without him, that there are people looking for us. Hell, it's been all over the news."

They leaned in a little, took healthy slugs of their drinks. Blake was walking a mental balance beam. She hadn't brought up the indictments. But what did she mean by "people are looking for us?"

"All I know is I can't stay here now," Lauren said. "I've gotta disappear somehow."

"Guess that goes for me too. Any ideas?"

"You mean the two of us? Together?"

"I can't go back to the Keys, told your friend that's where I came from." What Blake didn't mention was that the Keys might not be good for his health if Lauren did get arrested and the higher ups in the drug business decided he was a liability.

Their eyes met. Lauren's expression turned electric. "Culebra," she said. "We sail off on *Breezeway*, over the horizon, nobody knows where we went."

"Where've you been keeping her?" Blake asked.

"On dry land in a boatyard ten minutes from here. We could have her ready in two days."

"There's the 'we' again," Blake said. "Do we go as friends or lovers?"

"What? Who cares? How about fugitives? Is that a good term? Somehow the other stuff will work itself out I suppose. But right now it's irrelevant."

Blake had a reason for asking. He'd come to Fernandina Beach with the intention of killing Lauren, without having any clear idea how. Shooting the thugs on a marauding boat at sea was self-defense, instinct. The aftermath took care of itself. Three guys with automatic weapons found dead on a drifting boat: obviously a drug deal or a hijacking gone bad. Unlikely anyone would waste much time looking for whoever killed them. He'd been trying to picture shooting Lauren with his Glock and couldn't. It horrified him no end. And apart from the overwhelming psychological obstacle, there were practical considerations. Killing a person with a gun was fraught with risk: gunshots someone might hear; lots of blood, getting rid of the body—all with a hundred ways to screw something up. Culebra would be a way

DROWNING

to postpone coming to grips with his dilemma, at least for the time being, or maybe indefinitely. Like Lauren said that one time, a good place to crawl inside your shell and hunker down.

"Okay, captain," he said, "I'm in. I've got like nine-thousand in cash. I can pay my own way. Hell, we could both live on that for quite a while." He raised his glass in a toast: "To Culebra."

"To Culebra," Lauren toasted in return. She wondered about her vulnerability on the five-day trip between Northeast Florida and the Spanish Virgin Islands. If Blake meant her harm, to silence her, that would be the interval in which to do it. No way she could stand up to him physically. If he'd kept his gun, it wouldn't matter. Still, she had no choice but to go along in this latest scuttling of the cockroaches. And as she and Blake planned how to dodge back out of the light and into the dark recesses under kitchen cabinets, she knew she'd had enough. She worried about Blake: Was he thinking about wasting her? Would his drug dealing catch up with them? And she worried about the authorities closing in on them. It was too much. A negative feedback loop, a treadmill in a rat's cage. There had to be an off ramp ... somehow.

Suddenly, out of nowhere it seemed, a flash of inspiration bolted through her brain. She'd been paid well in the past for just such inspirational brilliance in helping clients squeeze out of tight spots. She recalled a book Rachel had loaned her. It had been sitting on an end table for days. Written by a local author, it was a murder mystery set on Amelia Island. It contained the seeds of her deliverance.

Blake was nearly finished with his drink. "I'm starving. Let's go get something to eat. On me. What do you say?"

"No. The less we're seen together the better. You get up and leave, then I will in a few minutes. Meet you at the boatyard tomorrow at nine. It's called Tiger Point Marina."

When Lauren got home to Rachel's apartment, she did some online searching. My God, they sold the things on Amazon. But here was a YouTube video on how to make one. She watched, it seemed simple enough. A few blocks from Rachel's place was a hardware store whose character and feel harkened back to the days when nearly every town had one just like it, before big-box retail homogenized and devoured a whole genre of personalized and specialized retailing. Its merchandise offerings featured, in addition to an excellent selection of marine hardware and fittings, a little bit of almost anything anyone might need.

The next morning, Lauren walked into the store and bought: a one-inch wooden dowel, a four-foot length of thin wire rope, washers, and a few small hand tools.

30

It was morning of the fourth day out of Fernandina Beach. A moderate breeze from the northeast ushered *Breezeway* along on a southeast heading, settled comfortably on a beam reach. Blake, having done the four a.m. to eight a.m. shift, turned the helm over to Lauren. "I've been holding her on one-three-zero," he said. "We're making better speed now that we're out of the stream. I figure we're about eighteen hours away." Having spent more than his share of time on deck over the last three days, the sleep deficit was catching up with him. He yawned and shuffled toward the companionway.

Lauren took the wheel and watched him make his way forward toward the v-berth. She wondered, as she had at every change of watch, whether the next time he emerged at the top of the stairs he'd be carrying a gun, pointed at her. Having seen Blake's proficiency and what the bullets did to the hijackers, she had no doubt those would be her last seconds on earth.

Yet a nagging residue of doubt, the contradictions in who Blake really was, tore at her. Was he really capable of coming to the top of the stairs and shooting her in cold blood? Blake? Sweet, clueless, shiftless Blake? But there was also the Blake who had shoved Tim backward, causing his death—or so they'd believed at the time. Was it really an accident, the way he'd described it? And though ultimately she went along, it was Blake's suggestion that easing Tim's body overboard would be to their advantage. Blake had been in prison on a serious charge. He'd described to her the survival-of-the-fittest culture inside the walls that kept everyone's head on a swivel. And then of course there was the incident with the hijackers: the swiftness, sureness in the way he cut them down.

No, she thought, waiting to discover whether Blake was actually so sweet or clueless, agonizing over the contradiction, could get you killed. When she weighed it all on a scale that measured only logic, removing all emotion from the equation, she knew what she had planned was the only rational choice.

As the noon hour approached, from behind the wheel Lauren could see Blake stirring below in the saloon. He was groggy, lethargic, puttering around, scratching his head, stretching, unfocused as he drifted uncertainly among small tasks. She locked the wheel, and as smoothly and quietly as possible climbed onto the cabin top, positioning herself over the companionway hatch opening.

Blake heard her movement above him and glanced up into the cockpit. He called out: "Everything okay?"

"Yeah," she called back. "Traveler's jammed."

He was conscious of not interfering or questioning her competence. "Need any help?"

"No, think I got it."

"Okay. Be right up."

She crouched, poised. In another minute his head appeared as he climbed the steps. When he was two steps from the top, she sprang. Looping the wire rope around his neck, she pulled hard on two wooden handles, snapping the loop taut. A garotte. Favored by assassins and executioners as far back as the Roman Empire, the simple device was unsurpassed as a weapon of deadly efficiency.

Lauren pulled the handles with all her might. Blake struggled and staggered, clutching at the wire around his throat. By the count of ten his world was going black. He slumped, trying in vain to support himself against the veil being drawn quickly over his senses—hearing, sight, touch, balance, awareness. Keeping her death grip on the handles, Lauren followed his collapse to the cockpit floor. By the count of thirty he was unconscious. She tried pulling the wire rope even tighter, though there was nowhere for it to go. It was sawing a shallow laceration in Blake's neck. Her arms began to ache. In ninety seconds, his brain had been deprived of oxygen long enough to kill most victims. Still, she held on—three minutes, four, then coming up on five. Finally, her arms gave out. She loosened the loop enough to relieve the cramping and fatigue in her arms.

She watched, and waited, ready to yank the wire rope tight again if need be. She watched his face, blanched now, fish-belly white, devoid of life. Unable to force herself to touch his neck, she grasped his wrist instead to feel for a pulse. As far as she could tell there was none, and when she let his arm go it flopped lifelessly. The sight broke her heart. Blake's beautiful blue eyes were empty, staring, a cold, dull gray. She broke down in a torrent of grief. Sobs and gasps wracked her, she moaned and bawled, head in hands, shoulders shaking. "Dear God, Blake," she sobbed, "I'm sorry. I'm sorry, sailorman."

She recalled standing on *Breezeway's* foredeck with him after a rough training sail across the Chesapeake. They'd been teasing each other up to the edge of an affair, and Blake issued a caution. "You know," he'd said, "things get complicated. It can change lives." She'd chided him, scoffed at his hesitance. Now, she keened, "Good God in heaven Blake Wentworth, you were right." Their affair had turned a circle of lives into train wrecks, not just the two of them but Tim's family and hers. And, looking at Blake's corpse, whoever he belonged to.

Her crying cloudburst eventually blew itself out, like a storm. She gathered herself and set about completing her ghoulish business. The boat, its trim and wheel unattended, had luffed up into the wind, sails slatting and flapping. She sheeted those home, effectively stalling the boat. The chore remained to drag Blake's dead weight from the cockpit floor up to and over the coaming, until she could push him over the side. She did this with ropes and winches, gradually, pushing, grunting, cursing.

Blake's body rested partially atop the cockpit coaming and toe rail running fore and aft at the edge of the gunwale. Lauren was determined not to make the same mistakes she and Blake had made with Tim. She retrieved a small ten-pound anchor meant to secure the dinghy to a shoreline or beach. Rarely used for those purposes, now it suited hers perfectly. She wrapped several feet of the anchor's line around Blake's ankles and tied it fast. Unfastening the hooks securing lifelines to stanchions alongside the cockpit, she pushed and wrestled Blake's body closer to the edge. As she did so she was struck by a gruesome flashback to the night she'd helped Blake do to Tim what she was about to do now. The memory, the imagery, sent a wave of revulsion through her. The evil had come full circle, she believed, and settled in her soul. She'd never been a religious person, but felt sure somehow that there were spirits or fates that would visit her to exact a price. Maybe they already were, she thought, and that price was in the form of a torment gnawing insistently at an open wound deep within her.

She pushed and shoved a bit more. As the boat rocked, Blake's body teetered at the edge. She tossed the anchor over, waited for the next wave, and pushed. She saw the top of his head as it sunk straight down, plummeting quickly out of sight.

She made her way to the small, out-of-the-way bar where she and Blake had stopped during their brief stay in Culebra. It was as she remembered—modest, well-worn, with a haphazard, what-the-hell decorating motif that had long since abandoned any pretense of a central theme, or a pretense to anything. She'd hoped it might be empty. Damn. No such luck. There was one other patron sitting there.

She sat on the opposite side, keeping her reflective sunglasses on. Seated across from her was a man, approaching middle age, wearing a baseball hat. He seemed overly glad for the company and his attempt to make eye contact with her was overt, awkward, and to Lauren, unwelcome. The bartender approached Lauren with a distinct lack of enthusiasm. "Rum and coke, por favor," she said. The bartender acknowledged with a faint nod and busied himself with her order. When he imagined Lauren might have looked at him, the man sitting opposite her smiled.

The bartender placed a coaster on the bar and set her drink on it. The man across the bar raised his beer bottle in what was either a toast or a form of greeting. Lauren didn't respond.

Finally, the man spoke. "Are you on that Island Packet anchored off by itself?" Lauren nodded with as much as noncommittal indifference as she possibly muster.

"Reason I ask is," the man said, "well, I retired from the Coast Guard about six months ago. I was a senior crew chief on a helicopter. Flew out of Brunswick, Georgia. On one of my very last missions—it was search and rescue—we came across a boat looked just like yours. I remember cause there was a pretty little gal at the helm."

Did he just say that? Lauren wondered, noting the southern accent. Did he really say pretty little gal? Do people still talk like that? She offered no reaction to the man's conversational foray. This guy was acting out one of her concerns—a woman by herself being hit on by every male aspirant, single or otherwise, most of whom seemed to believe it couldn't hurt to try no matter how unappealing they were or how slim the odds. Maybe this guy was just being friendly, but she wasn't in the mood.

"You on that boat all by yourself?" This was a question fraught with all the wrong implications. Again, she tried to telegraph icy silence.

"Reason I ask is, seems like a lotta boat for one person, specially a gal."

She paused for a moment, and then said in a low voice, "It's the way I like it. Plenty of space, room to be by myself. Privacy, seclusion. Nobody bothering me. And I can handle anything that comes along."

She hoped the guy could take a hint, that the frostiness of her tone and the words would be enough to avoid having to tell him to buzz off. It seemed to, for a little while anyway.

"You know," he said as he picked up his beer and drained the last of it. "When I think back, I can almost remember the name of that boat. It was breeze-something I think." He plunked some dollar bills on the bar and slid off his stool, looking at Lauren for a reaction. Her shrug was minimal, barely noticeable.

He ambled away, then stopped and turned back. "Sea Breeze?" Lauren's gaze behind the reflective shades stayed straight ahead. "No? I swear it was breeze-something. Breeze ... breeze ... oh, well. It'll come to me. Nice talkin' to you." He walked off down the street.

ABOUT THE AUTHOR

During the interval between his working years and golden years, Tom has transitioned from a career as a copywriter and creative director in ad agency settings, to freelance creative maven—to writing fiction. In effect, he's gone from making a comfortable living writing drivel to making chicken feed writing novels. Fortunately, the former more than paid the bills, the latter is an avocation. He is the author of five novels, four of which are set to varying degrees on or around Amelia Island, Fla. The first novel, his initial foray into fiction, is set primarily in Heaven. Tom and his wife Susan, a noted watercolorist, and their faithful dog Sunny, make their home on Amelia Island.

Made in United States
Orlando, FL
30 August 2025